Gnats, Humidity and Murder

Gnats, Humidity and Murder

EVERETTE HALL

Archway Publishing books may be ordered through booksellers or by contacting:

Archway Publishing
1663 Liberty Drive
Bloomington, IN 47403
www.archwaypublishing.com
844-669-3957

ISBN: 978-1-6657-5772-0 (sc)
ISBN: 978-1-6657-5774-4 (hc)
ISBN: 978-1-6657-5773-7 (e)

Library of Congress Control Number: 2024904383

Print information available on the last page.

Archway Publishing rev. date: 03/28/2024

CONTENTS

ONE

Change Is Coming

Amid the oppressive heat and relentless swarm of buzzing gnats, Bill Allgood sought refuge from a night so saturated with humidity that it pressed in from all angles like a proverbial "ton of bricks", squeezing all ambition and hope from any normal soul. The evening of July 1, temperatures had been beyond oppressive. And after a long day of sweating outside, fighting the insanely persistent humidity and gnats, he had come in only to fight with his wife inside the large, white-columned, plantation-style home. Even though the sun had gone down, the temperature was still in the nineties, but it seemed a lot hotter, almost suffocating.

He escaped his trouble from the outside and inside by immersing himself in what had been his father's private shower, where hot water poured over him, cutting away the grime of the day as it ran down on the white marble tiles in the stall, causing steam to fill the room.

Bill had inherited the house and plantation from his father years ago. The bathroom of choice that evening was on the main floor by the old man's office. He remembered, as a child, being prohibited from entering the room and especially could not go into the throne room. *Take that, you old bastard*, he thought. He deliberately showered there in further defiance of his father's prohibition of his use of that bathroom.

Hit by a growing urge, he stepped out of the shower, not bothering to dry off, and settled on father's facility, proud of the imagined contortions of the old man's face if he could only see him now, violating the old man's most private space.

The past few weeks had brought him to the edge of an emotional and physical collapse. But he knew if he could hold it together for a while longer that all his problems would not only be solved, but he would be wealthy and powerful beyond his wildest dreams.

He took that moment to bear down. He thought of what his uncle Buck used to tell him. "Boy, after a good shit, you feel like a king. When you stand up and buckle your pants, it's like you are a size smaller." He did not understand that at the time, but now that he found himself in his fifties and half as round at the waist as he was tall, he understood fully what Uncle Buck had meant.

As that thought went through his head, he felt movement from the depth of his bowels. He remembered his uncle Buck telling him, "Real men do not look," but he couldn't wait to admire the product of this hard effort that had given him so much joy and comfort.

He smugly thought to himself that all the hard work over the last year would reach a satisfactory conclusion in the next few weeks. *It's all coming together*, he thought as his peripheral caught a shadowy figure outside the door to the office. Startled, he yelled, "Hey!" immediately thinking, *What a stupid thing to yell.*

Bill Allgood saw movement out of the side of his eye, Instinctively he started to rise. He then saw a flash and heard the bang simultaneously. As if in slow motion, he felt a sting and saw blood trickle down his leg. Instinctively, he jumped up and ran toward the door, crashing into the shadowy figure, who had frozen with the realization that the planned course of events had changed.

For no reason, the thought ran through his head that even at that time of night, the humidity hung in the air so heavily that it was slowing him down. As he pushed past the figure and made it across the room, he heard two more bangs and felt stings on his right upper arm.

As he turned down the old pine-board hallway, he slipped. Regaining his balance, he heard two more bangs and fell forward as he felt the pain in the middle of his back. In his mind, he could see himself twisting and turning as he fell, landing. He realized he was lying on his back, naked on the hallway floor. He could feel or see (he was not sure which) darkness closing in on him in an ever-decreasing circle. He realized he was lying there exposed and embarrassed. The next to last thought he had was *I did not even get a chance to look in the bowl.* Then he thought, *I will never get out of Pear Valley* as he saw a light at the end of a long dark tunnel. The next shot was in his chest.

The shadowy figure stood over him and took a shot directly into Bill's groin. As Bill was moving slowly toward the light in the dark tunnel, he heard, "Even dying, you bastard, you mess up a great plan." Bill's open but lifeless eyes gave no indication he ever felt that one.

The blood seeped along the pristine wide-planked pinewood floor, penetrating the cracks and covering the silk area rug. Six hours after the last shot, the blood had begun to solidify around the victim, who had grown cold and stiff. The stench of gunpowder and decay filled the room as the morning sun rose over the pecan trees.

At sunrise on July 2, 1974, Jerry Roberts, foreman for the Allgood ranch, stepped out of his office trailer holding a green coffee mug in his right hand. Despite the thick, hot air, Jerry savored his first steaming cup of revitalization. And as the sun rose over the pecan trees to the east, Jerry's worn work boots crunched the gravel beneath him, marking the beginning of his daily farm survey. With his plaid shirt, bone dry minutes before, now moist, clinging to his thin frame, he wiped the sweat from his brow with the red handkerchief he carried in his back pocket and repeated to himself, *It pays the bills. It pays the bills.*

The Allgood farm or plantation, depending on where you came from in the country, was a majestic place. There were pecan trees standing by the hundreds along the eastern end of the vast property. The immense fields where the hay was grown for the livestock had been planted toward the southern end. To the north, grazing land stretched as far as the eye could see. In the center, several white barns with signature red roofs housed livestock and personnel. And to the west, a gravel drive connected the farm buildings to the owner's traditional southern home, complete with a large wraparound porch.

Twenty years prior, a young, naive Jerry Roberts had boarded a ship from Ireland to the US with his buddy Tim for a fresh start after his parents passed away. The two had hitchhiked south to the Carolinas, where they worked in the tobacco fields. But the work had dried up by the end of their first year. Tim fell in love, left with a college girl, and moved to Florida. Jerry took a train south to Georgia, where he heard some farms needed workers.

After hitchhiking for two days, Jerry landed at the Allgood plantation. Wade Allgood, a widower, was trying to run the operation with his no-good twenty-five-year-old son. It wasn't working. So Wade hired the nineteen-year-old orphan and gave him a shot. Seeing his work ethic, Wade took a liking to Roberts and started grooming him to take over as foreman. Allgood's son Billy would sarcastically tell Jerry, "You're just another one of my father's pet projects." Thankfully, Billy didn't spend much time on the farm, and he let everyone know his disdain for farm work. He had his sights on far more lucrative endeavors.

By the time Wade Allgood passed away, Jerry had been his foreman for over fifteen years. Unfortunately, Wade left all his assets to his miserable son. Billy, who demanded to be called Bill after his father's death, was all too happy to allow Jerry to keep doing the day-to-day running of the farm. Yes, as Bill happily piled it on with Jerry's workload, he simultaneously cut his pay. "Jerry, my father spent far too much to run this place. You understand we need to cut things so it will continue to run and give you a job, right, buddy?"

Jerry fumed and plotted his exit to leave Georgia for good until his wife came home later that week with a death sentence diagnosis. With medical bills mounting, Jerry swallowed the bitter pill Bill Allgood administered. But he would discover that was just the first of many doses to come.

Bill routinely drained the farm's operating funds, making it harder for Jerry to maintain the farm in the way Wade wanted. Just making payroll some weeks was a struggle. And the more responsibility Allgood piled on his foreman, the less he wanted to pay for it. Then seemingly overnight, Bill had a change of heart and offered to cut Jerry in on a business opportunity, or so he said. But by no means was this anything other than self-serving. The added cash in Jerry's pocket only imprisoned him more under his ruthless boss. The Charlie Daniels song "The Devil Went Down to Georgia" haunted Jerry, as he had sold his soul for the love of his life.

And so, on that sweltering but fateful summer morning, Jerry went to work like always, coffee in hand on his rounds. His first stop was the horse barn. He opened the barn access door and found Colin, a new hand, washing down the stall of a mare they had lost the day before. No one knew how the horse had died, but Jerry expected the vet's report later that week. Colin had found the whitish mare with beige undertones, named Blue, already stiff and covered with gnats when he'd gone to saddle him up for his owner's morning ride.

The equine beauty belonged to the even more gorgeous Sandra Allgood, a gift from her philandering husband Bill on their wedding day. Sandra rode Blue at the same time each morning, sometimes not returning to the barn for hours. Most workers assumed riding gave her an escape from an unjust, unstable man. Her love for that horse was evident to all, and her reaction to his death had been gut-wrenching for Jerry and all that witnessed it.

Sandra had told Jerry, "I know he poisoned Blue!" Jerry had hustled a crying Sandra into his office to avoid others overhearing her words. Once inside, she looked at Jerry. "I'll get my revenge!"

Jerry shook his head, clearing his thoughts as he watched Colin continue to clean without acknowledging him. "Colin, when you're done here, come find me. I have a few projects we need to get started on."

"Yes, sir," Colin answered without looking up. No one who worked at the Allgood farm had a particularly happy existence on any given day. Emotions trickled from the top. Bill Allgood oozed dissension and indifference. And despite Jerry being congenial, most workers still feared him. There was a false perception among the hands that Jerry had a close relationship with the boss. Jerry was smart enough to use that falsehood to his advantage.

Jerry continued through the barn to find several other workers feeding the livestock. And as he rounded the corner, two others were cleaning the equipment to mow a few of the vacant fields and bail the hay. He gave them a nod, then rounded another corner to look up toward the main house where Bill Allgood would typically emerge and stroll down the gravel drive to meet Jerry midway for their daily conference. "A pretense of interest," Jerry said when he explained the demanded daily meetup to his wife.

On July 2, 1974, Bill Allgood never made it to their meeting.

Jerry poured the remainder of his coffee out after a mosquito landed in it. "Just my luck," he muttered to himself. After wiping his brow for the hundredth time, he checked his watch. Still no Bill. "Maybe that luck is changing," he joked to himself as he looked around. Then as if on cue, a high-pitched scream flew out an open window of the main house, a scream that would ultimately wake the entire Pear Valley from its slumber.

TWO
The Suttons

July 2, 1974

D riven to the brink by the backwardness of south Georgia and the psychological cloud the humidity and gnats visited on one's soul, Ruby hit him with a teary-eyed "Mommy called this morning; she doesn't understand why we aren't coming home for the Fourth," Ruby stated as Jack joined her on the front porch for his morning coffee while struggling to put on his shoes and fix his tie.

Jack and Ruby agreed to stay in Pear Valley for the upcoming holiday despite some sadness over foregoing the Fourth of July events back home in Atlanta. Ruby's family tradition included the Lanier Yacht Club for fireworks on July 3 and Stone Mountain or Lenox Mall for their fireworks on the Fourth, which were spectacular. But after just moving to their new home, Jack wasn't eager to return to the Buckhead elite anytime soon. They needed to assimilate to their new life, and he could sense his new bride struggled with a case of homesickness. And of course, her mother, Melanie's, pleas for Ruby to come home weekly weren't helping the matter.

"Ruby, we need to show our faces here in town. If I'm going to grow my caseload, I have to get to know the community more,"

Jack answered before grabbing a piece of coffee cake Ruby had laid out for them that she bought at the local Piggly Wiggly.

"I get it, but I don't like it. This heat and these infernal gnats are driving me crazy, and this infernal little town and people are like they are still living in the 1950s."

"We've only been here a month! Give it time," Jack said as he grabbed his cup for a final sip before kissing his bride. "I love you, but your husband has to go to work."

Ruby gave him a smirk and then opened her mouth to say something sarcastic when the sound of sirens wailed and two police cruisers flew by. Jack headed down the front stairs but then turned around. "Doesn't seem to be boring this morning!"

Ruby grabbed her coffee cup and picked up the paper before she sputtered, "Probably a cat stuck in a tree!"

—⁓—

In a wedding Ruby's family hoped would never happen, Jack and Ruby Sutton were married in the First Baptist Church of Atlanta on April 21, 1974, on Ruby's beloved maternal grandmother's birthday. The weather, a perfect seventy-five, with clear blue skies, wrapped the bride and groom in good fortune. Jack's mother joked that Ruby's parents had ordered the ideal climate for their one and only child's wedding, saying in a mockingly high tone, "Anything less would have been unacceptable for our Southern belle."

Jack chuckled and then gave his mom a stern "Mother." Directing her to keep her thoughts on Ruby's family to herself. Jack knew his mother had come to love Ruby as a daughter, so he let the indignation toward his future in-laws slide most of the time. Truthfully, he couldn't blame her for having the same reaction as he did to the Cartwrights. Especially since Mrs. Cartwright made the obvious gesture of scrunching her nose like she smelled something foul in their presence. Mr. Cartwright remained removed mostly, except when giving Jack his one directive in regard to Ruby. "If baby doll wants it, baby doll gets it," certainly a perverted parental view of being supportive.

The wedding had been the season's social event for the Atlanta Buckhead/Morningside/Peachtree Battle community. Held at the swanky Piedmont Driving Club's ballroom, the reception hosted over three hundred close friends and family—mainly from Ruby's side. Ruby had arrived at the reception in her Cinderella-inspired ceremonial gown for pictures with Jack as well as the ritualistic greeting of their guests during the cocktail hour before changing into the body-hugging, slip-style, milky-white silk reception gown. The second dress had been flown in from France by a designer retained by Ruby's mother. Jack beamed with pride for his beautiful bride as she wowed everyone with her beauty and grace.

Jack's mother had come up to him at the night's end and whispered, "I'm so happy you two found one another; she is a lovely girl." But she couldn't help but add, "Despite her parents."

Jack's father nodded in agreement and shook his son's hand, holding his grip and pulling him in for a hug. Not known for being demonstrative with his affection, Jack relished the moment with his dad before gathering his new bride and heading off to start their lives together.

The lovebirds had met when Jack was a student at the University of Georgia and Ruby attended Wesleyan, an all-girls college in Macon. Ruby studied journalism and won the Georgia Press statewide award for college journalists based on her war and civil rights protest articles. The awards dinner was on the Athens campus, and they had met at one of the receptions.

After they graduated from their respective schools, Jack went to law school at Emory University and Ruby worked at the *Atlanta Journal-Constitution*. Initially, she was covering the society section but had hopes of hard news. Due to his ROTC commitments in Georgia, Jack had to serve six months at Fort Benning in the army upon graduation. But the distance only made the reuniting sweet for the two until the question of where Jack would practice law came up.

Ruby's father had wanted Jack to come work at his law firm. "Son, once you finish your ROTC commitments, I have a corner office with your name on it. And a paycheck to help you take care of my baby doll!" Stone Addison Cartwright III was a robust man with an equally sized voice and wallet. He didn't hide his feelings any more than his wife, Melanie, did. He was just more vocal and forthright. Weirdly, Jack respected him for it.

Ruby had all but begged Jack to take her daddy up on it as staying in Atlanta was *her* goal. Her friends, family, and career were there. Jack couldn't blame her. But still, Jack refused Stone's offer repeatedly, "I appreciate that, sir, but I don't want a job that's handed to me." Ruby's father said he respected Jack's decision, but her mother spat out a puff of air followed by an exaggerated eye roll and a dramatic head turn.

While in the ROTC at Fort Benning to fulfill his reservist commitment after law school, Jack served as a tank commander. However, the most action he saw was when he drove the tank under a tree in an artillery course and dislodged a hornet's nest that fell into the open hatch of the tank. In that crisis, he gave the "De-ass the tank" order to save his men. It became a legend in that division of the reserves as the best order a college boy and first lieutenant had ever given. This event was the most action Jack ever saw during his time in the service.

Once finished with his military obligation, Jack returned to Atlanta to search for a job. One evening, he went with Ruby to the Daughters of the Confederacy Ball she was covering for the paper. And while Ruby trailed the hoop skirts for interviews and photos, Jack milled about. That's when Jack met the state senator from Callaghan County and the president pro tem of the Georgia State Senate. Mr. Truitt was also an esteemed attorney. Once the legislature session finished in April of each year—with the traditional shouting of "Sine die!" to close the legislative session—Mr. Truitt would return to Pear Valley, where he maintained his law practice and other businesses. While in Atlanta, it had been widely known that the senator attended many social events, especially when fine food, strong bourbon, good-looking women, and an opportunity to flex his political clout were present.

After the chance to meet with Mr. Truitt, who had a tremendous reputation as a trial lawyer and political orator, Jack found himself out of options in Atlanta. Although Mr. Truitt had not suggested Jack contact him, Jack reached out when his prospects all dried up. Senator Truitt was exceptionally well-placed and well-respected in the capital. Given a chance, spending time with him in the southern part of the state would be a great place for Jack to start his career and gain experience. Despite fearing Ruby's unhappiness, Jack convinced himself he would eventually sell the opportunity to Ruby if the offer letter came. He practiced his sales pitch in his head. *Whether I practice there for the long haul or come back to Atlanta, I think Pear Valley will give me the opportunity to learn to be a skilled trial lawyer and be able to take care of you myself instead of relying on your family.*

Unexpectedly, at the same time, Jack received an unsolicited offer for a job at the prestigious Atlanta law firm Jones, Spalding, and Kirkpatrick. He knew instantly that the letter was due to Ruby's family connections, and Jack became heated upon reading the letter. But despite the not-so-subtle pushes from his in-laws, Jack remained steadfast in his decision to make it on his own merits.

Jack's dad, Allen, had sat down with him shortly after the offer from Truitt came through. "Son, are you sure about moving to such a rural area?"

"Dad, I love Ruby. But if we stay here, I'll be swallowed up by her family connections and expectations. I'm not saying we won't ever come back. But if we do, I'll have already established myself and my career. I want to be my own man."

Allen sat back in his easy chair and puffed on his pipe, proud of the man his son had become. "I understand. You have our blessing." Taking another puff and exhaling the blackberry-flavored tobacco, Allen asked, "None of my business, son, but are you sure Ruby and her family will go along with this move?"

Jack dropped his head and said, "Ruby's not happy about it, but she'll go. The Cartwrights are another story." He mused as he shook his head and dreaded the price he would pay.

The problem for Jack had been that he already had a few strikes against him. Primarily because Jack's family was not among the Atlanta social elite. Though they had developed a proper position based on hard work, they still didn't hold the prestige Ruby's parents had hoped for.

Jack's father had been a great athlete in his youth and received a football and track scholarship at Georgia Tech, where he studied engineering. However, he gave it up to marry Jack's mother, Mary. WWII had just ended when Allen met Jack's mother, Karen, a secretary, through introductions from a family member in Apple Valley, Georgia. Jack's dad couldn't let her escape so they eloped and had Jack a year later.

Unfortunately for Allen Sutton, Georgia Tech revoked his scholarship when they discovered he had wed. His dad worked his way through the rest of college in the co-op program because the Sutton family didn't have the money to help him. Jack's granddaddy was a machinist with the Southern Railway, and every penny he made went to food and shelter.

Jack was born in his father's senior year of college, and the young family lived in Atlanta, next to Perkinson Park. Eventually, they moved to East Point, a white middle-class neighborhood. His idyllic, working-class childhood filled with the love of God and country mirrored nothing in Ruby's white-glove and champagne upbringing. Ruby was a child of the Atlanta social aristocracy, a Buckhead debutante with family ties to Cox Enterprises and Coca-Cola, the elite of Atlanta.

So when Jack accepted Truitt's offer and then told Ruby, the couple experienced their first rough patch. Ruby folded her arms and glared at Jack. "You can't be serious?"

"Babe, I told you I wouldn't work for your father or one of his cronies."

Ruby paced next to the Olympic-sized pool in the backyard of her childhood home, adorned by perfectly manicured plantings. The sculpted hemlocks outlined the swimming area like an English garden and were accented by Ruby's parents' favorite flower, Cherokee roses, also known as the state flower of Georgia. But despite the picturesque setting, the mood threatened a deep frost that would kill the blooms for sure. Ruby stopped and folded her arms. "No, you didn't, but I never thought that meant moving to some small town in the middle of nowhere!" Before Jack could respond, she continued. "We won't be able to see shows anymore at the Fox Theatre or attend the social events at the Piedmont Driving Club. Our friends will forget all about us!"

"Then they aren't our friends," Jack came back at her.

Ruby ignored his remark and continued. "Or sailing at the Lanier Yacht Club on Lake Sydney Lanier. And what about the family we talked about having? You don't want to raise kids there, do you? So far away?" She slammed her arms against herself for emphasis.

Jack moved in closer and placed his hands on her arms, pulling her into him as his eyes met hers. "Nothing has changed. I love you, and I want a family with you just as we've planned. But I'm asking you to give me time to prove myself as a lawyer on my own. I promise we will come back here, babies in tow if we're blessed."

With a full-on pout, Ruby's eyes cast downward, and like a good Southern woman, she picked her head up just as quickly to stand by her man despite her disappointment. "OK."

Shortly thereafter, Ruby and Jack broke the news to her parents. Her daddy started to object, but she said firmly, "Daddy, I want this for us." Stone melted and reminded himself, "If Gal baby wants it, Gal baby needs it." And deep down, he was impressed with Jack's tenacity and desire to make his own success, and he felt a fatherly sense of pride. But he would never admit that to his devastated wife.

So to employ some compromise for Ruby's sake, Ruby's grandmother stepped in and bought them a house in Pear Valley as a wedding present, as she called it. Grandma hadn't told them until the day of their wedding, but as Jack went to open his mouth, she cut him off. "My only granddaughter will not live in a home beneath her standing!" Jack knew better than to cross her, and he relented, opting for familial peace.

Jack had reconciled that his concession on this one issue would help him get his way on the ones that mattered. But also, it would save money since Mr. Truitt had not proposed a handsome salary at the start, saying, "Once you prove yourself, son, we will see about more money."

The home Grandmother Cartwright gave them was located at 418 Georgia Avenue, Pear Valley, near the Robert E. Lee Park entrance just four blocks off the town square. While it was a 1930s-era house, Grandma had it spruced up, including all the furnishings, and even added central heat and air-conditioning, which was rare in 1974.

So six weeks after their announcement, Jack and Ruby packed their belongings and made the move south. The move hadn't been too bad since Ruby and her mother had already made several trips during those six weeks to prepare the home as much as possible. Jack had taken it as Melanie's way of making sure she had her input on things, even though she constantly complained about the move. But all in all, Jack had begun to learn how to pick his battles with the in-laws; he was nothing if not a fast learner.

THREE
Pear Valley

July 2, 1974

B rad Lavender sometimes shook his head as he looked in the mirror to shave. *What am I doing in southwest Georgia, the land of gnats and humidity, in a Podunk town called Pear Valley, working as a reporter?* he thought as he lathered up. Most folks who knew he had been a big-time reporter in Miami at the *Floridian* wondered the same thing. Brad had been in Pear Valley for over a year now. He got the head nods and "How's ur mama and them?" type clichés, but he was still a stranger, someone to be watched and not trusted. Even though Brad was originally from Birmingham, blond, and fair-skinned, the locals gossiped that he must have some Cuban blood in him.

In Miami, Brad had been somebody. He had won national fame when he broke the story of how Walt Disney bought up the land in a small town, Kissimmee, Florida, with the plan of building a kingdom there. The Disney people went to great lengths to make sure local politicians, real estate brokers, and vendors did not disclose a word of it. But Brad's dogged pursuit of the truth and his well-formed contacts in the area brought the story to light.

When the story broke, his editor got a call from the chairman of the *Floridan's* parent company, Blackwater News, threatening both their jobs. Fortunately, the story went national, and in the multimedia, the spotlight on Brad and his editor dissipated.

That success was more than five years in the rearview mirror. Now he was in this typical small Southern town boasting magnolias, camellias, pecan trees, odd accents, chewing tobacco, pigs, and small farms. The town elders incorporated and founded the town in December 1776; as soon as word about the signing of the Declaration of Independence made its way to southwest Georgia, the town acted on it.

Being in Pear Valley proved torturous enough, but having left so much behind in Miami made it worse, despite leaving for self-preservation purposes. Today's "hot" assignment, according to his editor, involved interviewing the head of the local museum on the town's history. While the national and town bicentennial celebrations were two long years away, the town leaders were primed to get started on planning and getting the word out.

Brad shook his head and winced as he cut himself with his razor. "Damn it!" he sputtered, dabbing his cut with toilet paper. Minutes later, Brad stepped out of his house, got in his Dodge pickup, and checked his mirror to confirm the bleeding had stopped. He put the keys in the ignition and started Ole Red up. As the truck spit and rumbled to life, Brad did a slight prayer the truck would make it through the year. He had originally bought the old truck as a way to blend, fearing his two-door Volvo would incite more negative press among the locals.

The dealership gave him a fair trade-in on the Volvo as the salesman assured him that in small towns, you were a Chevy, Ford, or Dodge guy when it came to pickup trucks. "Boy, this truck has been used but loved, and it will prevent you from doin' battle with them boys at the gas station. You understand what I'm sayin'?" Brad, having grown up in Birmingham, knew what he meant and gave him a polite nod. The venom that existed between the camps was the same as that existed between the Alabama and Auburn fans or the often spirited arguments between the Baptists and Methodists. The Baptists focused on "Once saved, always saved." But according to the Methodists, to be saved meant you were only good until you "backslid" and lost your faith. Both arguments had been known to split friendships and homes.

As he drove down the street, he had his window down and his left elbow resting on it, with his right wrist hanging over the top of the steering wheel. He had learned this is how you drive in South Georgia, so when you see a friend, acquaintance, or enemy, you will throw your right hand up with two fingers extended. Definitely a must in the local tribal greeting. If you did not give the gesture to someone, they started to wonder what you had against them and plot against you. If you threw up one finger, you probably would get shot.

The local country music station, WPVC, played on the truck's radio. They were playing "Kawliga," which was heading to number one on the country charts. Brad nodded his head along with the music and wondered if the local station, like most stations around the country, knew the singer was the reverse of Elvis—a black man who could sing like a white man. Brad had met the singer, Charlie Pride, in a show in Miami two years before. He was a great guy who understood the irony of it all but wanted to make great music. And he did.

Brad drove past the office of local state senator and lawyer Frank Truitt. Truitt had been one of the first local leaders he had interviewed when he got to town. Quite a story of a local boy who did good. As he drove by, he saw Truitt getting out of his 1974 Cadillac Fleetwood Brougham, a statement of success and stability for the senator. Brad threw up his hand as a greeting when he went by. The senator acknowledged him by touching the brim of his gray Stetson Rancher and nodding to him.

Brad continued to drive into the heart of the town, where there was a square full of lush green grass, crisscrossing cement sidewalks, and a Federal-style brick city hall where the police, courts, and municipal offices resided. Brad's destination stood across the street from the courthouse that was the center of the square. The history museum where he parked had been founded in the late 1800s and, in keeping with the grandeur of the time, was named Pear Valley, Callahan County Historical Repository.

When Brad entered, a little bell chimed above the doorway to announce his presence. No one came to greet him so Brad perused the list of the town veterans with a recounting of their bravery. A separate, distinct plaque served to enhance the reputation of the current locals, with direct lineage being outlined.

The museum, which prided itself on listing the bravest among them, however, did leave out one soldier, a private named Ethan Conger. Conger's service, to be honest, wasn't all that glorious. In his first battle against the British, he became confused, pointed his rifle the wrong way, and shot his commanding officer in the buttocks. The commander was so enraged that he swore to have Conger court-martialed and executed. So the private, figuring discretion and retreat were the better part of valor, deserted and headed for Florida, where he was eaten by an alligator in the Okefenokee Swamp, as the story was told.

Out from a door in the back of the room, a short, round man hustled toward Brad with his hand extended. "Mornin'. You must be Mr. Lavender. I'm Anthony Keel."

Brad reached out to shake his hand and said, "Good morning. Please call me Brad. I appreciate you letting me interview you and learn more about the town."

"No, Mr. Lavender, we appreciate you wanting to write our story. With the bicentennial of our great country and Pear Valley coming up, it's very timely and will help people remember the past." Keel started to walk down the hallway, his hands clasped behind his back like he was instructing a class as he continued. "With all the hippies, free love, Woodstock, and the like, the world has gone crazy. I think it started when the Beatles flew over here with their long hair and took the country by storm. That was the day the music really died." Catching himself, Keel said, "I am sorry. I digress. I was just reading in the Atlanta paper where there was more protest over the Vietnam War and I'm still a little worked up. Please forgive me."

Waving it off, Brad said, "No worries. I know how you feel." Brad smiled, then added, "But please, call me Brad."

Keel nodded in agreement, then waved Brad toward a chair opposite his desk.

"We want to run a nice piece in the July 4, 1974, edition, and featuring the museum is a key part of what we want to do. Thanks to the workings of Mrs. Fanny May Smith and her committee, the paper is planning to do a series each month over the next two years leading to the big day. I've already gotten some information from her for the article but thought you and the museum would round out the piece."

"Well, thank you, Mr.—sorry, Brad. Where should we begin?"

Brad took out his small notepad and started. "One of the puzzling aspects of the town is the name. There does not seem to be many pears, and certainly not a valley. I heard several different versions from Chamber of Commerce President Horace Brumlow."

Keel chuckled. "Good question. The county is primarily flat land with remnants of southern wiregrass and free of pears. Horace is probably not a fan of the real reason and wants to give a good impression. He tells several stories and invents new ones freely and often." Looking up, Mr. Keel said with a smile, "Now don't quote me on that part. Horace tells many intriguing and interesting stories with such great conviction no one would ever dispute them to his face. So I think it best you quote those stories if you use them."

Brad nodded in recognition.

Looking left and right as people will do when they are telling something of interest but don't want to be the source of it, Keel went on. "However, a few elders knew the true story. It goes something like this: When the town had been settled, a particularly well-endowed young lady had been walking down the main street past the general store where many townspeople gathered. On one of those humid Southern days, she had allowed the top buttons of her dress to loosen, revealing the glistening perspiration nestled in the valley of her bosom. The site had stirred even the most reserved men. So of course, the old perverts sitting, chewing tobacco, and playing checkers couldn't resist gawking. After a long pull of his sweaty glass of sweet tea, one of them blurted out, 'Thar shor is a valley between that pair.' And from that day on, the name, Pear Valley, spread faster than melted butter on bread."

Brad laughed out loud at the history lesson. "Well, Mr. Keel, I will work it into the story, maintaining the dignity of the town and of Mr. Brumlow."

"Brad, please call me Anthony."

Brad inquired into the early relationships with the Creek Indians since he had seen them featured in the displays. Mr. Tanner told Brad that when the Europeans arrived, they lived cohesively with the Creek Indians until conflicts broke out in the 1780s. In short order, thankfully, peace treaties were signed, and relative peace existed until the 1800s. During that period, the government head in charge of the relationship with the Creeks was a man named Benjamin Hawkins. Benjamin did a fine job; his efforts were noticed, and he was asked by the US president to go to Washington. In his reply, he was said to have written, "God willing, and the Creek don't rise." Benjamin's name is properly displayed in the museum next to a drawing of the stout, balding man.

As they talked about the town and its history, Mr. Keel not only educated Brad on the facts but also about some of the people along the way and presently. After a series of looking right then left, Anthony went on to tell Brad that in the second half of the twentieth century, most self-respecting Southern towns boasted of having a small percentage of eccentrics. Pear Valley exceeded that expectation.

For example, there was a banker who was an all-around nice guy, but he believed in the lost continent of Atlantis and told folks the Atlanteans—of the submerged continent of Atlantis, not the state capital Atlanta—would soon end their hibernation and start traveling to the shores of the nation. Then there was the local mechanic who did not believe that man had landed on the moon. He and his helper would debate the issue on and on, usually with a beer or two being consumed unless there was some white lightning available, which would cause the conversation to go through the night and into the next day. And of course, the wealthy widow who lived to host elaborate "Clue" parties where invited guests would figure out who killed the victim, what room, and what murder object. Winners were given small trophies by the hostess, which became treasured items in the town.

Generally, most viewed Pear Valley as a pleasant, if not slightly dull, place to reside. But life in this unassuming Southern town represented a complicated quilt where many folks favored the saying "bless your heart" to sugarcoat their rancor. Or how they would show up on your doorstep with a casserole under the pretense of being neighborly but were instead being driven by downright nosiness.

Mr. Keel had started to show Brad an exhibit on the history of the courthouses in Callahan County and surrounding areas when they both were startled to hear a police siren passing in front of the museum. Pear Valley was not a town where that was heard often.

Brad started to excuse himself, but Mr. Keel nodded and extended his hand toward the door. "Go, young man. I can take all day with history, but it looks like some might be in the making. Better to catch it in the present."

Brad, thankful for the old man's situational awareness, ran out shouting over his shoulder his thanks and promised to return. He jumped in his Dodge and backed out of the spot, quickly following in the direction of the police car. He reached over and turned on his latest acquisition, in addition to the truck: a citizen's band (CB) radio. This had become the fad since the "Convoy" trucking song hit number one on the charts, and the *Smokey and the Bandit* movie with Burt Reynolds was released earlier in the year. The song talked about "Breaker, breaker 1-9" to chat, but the CB emergency gossip channel was channel 16, and Brad turned to it as he flew down the road in pursuit of a story.

Over the CB radio, the local service station chimed in, "Yeah, they are on their way out to Bill Allgood's farm. Someone said they had found a dead body out there." Brad pushed the pedal to the metal and followed not far behind the sheriff's car.

The county historian Fanny May Smith came into the museum shortly after Brad had left, like a small hurricane bent on finding Mr. Keel. She flew through his office door as he hummed "Dock of the Bay." Looking up from the history book in his hand, Keel asked, "Yes, Fanny May, what can I do for you?"

"I am on the committee for the bicentennial, and while it is two years away, you can never start too early with preparations. 1976 will be the two hundredth anniversary of the founding of Pear Valley. When the town's fathers heard the Declaration of Independence had been signed, they thought they should incorporate the city and did so before the year ended. I want to make sure the committee is ready, and it is an event of two centuries," she said.

Keel nodded. "Yes, Fanny May, I know all that. We certainly

can't let that pass without some mention. I assisted the chamber in picking you for the committee, and I just had one of the reporters in here from the *Observer* to start a two-year series leading up to the country and Callahan County founding."

"Excellent. What reporter did you talk with?"

"Brad Lavender."

"Small world. Mr. Lavender interviewed me on it early this week. He also was working on another feature on the championship basketball team that Judge Throwbridge and Attorney Truitt played on. We went down to the high school, and I gave him a pile of old school annuals and newspapers to go through. He is a real history buff and was really interested in writing about it all," approved Fanny May. She followed her explanation with a smile and a nod, clearly proud of herself.

"We'll have a meeting of the committee in the next few weeks. We can open it to additional volunteers and see how many people we get. I think I will also ask Lady Daisy to join one of the commissions. She'd be perfect."

Fanny May's eyebrows shot up. "I'm not sure, Anthony. She's a little, a little—"

"Unique."

"That's one way of putting it."

"But she is an out-of-the-box thinker."

"That's certainly true," Fanny May said with an added rolling of the eyes.

"I'll bet she will come up with some very good ideas for the celebrations, and she always loves a challenge. She'll probably think of things that no one else will."

"I don't doubt that," Fanny May said with a frown. "She will probably suggest painting the town red, white, and blue to celebrate the red, white, and blue."

Keel slapped the desk with his hand. "Well, that's not a bad idea. It would be unique. We'd get publicity from all over the nation if we did that." He paused for a moment. "Well, maybe not the whole town. How about a street or two? That would have the same effect. We'd probably get reporters from Atlanta, Augusta, and all over the South to cover that, maybe from all over the nation. Then we can ask Brad to help us with the reporters. He probably has connections."

"We could throw that out as a suggestion," Fanny May said, although she didn't sound too enthusiastic about the idea.

Keel nodded his head.

"Maybe more, but we will be open to suggestions from all citizens, and we'll incorporate the best ideas to make it the best celebration ever. The whole year will be a time to remember. Not just a day or a month but the entire year."

"Yes, ma'am," Keel agreed.

FOUR

Something's Not Right

From the day Jack started work, Frank asked him not to refer to him as Senator Truitt. The senator indicated that he much preferred to be called Mr. Truitt in the law firm because he did not want people on the other side of his disputes to necessarily associate him with his role in politics. But in another breath, Truitt boasted that while "in office," he could take someone to the cleaners in a divorce and still get their votes because he got their road paved. Frank Truitt was a player, and he flaunted it.

The Truitt firm consisted of Frank's longtime partner, Mosely Brown, and a relatively new lawyer named David John, ten years Jack's senior. Although Jack felt welcomed by Brown, John, although more his age, maintained his distance but was cordial in his interactions.

Jack's first few weeks or so were all about getting his feet wet and learning the lay of the land. So most of what Truitt or Brown assigned the young attorney were title checks. These assignments weren't riveting or exciting work, but Jack was thankful for the start and eager to prove his worth.

And on that morning of July 2, when Jack walked into the office, Frank Truitt met him in the front hall and declared, "Son, buckle up because the honeymoon is over. You will be getting case assignments from me to handle in July. So let that pretty little wife of yours know there will be some late nights."

Excited for the opportunity, Jack gave a measured "Yes, sir," which was followed by a weird twinge in his gut.

Mosely Brown came through the door at that moment. "Morning, all. You hear what all the commotion's about? Sherriff went screaming by me as I made my way in, followed by his deputies."

Truitt pushed his hand in a downward motion as he headed back into his office. "Ah, they're just heading out for their morning doughnuts."

Moseley continued toward his office, adding, "Ah, I don't know. This one seemed like something."

Jack gripped his briefcase tightly, took a deep breath, and walked back to his office.

—◊◊◊—

Brad made his way out of Pear Valley's downtown square. He turned right on US 319 and State Highway 93 toward Sale City, about five miles outside of town; he turned left on a dirt extension that led to the Allgood Farm. The county may have had names somewhere in their records for these roads, but they were not marked with proper signage. However, the locals always referred to the dirt road as Allgood Farm Road because, well, the Allgood Farm was on it.

It had been a dry June, and the road had not had a scraper on it in a while. The hard red Georgia clay and dark sand had formed multiple ridges in the tracks where vehicles ran. Brad had memories of these from his Alabama days, and as he recalled, his mother referred to them as washboard roads. As his truck shook and bounced its way closer, he remembered why. The truck seemed to have a mind of its own as it vibrated up and down and swayed side to side so much that the truck meandered toward a ditch. Brad had to correct by countersteering down the entire road at fifty miles per hour, which given the conditions felt more like ninety miles per hour.

He approached a curve at a large oak that, according to the radio communications, would signal the Allgood place was right after it. As Brad drove midway into the curve, he slammed on the brakes, sending up a cloud of dirt and dust into the thick summer air. The road and yard ahead were littered with sheriff's cars, two ambulances, and several local municipal vehicles. One of the sheriff's cars was draped across the road, blocking traffic, but no sight of any officers.

There were a couple of cars sitting in the road ahead of Brad that looked occupied. He thought about pulling to the side of the road, but the ditches were three feet deep with a sharp, crumbling drop-off. He thought, *All I need is to be the city slicker from Miami who fell off into the ditch and had to be pulled out.*

About the time the thought flashed in his head, he saw a turnoff road right before the road blocked, and he seized the opportunity. The tertiary road led to a tobacco barn. That time of year, the tobacco was just being cropped, strung, and hung in the barns. The barns would have heaters in them, and they would be lit to dry the tobacco out. While some of the workers, mostly high school kids, worked on cropping and stringing the tobacco. Brad spotted room for him to pull up and park his pickup.

Brad grabbed his camera and notepad and jumped out of the truck.

"What's going on, mister? We heard there was somebody dead!" shouted one of the high school kids sitting under the shelter.

Over his shoulder, Brad yelled, "Not sure, but I'm about to find out!" He ran across the road, through the line of trees, and down to where the sheriff's cars were. He passed a couple of vehicles before he got to the sheriff's cars. One was a red Ford pickup that had two guys in it—no one he recognized. They were watching the cluster of folks by the house. The other was an old Ford Maverick that Laquita Roberts, the rural delivery post person, used.

Unlike the postal trucks in Miami with right-hand drive, rural mail carriers drove a regular car from the right side, usually their personal vehicle. He always wondered how they did that without causing all kinds of chaos on the roads. She was sorting mail and looked up and saw Brad. "Would you tell the deputy to move his car so I can get on down the road? Oh, and would you stick this in the Allgood mailbox when you walk by since I won't be able to get close to it?"

"Of course," Brad said with a smile as he took the mail, slightly amazed at her lack of awareness.

He walked up to the last car where Deputy Brian Haughton stood. "Laquita wanted to see if you would pull up a little so she could get by and go on with her deliveries." He had seen Haughton around town and shared a beer with him in the past.

"Hey Brad, you out here to get the story?" he asked with a grin.

Brad responded, putting the camera up with his one free hand, and took a photo. "Yep, and now I have a photo of you doing crowd control for the paper." They both chuckled. "What happened?" Brad asked.

Haughton replied, "You didn't hear it from me, but Allgood's dead. But I was told to stay out here and keep the public out, so I don't have any details."

"Can I go on in since I have your crowd control photo?" Brad asked with a knowing smirk.

"Yeah, but ask the sheriff before you take any photos," Haughton replied with a grin. He moved to pull his car up to let the cars pass on the one-lane dirt road.

As the deputy backed out and Laquita started pulling forward, Brad walked toward the mailbox to put the mail in. As he was walking, he looked down and shuffled through it. He saw a letter to Mrs. Allgood from a local dress shop, a Georgia Farm Bureau newsletter, a copy of *True Grit* magazine, and a letter from the Winthrop Aircraft Corporation, which appeared like one of those cellophane windows that could have been a bill or check. There was also a smaller invitation-looking envelope from Winthrop to Mr. and Mrs. Frank Allgood. He pretended to drop the envelopes on the grass and snapped a photo before picking them up and depositing the mail into the mailbox.

The envelopes from Winthrop interested Brad because he knew Allgood had a hand and interest in bringing that company to the county. They specialized in short take-off and landing (STOL) aircraft and were relocating to Callahan from Ohio. Brad knew they had an announcement coming up with Pear Valley Chamber of Commerce and made a note of it in his head. *You can learn a lot from people's mail*, Brad thought.

A murder in Pear Valley was unheard of, and the law's actions reflected that as they mulled around the scene like children lost in the woods. Inside the house, the sheriff hoped it would be a routine case of lethal domestic violence. *That* he knew how to handle. Pear Valley was sleepy but not immune to familial strife.

Unfortunately, the situation at the Allgood residence conformed almost perfectly to the old legal joke about someone leaving a suicide note but shooting themselves seven times with a six-shot revolver. The entire department was over their heads. Everyone in that house knew it too, including Sandra Allgood, wife of the deceased.

A young and inexperienced deputy, Tom Kronenberger, walked toward Sheriff Jones as he stood over the body. "Is she giving anything more?" the sheriff asked before tilting his head toward the living room through the open doorway in the dining room.

As the two stood next to the bloody mess, the deputy said, "Nope. Claims she heard nothing. Says she woke up and found him this way. Trying to get her to speak or form a damn sentence's impossible! Like she had hangover brain fog."

"She didn't hear shots? How's that possible?"

The deputy bent down to look closer. "And boss, why is she all covered in blood?"

"Claims she fell in it when she came down here and found him. Seems the poor bastard was shot first in the bathroom. I bagged a suicide note I found up there, but this ain't no suicide."

The deputy shot a look at his boss and then looked down at the victim. "Sheriff, he was shot in the genitals?"

"Crime of passion. The killer sent a message last night. Most of the time, it's the spouse." They both looked up toward a catatonic, number one suspect seated in the next room. Sandra Allgood sat at a perfect right angle, blood-soaked hands resting on her linen pants, hair and makeup smeared on her tear-soaked face.

"Why is she dressed like she's going out if she found him when she woke?"

"She said she woke up that way."

The deputy leaned in. "She does look shocked and upset."

The sheriff stood to relieve the pain on his arthritic knees and looked at his impressionable underling. "When you were little, Kronenberger, did you do something your momma said no to?"

"Yeah, all the time."

"And when you got caught, how did you react?"

Tom thought for a second and then shot the suspect another look. "Like her, minus the blood."

"Exactly. Now go wait outside for the coroner," the sheriff commanded as he stared at the victim.

The deceased, Bill Allgood, had been a known philanderer,

a crooked businessman, and as nasty as a rabid junkyard dog. Everyone in town gossiped about his younger, attractive wife as only interested in his money, given his lack of redeeming qualities. There were rumors that she dipped her pen in someone else's well. But Bill wasn't one to share. So that only added to the gossip and soon-to-be whodunit speculation.

The sheriff broke from his thoughts and meandered back into the living room. "Mrs. Allgood, the coroner is taking your husband. We will be done here in a short bit," the sheriff said, standing in front of his mute but potential suspect. She hadn't moved a centimeter since the cops arrived. "Is there anyone you'd like us to call?"

Jerry walked into the front room as the screen door slammed behind him. "Sheriff, I don't think she can talk right now. I think she's in shock."

"I can see that. But we need to do an investigation here. Jerry, did you ask your boys if they heard anything last night? They would've heard the shots if nothing else."

"Around here, shots at night aren't unusual. Bill shot his gun all the time. He uses the back fence for target practice. Besides, the boys were in town until midnight. Yesterday was payday."

"And you?"

"I wasn't near here either. I was home." Jerry sat next to Sandra and put an arm around her. "She needs to rest."

The sheriff scrubbed his facial hair and added, "I'll keep one of my guys posted out front. Do you want me to call anyone for you, Mrs. Allgood?"

Sandra Allgood shook her head no and then curled up on the couch in a fetal position. The sheriff looked at Jerry then moved back toward the dining room and stood at the doorway, watching the coroner pack up the body. He glanced over his shoulder to see Sandra shaking and crying as Jerry tried to console her.

The deputy leaned in. "Do we just leave her like this?"

With his hands on his hips and exaggerated breath, he said, "I want you to tell Haughton to stay on post in the driveway today and arrange relief. On the off chance she didn't do it, then we have a killer on the loose, and I don't want that on us."

The young deputy fidgeted. "You think she may be innocent?"

The sheriff became annoyed. "No. But I'm covering our asses because this is going to trial." The one thing the sheriff knew for sure was the woman shaking and crying in the living room would be tried and hung in the court of public opinion. Even in his own opinion, she looked guilty as hell, but then something seemed off. *A woman loses it, shoots her cheating, ruthless, no-good husband with a final shot to his balls, and then writes a suicide note leaving it in the bathroom. But she was too smart to think that would be plausible with him being shot so often and ending up naked in his dining room. A crime of passion gone wrong? Did she forget she wrote the note?*

"Sheriff?" The coroner came from behind, breaking his thoughts. "I found this under the body."

After his exchange with Deputy Haughton, Brad started walking closer to the house. Chief Deputy Tom Kronenberger approached him. "Morning, Brad."

"Morning, Tom. What you got?" Tom and Brad had met a few times at the courthouse, and they even shared coffee one morning. Brad made an effort to be seen and mix with the local authorities. He had found out that Tom was an Alabama football fan like himself, a rarity in southwest Georgia where you were either a Bulldog or a Seminole. So he used that tidbit to his advantage whenever he could.

"Is this on or off the record?"

Brad smirked. "That depends on what ya got."

Tom laughed. "Well, then, Allgood's dead. But we have no specifics to share at this time. That's our on-the-record statement."

Brad pushed. "And your off-the-record statement?"

Tom took a breath and placed his hands on his hips. "Fella was shot several times, but there's a suicide note. Don't make no sense. Wife's there but acting all groggy and not really able to give us anything."

"Can I go take some photos?"

"You can get some from out here, but Sheriff Jones don't want you in the house. So stay out and be subtle. You understand?"

"Will do," Brad agreed. "Can I call you later for more details for the record?"

"Sure," Tom responded in a tone that Brad knew he would have to chase him down like a greased pig at the Fourth of July celebration.

Brad went about taking shots of the house. It was a classic old Southern farmhouse. Not the columned mansion like in *Gone with the Wind* but just a big old Southern home with a porch across the front and wrapped around one side. It was wide plank sided, painted white years ago, but now looked more like the manila paper they gave kids to use in school. The chipped paint and rotted wood spots solidified Brad's assumption that it had not been updated in a while. The shrubs and gardens, while clearly magnificent at one time, were in need of good shaping. *But is it a lack of care or lack of money?* Brad wondered as he snapped a picture.

Brad saw the sheriff coming in and out with several deputies. One of the deputies left with what appeared to be bags of evidence and drove off back toward town after having talked with Deputy Haughton, who seemed to stay behind on yard traffic duty. Two attendants came out with a stretcher that had what appeared to be a body in a body bag on it. He had seen too many body bags before, covering soldiers being brought home from Vietnam, and the sight caused him to take a breath.

As they loaded the body into the coroner's vehicle, one of the EMTs got out of the second ambulance and looked like he had retrieved some supplies. He went back inside the house. Brad wondered if someone else was injured, maybe Mrs. Allgood. He had seen her around town before and never understood what she saw in Bill Allgood unless it was the money, of course.

Brad walked closer and approached the sheriff, who was standing at the bottom of the wood steps talking to another deputy, Rodger Franklin.

As he approached, he heard the sheriff say, "Well, be sure to get a sample." At that time, Sheriff Jones saw him approaching and said, "Brad, didn't Haughton tell you not to come in here?"

"He did. I just saw the coroner leave and wanted to ask you a few questions."

"Not today, boy. Just go back to the edge of the yard before I have to escort you out."

"I will, Sheriff. Just wondered if Mrs. Allgood is OK."

"What part of getting back do you not understand, boy?"

Raising his hand defensively, Brad started baking away. "Sorry, just trying to get some information."

"You and me both," Jones said under his breath.

Brad went back to the edge of the property and kept taking photos until everyone finished up. Haughton came over. "Sorry, Brad, but the boss is not too happy you're still here. You need to leave."

Brad went back to his car, noticing the Ford pickup he had seen earlier pulling away. The force of habit made him look at the tag. All he could get was the first two numbers: 25 with a dash, then some letters he missed. Each Georgia county was given a number for its tags as the first two letters on each license plate. He knew from a past story about a dog fighting ring that 25 was for Cook County. *Peculiar*, he thought as he got back to the car. By that point, the farmhand in charge of the tobacco crew was yelling at his men to get back to work. Brad got in his Dodge and headed back to town.

FIVE

Independence Day 1974

On July 2, Diego drove from Waco to Jacksonville, the city of bridges, where he received a tip that one of his dealers had been cutting their product into a third more. And from that cut, the dealer sold the lesser product through the system, keeping the extra for himself and his pockets. As Diego neared his destination, he could smell the blood of this snake about to be spilled, and he smiled with excitement.

Diego had been in the cartel since he was five years old; they were family. He had been abandoned at the US border by his father with nothing but clothes on his back and a note around his chest asking for the child to be smuggled across the border. Only the cartel found him and quickly saw him as useful. Diego had a fierceness about him, even at a young age. He reeked of potential.

Owned by the system, he had been brought up to be loyal and true to the only family he would ever know. Luis, his older cousin, a member of the cartel, had always acted as Diego's protector from the beginning. But Diego's ruthlessness progressed with his age, and it moved him up in leadership fast. As he advanced past his cousin, Diego requested Luis to be his guard. Luis accepted, not that he had a choice, but he knew Diego would do anything for him, and he would do anything for Diego; their family loyalty went deeper than bloodlines.

Tasked with fixing this problem in Florida, Luis sat next to Diego as they entered Jacksonville. "When we're done here, what next?"

Diego cracked his neck and opened his window. "We head to that shit town in Georgia to deal with some more disloyal fuckups."

Knowing the dealer's location, Diego only had to give Luis the sign and then slow down enough for Luis to grab the man off the street. Luis's strength and speed were an impressive combination as the man had barely realized what was happening before Luis had him hog-tied and weeping in the back of the van. Once they arrived in Brunswick, Georgia, they turned off I-95 and proceeded on Highway 82 West through Waycross and on toward Homerville, where Diego's sister lived and ran a restaurant. But before they entered Homerville, the men turned onto a gravel road, barely seen through the thick trees and overgrown brush, that eventually led them into the middle of the Okefenokee Swamp.

Diego, a man of few words, nodded to his cousin.

Luis jumped out of the van, dragging the dealer behind him as he whimpered and cried. The lack of machismo in facing death by these gringos disgusted Diego, who by then had exited the vehicle and waited for Luis to pull the loser into a standing position. Diego closed the distance between him and the piece of shit who had taken from the family. Diego lifted his pointed cowboy boots and kicked the guy in the balls, making the dealer fall to his knees while letting out a muffled scream from behind the tape. Diego leaned over him and ripped the tape off in one fast motion, taking layers of skin with it.

"Ahhhh! Please don't hurt me!" the dealer screamed as his lips bled profusely down the front of his shirt.

"You have the cajónes to fuck with us, then show them now. Stop being such a pussy, you fucker!"

The dealer screamed and cried like a petulant child as Luis took the machete and hovered it against his neck, and then dragged it down to his genies. "You want to lose your head or your balls first?" With the dirtbag whaling, Diego gave the nod.

The deed was done. Silence.

Luis kicked the body parts into the swamp as the gators moved in from all sides.

Diego looked at Luis, who stood watching the feeding frenzy. "Luis, vamonos. I'm starving."

Luis smiled and said, "Stuffed tamales? Your sister makes the best-stuffed tamales."

"Whatever you want. Tomorrow is, after all, what these gringos call Independence Day. So we celebrate freeing ourselves from these lying pieces of shit!"

—✺—

Ruby liked it when the Fourth fell on a Thursday; it tended to make the celebration extend into Friday because, with just one day until the weekend, people generally slacked off. It led to life just being a little more relaxed.

Jack, enjoying his day off, sat on the front porch watching the neighbors walk by. He gave a friendly wave to some as Ruby came out with their morning coffees, the screen door slamming behind her.

"Are you looking forward to getting out and meeting all the townspeople today?"

Jack sat with the *Pear Valley Observer* on his lap as he took the coffee from his young wife. "I guess."

"What are you reading about?"

"The Allgood murder."

"Any new developments."

"Nope."

"I heard he was an SOB."

"Me too."

"So that means the list of suspects could be long?"

Before drinking his coffee, Jack looked at his wife with a quick side-eye and a smirk. She was ready to gossip through their morning routine, and he knew he had stepped right into it. Ruby's attention had been piqued by this murder, and her journalist side emerged. Jack was thrilled to see it since it took her thoughts away from missing Atlanta. So he thought he would sprinkle a little water on it to help it grow. "This writer is pretty good." Jack tapped the paper in his hand, pointing to the headline about Allgood. "I heard through someone at the diner in town that he had worked for a big paper in Miami."

"Why would he come here?" Ruby asked sarcastically while unknowingly taking Jack's bait.

"That might be the more interesting story to follow up on," Jack said, dropping the paper to shoot his wife a coy smile. She returned an eye roll before drinking her coffee.

Placing her cloth napkin on her lap, Ruby changed the subject back. "So tell me what you heard about Mr. Allgood. I overheard a few ladies at the Piggly Wiggle talking, and it seems almost everyone in town thinks he was shot by his wife and deserved it."

"Yes, it's all Mosely talked about yesterday. Unfortunately, we have to go to the funeral for that this coming Saturday."

Ruby stopped before sipping her coffee. "We didn't even know him!"

"Ruby, I'm trying to make a name for myself. People need to be able to place a face with a name," Jack said, snapping the paper for effect.

Ruby continued ignoring her husband's irritation. "What did Mosely say about the man's death?"

"Not much, just speculation at this point. Not exactly a high-crime area, and there was supposedly a suicide note." Jack dropped the paper to his lap and looked over at Ruby. "Which is odd because the man was shot multiple times. Not typical of suicide unless the guy's incredibly stupid," he offered with a smile before drawing the paper back in front of him.

"But the wife," Ruby said as she made air quotes, "found him. And she was home all night. I would think if someone shot you many times, I would hear it."

"Well, he either committed suicide or was murdered by his wife, if you believe the local gossip. And I can almost guarantee most of what gets talked about at the Fourth of July celebrations will revolve around the great whodunit mystery." Jack laughed before closing the paper, accepting the futility of trying to read when Ruby wanted to talk. "And you thought it would be boring here."

Ruby cocked her head to one side. "You realize one woman killing her husband—"

"Ah, *allegedly*," Jack pointed his fork toward Ruby.

"Even worse, one alleged spousal murder doesn't make this sleepy town exciting!"

"Well, it could, at least temporarily. Do you remember that banker guy? You know how he talked our ear off when we opened those accounts? He went on and on about Atlantis. Well, what if his theory on zombies is right? And maybe it's not the wife or the suicide. It could be the walking dead, like he said, or aliens. Then it'll get interesting."

Ruby laughed at her husband's attempt to lighten the conversation and get away from how much she missed Atlanta. "The man is a nut. I'm pretty sure he spent the sixties smoking pot in the back of a VW van!"

As Ruby got up and headed inside, Jack called after her, "It's always the ones you least expect."

—◦◦—

Sandra Allgood's head pounded like a Clydesdale trotting on cobblestone. She hadn't yet recovered from the last few days mired in the death of her husband and her love, Blue. And as she rolled over in the most uncomfortable guest bed, she stared down the hallway where Bill had taken some of his last steps. The smell of cleaning fluid hung in the thick summer air, a constant reminder of the scene she had woken to two mornings prior.

Her phone rang, making her jump. Grasping her chest, she rolled over and answered before the maid got to it. "Hello?"

"How are you?" Sandra's lifelong friend, Robin Dyer, asked.

"I don't know how I am. I hate being here but don't know where to go."

"Come with me to the Fourth festivities today. You need to get out of that house."

"Are you kidding? The town gossipers will pick me apart. I don't feel like having everyone staring and judging me."

"Honey, how is that any different from before, honestly? Just think to yourself, *Bless their Hearts*. It's the Southern way."

Sandra replied, "I guess," and slowly rose to a seated position on the bed. "I miss Blue. If he were here, I could escape," Sandra started to weep into the receiver.

"Do you remember when we were kids how when my parents would fight you made me walk all the way into town to get my mind off it?"

"Yes."

"Well, let me do the same for you. You've lost a lot in one week. Please, it will make me feel better too. Like I did something good."

Sandra wiped her tears. "You always did the right thing. It's why you never ended up like me." Silence lingered over the lines and spoke volumes of a shared history before Sandra whispered, "I love you, but I'm not ready to go out."

"Well, then I'll just come over, and we'll watch *1 Adam 12* and *The Waltons* like we used to do."

"OK." Sandra placed the receiver back on the hook, but the slightest movement proved difficult. She laid her head back down on her feather pillow. Closing her eyes, she relived her happier times.

In her younger, more carefree days, Sandra's friends always called her Sandy because she was light and airy like a grain of sand. Probably because Sandra had no care in the world back then except for finding enough work to pay the rent. She and her best friend, Robin, had dreamed of a life beyond their meager upbringing and equally low-rent district residency. And as the two waited tables and did other odd jobs, they plotted to find men to pull them out of poverty and into luxury. They daydreamed about how they would travel the world together, shop, and dine without care. But those dreams assumed happiness would follow, like water from a faucet. But reality proved different.

The tall, shapely, raven-haired beauty had met Mr. William J. Allgood at a function she and Robin worked at. They had gone to the state's capital to work for Senator Truitt's campaign fund-raiser in hopes of finding Mr. Right. And before the dinner service started, Sandra had her eyes set on one man.

"Robin, did you see the guy that just walked in?" Sandra asked, nodding in the direction of the entrance.

Robin, determined to earn her wages, kept passing out appetizers. Then finally she whispered, "He looks old," before dawning a broad smile on the wealthy elderly couple interested in her crab puffs.

Robin and Sandra headed to the kitchen to refill their trays as the couple moved on. "Robin, the older ones are better. They're established and aren't just looking for one thing."

Robin put her tray down. "OK, so go and take your tray by him, and I guarantee once you get a closer look, you won't even be able to think about kissing him. I've got my eye on a few young attorneys working the room."

Pushing up her underwire bra to try to enhance what she had in that category, she said, "OK, you're on. Let's see who ends up the lucky one tonight."

By the time the attendees cleared out and the servers were clearing tables, Robin and Sandra hadn't gotten within feet of their intended targets. "Did you get close?" Robin asked.

"Nope, and to be honest, my feet are killing me right now. I'm ready to go home," Sandra said, sitting on an empty chair as the busboys broke down the tables.

"What about that guy right there? Isn't he cute?" Robin asked, pointing her head at one of the young, tall, skinny bussers.

"Ooo, he's a babe but broke like us," Sandra replied with a laugh.

"Well, the cook asked me for dinner, so I'll see you at home."

"He's like seventy!"

"No, one of his trainees. You saw him, the adorable one," Robin said, heading toward the kitchen. She gave her friend a knowing wink and pushed through the swinging door.

Sandra took her shoes off and rubbed her aching feet as a deep voice from behind asked, "Can I help?"

When Sandra turned around, Mr. Right dawned a big smile. But despite what Robin said initially, the man didn't look old, weathered, or too repulsive to kiss. Instead, he looked handsome. He stood at least six feet with tanned, smooth skin and a head full of dark wavy hair. His aqua-blue eyes homed in on her, and she responded with her best Georgia peach smile.

"Not sure how you can help," Sandra teased. Even in her waitress uniform, Sandra was stunning, and she knew it. The dark-haired beauty with piercing green eyes and a body with more curves than a mountain pass could make a dead man swoon.

"I can take you to dinner and let you relax. What do you say? You have to be hungry," William J. Allgood said with a sweetness sugar couldn't deliver. He added a wink as he slid into the seat next to her, flashing a coy smile.

From that first dinner, Bill had swept Sandra off her feet. A whirlwind courtship ensued. Within a few months, the two went to Vegas and got married. Robin had gone as her maid of honor, and a college roommate of Bill's, Tony Tanner, went as his best man.

The next several months started well, but then Sandra met the real William J. Allgood. Unfortunately, he was anything but the man she thought him to be. Bill fed on her insecurities and used his abusive words and actions to help them grow. He had been especially cruel in the months leading up to his death. But she never would have expected to wake as a widow on July 2.

That morning, Sandra had rolled over in bed, fighting the pain. She felt groggy, unable to open her eyes even as the sun shone through the open Bermuda shutters of her east-facing windows. Lobbing an arm over her eyes to shield them, Sandra slowly sat upright in bed and stumbled down the short hallway inside her master suite to the bathroom. What she expected to find was her perfectly adorned white and black marble bathroom, crisp hanging white towels, and the smell of jasmine, all welcoming her to a hot shower. She didn't know how or when she fell asleep or why she was still dressed in the clothes from the day before, but she had to make it to her sanctuary. She would get herself together before the housemaid saw her.

As Sandra continued toward her bathroom, the room spun, and she leaned against a wall to her right until everything stopped moving. She didn't recall drinking more than a glass of whiskey the night before. But her body responded like she had downed several bottles. The previous night's events unfolded in her mind as she rested against the wall.

"How much did you spend on those new outfits I saw in your closet?" Bill had snipped when he first got home.

"I thought you wanted me to have something to wear on our trip to Atlanta."

Bill whipped around as he opened a bottle of whiskey. "You have enough! Take them back!"

Sandra started to turn and head out of the room as Bill grabbed her arm. She winced from the pressure. "We're having a drink, darling." His cold eyes glared at her, and she knew better than to resist as she felt the hard metal of his ring against her bare arm. When he calmed, he released her. "Get the glasses," Bill demanded, adding a slight shove for emphasis.

Sandra walked to the cabinet and retrieved the glasses. Bill then forced her to have a glass—or was it two?—of the Blanton's bourbon he had poured. The rest of her recollection was a blank.

As she snapped back to the morning after, still woozy and leaning against the wall, she noted the house had been eerily silent, but something made her head toward the stairs. She steadied herself and slowly to the top and looked over the railing before inching her way down the stairs, grasping tightly to the banister. Once down, she continued through the main hallway toward the side hall that led to the dining room. Suddenly her foot slipped out from under her on something cold, wet, and gelatinous on the hardwood floor. Her body landed with a loud thud. Lifting her blood-soaked hand to her face, Sandra let out a scream that would have won her an Oscar for a horror film.

Sandra snapped back to the present when she heard a knock at the front door and then Robin's voice. "Sandy, I'm here!"

Like most small Southern towns, the Fourth of July in Pear Valley was a big event. Everyone in the county and the surrounding area came in for the daylong festival and fireworks at night. The town was decorated in red, white, and blue ribbons, balloons, and flag buntings adorning the houses just off the square. There had even been strings of lights attached to the top of the courthouse and strung across the grounds and the road around the courthouse to the rooftops of the businesses around the square. It created a red, white, and blue tent—beyond impressive for such a small town.

The day's events were held at Robert E. Lee Memorial Park, a block away from Jack and Ruby's house. There were all kinds of food stations by the local clubs and churches. Many arts and crafts tables were around the edges selling their treats.

Ruby and Jack walked over at 10 a.m. to catch the greased pig chase. Ruby slowed her pace by the craft tables as Jack followed behind her. Emily Knight, a young student, was staffing her mother's quilting table. Emily was notoriously shy but brilliant, and Ruby made a beeline for her table. "Hi. Emily, right?" Ruby asked. The two had met recently after church, and Ruby had seen her younger self in Emily.

Emily dropped her head and nodded yes.

"These are beautiful. Did you make these?"

Emily lifted her head slightly and shook it, then in a low voice she said, "Mama did. She's over there if you want to ask her about 'em."

Ruby turned to Jack, waiting patiently behind her, shaking his head. "Thank you. I'll be back. I'd love one of these for our guest bedroom."

Emily dropped her head.

As Ruby and Jack walked toward the pig pens, swiping gnats along the way, Ruby said, "She is such a beautiful girl but incredibly shy. Reminds me of myself."

"Hardly!" Jack rolled his eyes at Ruby. "You're more the I-am-woman-hear-me-roar type."

"Honest, that was me in my teens. If I had married before college, like so many of my friends, that would still be me," Ruby commented as something else caught her eye and she took a quick turn.

Jack reached for his bride and pulled her back as she started to meander to another table with wooden figurines. "And no flub dubs right now. First, we have to catch the pig race."

"What exactly is a flub dub?"

"For a journalist, you should be more up on your history."

Ruby stopped and folded her arms. "Enlighten me."

Jack smirked. "When Mary Todd went a little budget crazy on decorating, Lincoln scolded her for purchasing what he called 'flub dubs.' See all this stuff: flub dubs." Jack gestured at the craft tables.

Ruby rolled her eyes and turned toward the squealing pigs. "Yes, and watching pigs race around in mud is much better than buying a piece of art someone put their heart and soul into."

Jack smiled at another couple who passed and took his wife's hand as they navigated the grassy and muddy terrain. The town council had an area fenced off for the kids to compete. The kids were divided into age and size groups. The object of the game required a child to catch and hold a pig. The animals went from little pigs to well-fed ones, and their sizes were matched with the separate age groups of the kids doing the chasing. The pigs had been covered with grease to make the competition more of a challenge, and the first kid in each age category who captured and held a pig won. The prize remained a mystery until the end.

All the spectators, including Jack and Ruby, stood around and watched, laughed, and cheered the younger generation on. Even Frank Truitt and Mosely Brown were there screaming for their grandkids. Jack gave them both a wave and received a head nod back. Sheriff Jones was on duty, but he remained focused on coaching his twelve-year-old son, Adam, a participant.

Ruby leaned over to Jack and whispered, "Shouldn't Sherriff Jones be more concerned with the only murder this town has seen in maybe centuries?"

"Darlin', even Sheriff Jones gets a reprieve from his duties on the Fourth. Besides, he seems oddly invested in his kid being the one to catch a pig."

Ruby and Jack laughed at the sheriff yelling instructions at his child, who seemed equally engaged in the contest. And when he finally held the squealing animal in his arms, he fell back into the mud but kept a tight grip. On cue, Sheriff Jones let out a hoot and howler for his son's triumph and then began to make the rounds shaking hands and basking in his son's glory.

The courthouse bell and the fire truck siren grabbed everyone's attention at noon. A couple of operators went to the grandstand, stood before the microphone, and waited for the crowd to quiet. They introduced the mayor and the head of the chamber of commerce, so both men could give a short speech. Then they also introduced the county beauty queens who were currently reigning.

Mr. Truitt was introduced as "the esteemed state senator," and Red Robinson as the current representative to the house. Both pontificated like true politicians until they were instructed to cut it short so the blessing could happen. The pastor then blessed the event and the food as people milled around to talk while the high school band and a couple of gospel and country soloists and groups performed a concert.

The conversation among those milling divided them up between those who thought suicide and those who speculated murder. "Did you hear she shot him in the balls?" "Are we sure she did it? She always looked depressed to me. She doesn't look like she could even handle a gun." "Oh, she did it all right; when a woman is scorned, she will do what she must." "We're all thankful she took that bastard out; he deserved it!" But no matter the side, the common theme that Bill Allgood was a no-good son of a bitch resonated among everyone, leaving many to speculate he had abused Sandra Allgood.

Jack walked over to Ruby, who had just left a group of ladies. He handed her a hot dog. "You should eat."

Ruby took the hot dog from her husband. "Thank you, dear," in a mocking tone. Ruby loved how Jack always ensured she ate, but she feigned her indifference to perpetuate the independent woman persona. The two started to walk as they watched all the activities while listening to the live music in the background. Ruby couldn't help but share the gossip she heard with Jack. "So the scuttlebutt is that William Allgood had it coming to him. Supposedly he was a mean man, not just to everyone he encountered but to his wife. Some said they thought he was abusive to her, and they don't blame her for killing him."

"Ruby, we don't know if she had anything to do with it yet. The DA hasn't filed any charges, and the sheriff hasn't even arrested her. Everyone needs to stop gossiping and let the law handle it."

Ruby stopped and chewed her bite of hot dog; Jack waited for her retort. "First off, this is the only exciting thing that's happened in this town for years. I'm sure. And second, he must have been awful for these churchgoing people to be glad the man's dead! Come on. You have to be a little curious!"

"I am. But I'm also a realist. We may never know how it really happened. Just as these people have no idea what happened inside that marriage." The two continued to walk in silence until Jack thought aloud, "Hey, do you know where the word *scuttlebutt* came from?"

"Nope. But I bet you're going to tell me," Ruby answered as she dramatically rolled her eyes at her husband.

"Come on. Where's your journalistic mind?" Jack loved to tease his wife when he knew something she didn't, but they both knew that Ruby was superior to Jack when it came to book smarts.

"My journalistic mind is on the whodunit case everyone else is speculating about. But I'm sure you'd rather tell me what that word means!"

Jack laughed at his wife's playful jab. "Scuttlebutt is from the 1800s, and it was the word for the drinking well on the ship. When sailors would stand around and drink, they would trade stories and gossip."

"See, even men gossip! Get with the program!"

The day continued with the greased flagpole climb, an ax-throwing contest, the sack and egg races, and various games. Jack watched the horseshoe tossing contest for a while. Many of the most respected old men in the community were in it. In fact, the final match included Judge Throwbridge and his clerk Don Simone against the local family doctor Furman and a local farmer who had supplied all the pigs for the greased pig contest, Jim Bob Bunch. Doc and Bunch eventually won, but Throwbridge joked he would file an appeal. Jack watched the legendary judge and was surprised to see this relaxed, fun-loving side to a man with a stern and exacting reputation. He was tempted to approach the judge but decided it was better to wait for their formal introduction, and he walked away from the event.

The evening concluded with fireworks and then an all-night gospel sing-along. Truly a great day that brought out the best in Pear Valley, even if slightly tinged with gossip. The day's events even served as an unofficial round-table discussion before the Allgood funeral on the sixth. After the talk that day, Jack presumed the service would be wall-to-wall attendance, beating out Christmas and Easter attendance at the local church.

After the news of Bill's death, Robin had immediately gone to Sandra's side. She wanted to be there for her friend but also wanted to know what had happened. Their history had been far and deep until Sandra met Bill.

Robin had not initially been around much after the Vegas

wedding. She had met the best man, Tony Tanner, who was to be her unofficial date for the trip, in the airport on the way to the ceremony. It did not take Robin long to figure out that Tony was gay and Bill and he were close. Bill clearly had a wide variety of tastes. When Tony hinted at secreting a time for him, Bill, and her to have a threesome in Vegas, Robin refused. And over the next day or so, she struggled with telling her friend. She could see how happy Sandy seemed, so Robin ultimately kept the proposition to herself.

Robin and Sandra spoke less and less in the months after Vegas. Robin assumed the two were in the honeymoon phase and that the distance would pass. On the few occasions Robin ran into Sandra and Bill, she sensed a coldness coming from them both. She figured Bill's attitude came from her rejection of him, but Robin noted a hint of despair in her friend's eyes. There had been far more going on at the Allgood home, Robin suspected, than anyone knew, and she waited for her friend to reach out when she was ready. Although Robin regretted having kept Bill and Tanner's proposition a secret as it may have spared her friend from what began to look like an unhappy union.

Robin walked out onto the porch and placed a glass of wine next to Sandra. "You need something to relax you," Robin said. She saw Sandra's attention had been diverted, and she was looking out toward the front yard. She strained to see what was catching Sandra's attention. "What are you looking at?"

Sandra stood up, walked to the railing, and leaned against it as if she couldn't hold herself up. "They're out there."

"Who? The cop?" Sandra kept her back to Robin.

"Yeah, they have Brian Haughton out there. Remember he was the little brat in the sixth grade when we were in high school. He is sitting out there for your protection." Robin attempted to distract her friend, whom she feared had started to mentally unravel. "Hey, let's give him something to think about," Robin joked as she came over to Sandra, grabbed her arm and turned her around, and started the Carolina shag, twirling her with her arm over her head. "That will make the little twit get a hard-on like when he was twelve." Robin laughed, settling into the white rocker on the porch.

Sandra gave an obligatory smile and slowly lowered herself into a rocker.

"Do you remember when we were in ninth grade and went to our first high school dance in the gym?" Sandra remained mute and stared back toward the road. "All those bitchy older girls made fun of my dress that barely fit me. I had had it since I was ten." Robin paused and waited for Sandra to look at her. "Do you remember what you did?"

Sandra turned and half smiled. "We danced like we were on *American Bandstand,* and every one of those bitches' boyfriends wanted to be with us," Sandra said, smiling for the first time.

"Exactly. I need that fearless, guilt-free, free-spirited girl back."

Sandra dropped her head and started to weep. Robin got up and put an arm around her friend. "I'm sorry. I'm being insensitive about your loss," Robin said, feeling sick saying the words, but her friend was in pain.

Sandra wiped her tears. "That's not why I'm crying. Thank you for being here and making me remember. I want her back too."

SIX
The Funeral

On Saturday, Jack and Ruby, over her protest, got up and walked down to the Lovein Funeral Home for Allgood's funeral.

Jack's thoughts proved correct, standing room only. The only funeral home in town was owned and operated by old man Don "Bo" Lovein. Bo always wore a wrinkled black suit that looked like he slept in it. He had a slightly hunched back and appeared as if, at any moment, he might keel over and need his own services. But Bo had built a funeral home monopoly in the region that had allowed him to become one of the largest landowners. You would never know it by seeing him, but Bo also owned the largest herd of breeding cattle.

Of course, rumor had it that he acquired the land by playing the widows. And many speculated that Bo, a shrewd businessman at heart who had a habit of creepily extending his forefinger toward the vein in your wrist when he shook hands, was checking your pulse. A weak or erratic heartbeat might signal to old Bo that he had a potential new customer.

In a small town like Pear Valley, funerals were as much of a social event as any wedding, if not more. You didn't need an invite to attend a funeral, and when a man is murdered, whom everyone suspects had been "done in" by his young wife, well, you can bet no one would stay home that day. The irony of the turnout was not lost on most, especially Ruby. If Allgood had died of natural causes, she suspected the turnout would have been far lighter since everyone seemed to think he was a son of a bitch. But on that Saturday, the crowds poured into the Lovein Funeral Home as if Jesus had arrived for the Second Coming.

Despite William Allgood having been a prominent farmer and employer of many, William did not participate in town politics and pretty much ignored the elders. That was until Bill took the lead in forcing the chamber toward a small, short, take-off airplane plant built inside the county line. The manufacturer was looking to move from Birmingham, and Bill thought they would fit in South Georgia with all the crop dusters and short runways. Moreover, it would add jobs to Pear Valley. But most sat back, speculating why Bill seemed suddenly interested in Pear Valley's success. No matter his motive, however, Allgood was proven right after he got his way, much to the annoyance of the townspeople. The company had decided to relocate, and it would be a boom for business in Callahan County.

Outside on the steps was where the powers that be gathered for their powwow before appearing to pay their respects. Of course, everyone knew better, but in the South, appearances were everything. The head of the chamber leaned in. "Think this was the one-time Allgood didn't win an argument." He made a gun out of his index finger and pretended to shoot. The others chuckled as Frank Truitt approached.

Frank, overhearing the comment about Allgood, leaned in. "You know, boys, I don't know anyone who likes to speak ill of the dead. But today, I'll personally make an exception."

Inside, Ruby shifted in her seat as Jack surveyed the room, waiting to see if his boss or Mosely showed up. He assumed David would be far too removed from the inner workings of a town where he had few ties, but that was all supposition since he and David barely spoke other than niceties.

Ruby whispered to her husband, "Quite the turnout."

Madeline Abrams, who fancied herself an expert at Clue, sat to Ruby's left and overheard her. "Don't mistake this for compassion, dear. This is 100 percent curiosity and conjecture at work. Like vultures checking out a carcass on the road." Ruby couldn't help but laugh.

Ruby gave the older woman a sweet, gentle smile as Jack squeezed her hand while his eyes continuously scanned the attendees.

Jack saw his and Ruby's attendance as an opportunity to meet potential clients. He thought, *You never know when someone might remember me from the funeral and contact me about drawing a will or dealing with a land dispute. There are more land dispute cases than divorces in a town like Pear Valley, where land is king, though a land dispute could lead to a divorce.* Jack stopped to focus on Truitt, who strutted in like the lord and master, with the crowds dispersing to allow the great senator to make his way to a seat up front.

When the widow entered the funeral home wearing all black and being walked to her seat by Doc Furman, the whispers flew, and you would have sworn the room had been invaded by cicadas. Sandra had her face covered and appeared to be holding a white handkerchief, ready for the tears to drop. Ruby had a perfect view of Sandra. Sitting next to the widow was an attractive woman about the same age who was trying to comfort her. She leaned over to Jack and asked, "Who is that with Sandra?"

Jack whispered back, "Don't know. Probably a friend."

By the end of the service, Ruby noted that the grieving widow hadn't used the handkerchief, not once. Instead, the handkerchief remained in her lap, presumably dry.

Jack was duly surprised when Mr. Truitt approached him outside the church. He took off his Stetson and nodded toward Ruby. "Ma'am." He then said to Jack, "Well, you know, boy, in one of these murders, it is almost always the wife, and this wife was twenty years younger than him. You remember that."

"Yes, sir," Jack quickly agreed as Ruby gave him an elbow to the rib cage, indicating her dislike for the comment. Jack was just happy the old man spoke to him. Mr. Truitt started to walk away after tipping his Stetson toward Ruby a second time. Ruby flashed her infamous Southern belle smile that would suggest sugar wouldn't melt in her mouth. Jack found humor in how his wife made other men swoon and see her as a soft Georgia peach. Underestimating her would be their downfall.

Truitt stopped and then turned back to add, "And boy, you'd better get a haircut. You look like one of those damn hippies ruining this great country. I let you look that way these last couple of weeks, but I am about to get you out in front of clients. I don't need you embarrassing me. You understand, boy?"

"Yes, sir," Jack sheepishly responded.

Truitt flashed a smile at Ruby and walked away, greeting other attendees like he was working the campaign trail. Jack saw him end up with the sheriff and his deputy, who were still hanging around outside the funeral home.

Ruby leaned into Jack. "Why does he call you boy? It's so demeaning."

"You're from the South, Mrs. Sutton; you know how the old boy network works. I'm paying my dues. If old man Truitt says to shovel shit, I shovel shit." Jackson "Jack" Lee Sutton understood that respect had to be earned, and he intended to win over Mr. Truitt and make his parents and Ruby proud, not to mention her folks.

"Doesn't mean I have to like it. And isn't a good lawyer supposed to base things on facts and not wild gossip. Aren't you supposed to remain impartial? Daddy would never have talked about his clients like that."

"She ain't a client, at least not yet. Although I bet she comes to him if the state files charges. Truitt may be a pain in the ass, but he is the best in town."

"Huh, and here I thought I married the best lawyer in this one-horse town."

Jack smirked while taking Ruby's hand as they walked ahead of the lingering crowd. "And when you've handled as many cases as Truitt has, you notice trends. You're overthinking him. He's a hard-ass on purpose."

"What did he mean he's about to get you in front of clients? Has he been locking you in a closet every day?" Ruby shook her head in annoyance.

Jack squeezed his bride's hand to tell her to relax. "Actually, Truitt assigned me to court Monday for the criminal case assignment calendar, which might mean a burglary or petty theft case to handle and get some court experience."

Ruby assented with a smile and changed the subject before her irritation grew even more. "I'm glad we're getting away tomorrow on our road trip." The two had decided to go to Ichetucknee Springs in Florida that Sunday to escape the fishbowl that Pear Valley could be, proven by the Fourth and now the funeral of the year.

"You and me both," Jack said as he waved to a group of ladies huddled in a gossip circle who had stopped to stare and wave at the young couple.

"Who's that?"

"Just the small-town rumor mill at work."

"No." Ruby gave Jack a love tap on his arm and nodded toward the far end of the parking lot. "There."

Jack looked over as two men leaned against an old red Ford truck smoking. "Oh, probably the gravediggers."

"Well, shouldn't they be at the cemetery?"

"Cemetery is right over there. They probably parked here and will wait for the service at the cemetery to complete before they go back over and finish."

Ruby got in the car, eyes still on the unsightly pair.

—⟋⟍—

Brad, while talking to the sheriff and his deputy, noticed the same red pickup that Ruby Sutton had. He recognized it from the Allgood place and found it odd to see the truck again if it indeed was the same one. He couldn't make out the plate from where he stood. He made a mental note as he continued his conversation. "So what do you think?" Brad said to Jones while keeping an eye on the truck as it exited. Brad had hit the sheriff by doing a piece on him for the *Observer* the next month, celebrating his twenty years as Pear Valley sheriff.

"Thank you, Brad. But let's talk about it as we get closer. Right now, I've got way too much on my hands."

"I understand. Speaking of which, anything you want to share?" Brad shot the sheriff a smirk.

The sheriff and his deputy, on cue, started to walk away from Brad, but not before tipping their hats and Jones saying a curt "When I do, I'll call ya."

—⟋⟍—

"Boss!" Luis yelled, coming into the trailer on the outskirts of town. Diego met one of his girls there when he was in town, and he left Luis to wait for him at the gas station around the corner. But when the girl's car peeled out onto the dirt road, Luis took his cue to head back to Diego with what he found out.

"What? You don't knock?" Diego asked with an added slap across Luis's face for emphasis.

"I saw her go!" Luis shot back as Diego buttoned up. "I called up north. Payphone sucks. I could barely hear, but it seems someone got to him before we did."

"Who?"

deep holes feeding the spring. Jack found an old roped tied to a tall oak that swung out over the water and had a go at it several times. Eventually, Ruby joined in the adventure culminating in them swinging out together and dropping off into the hole. After being worn out, they swarmed to the sandy beach and broke out the picnic.

Jack, eating his Masters-style egg salad sandwich, became serious. "Ruby, look. I know being down in South Georgia isn't your cup of tea. But thank you for letting me try to make a reputation for myself. I know I could've gone to your father's firm or one of his buddies, but I felt I needed to make my own way."

Ruby set down the watermelon slice she was holding and leaned over and kissed him. "I know, and I get it in some ways but not others. But I support you totally, even if you must work for that annoying Truitt."

He kissed her back, and they hugged each other tightly, the type of hug only two people who are fully invested in each other can give. But when they heard a church group floating around the bend, singing some gospel hymns, they returned to their lunch.

"I'm so glad to have you, Jack. I can't imagine what it was like for Sandra Allgood to be married to such a horrible man." Ruby thought for a second and asked, "Did you notice she never cried?"

"How could you tell? She wore that black veil. You couldn't see her face."

"She never once used the handkerchief in her left hand."

"Wow, you were paying attention. I wonder if the district attorney will charge her. I hear rumors it could go before the grand jury tomorrow."

"I guess, weirdly, they were lucky to not have dragged children into their mess."

Jack and Ruby finished their lunch and headed back home.

They had the Beatles and other music playing on the eight-track stereo Jack had put in. Jack was driving with his left hand and elbow resting in the window. He had his right arm around Ruby, snuggled tightly next to him. Kissing her on the top of her head, he said, "We may need to start thinking about actually starting that family we've always talked about."

She looked up and kissed him on his mouth, slipping her tongue quickly between his lips. "Well, maybe we should. We can at least start practicing." Jack pushed hard down on the accelerator, and Cindy's four-barrel carburetor kicked in with a deep moan as the speedometer crept up to eighty miles per hour.

SEVEN
Calendar Call

Frank Truitt instructed his newest attorney, Jack Sutton, to attend the assignment calendar session on Monday at the courthouse. Jack arrived at the impressive white structure that was set in the center of the town square, surrounded by magnolias, live oaks, azaleas, and camellias. The historic building had four large sections that were in a cross shape, with the front being on the short side of the cross. Up on top sat a robin's-egg blue dome that had a square base to support it. The front of the base housed a large clock that chimed every hour on the hour with a single clang at the half hour.

Jack was nervously hoping to get appointed to an interesting case to help bring in money and polish his trial skills and reputation. This would be his win-win day. Jack had been with the Truitt firm for two weeks handling the title searches, minor wills, and estate matters. The experience had been good, but he needed to do more to be seen and make a name for himself, like getting some actual court experience.

At the calendar call, the judge would initially hear any new noncriminal matters, such as divorces and challenges. Then he would assign criminal cases for the people who could not afford their own lawyer and schedule arraignments. Most issues would range from misdemeanors to minor felony matters, such as theft or assault. And the judge would make the assignments based on the case facts and the lawyer's skill level. The lawyers would get a small sum for the representation paid out of the county treasury, but it was mostly pro bono to build their skills and make names for themselves. Rarely a major felony like murder or such would be assigned. Usually, those went to more experienced lawyers to maintain the appearance of propriety, who would get a larger fee from the county. They might not be the better lawyer, but the court of appeals would not look favorably at a nonexperienced attorney being assigned a major felony case.

On that Monday, many young lawyers graced the courthouse halls with confidence and ego firmly in their hands as they watched some poorly skilled senior attorneys do far less for far more money. It was always recommended that lawyers show up early to claim one of the twelve seats in the jury box. Being "inside the bar" was a status symbol. It was a long tradition to sit there during motions and nonjury matters. The special seats helped the lawyers look unique to potential future clients in the audience. Because the judge traveled a three-county circuit, lawyers from all three counties would gather for an appointment. The firms were expected to send their young folks there so the judge would have plenty to spread the work to.

The other less talked about but ever-present positive of being in court on Mondays included the ability to be seen by the gallery with the hopes of their names being mentioned in and among the gossip. In a small town, talk fueled any and all action. Like Hollywood, in Pear Valley, any publicity was good publicity.

The gallery seating was designated for the public, the press, and the late-arriving lawyers waiting for their cases to be called. And on any given Monday, the court gallery filled with people who had time to kill, mostly seniors and busybodies. The gallery would eagerly watch the myriad of cases marched before the court as if it were a Broadway production. The entertainment factor proved significant for some folks in town and provided much fodder for salacious gossip. A good divorce case or a drunk and disorderly charge could set off a month of chatter among the fine God-fearing citizens of Pear Valley. A young lawyer who showed well for himself would be the talk of three counties and could build a reputation on these types of assignments.

Brad Lavender had arrived at the courthouse to see the proceedings also. He needed to cover the regular riffraff for the court docket column in the paper that went out on Tuesdays. However, that day, he hoped to visit with the sheriff and some deputies to get an update on the Allgood murder. He also wanted to stop in on the district attorney and see if he could get some information from him or the assistant DA. If not from them, Brad banked on the possibility of a well-placed smile at their young but homely secretary might reveal an interesting morsel he could work with. He had already heard a rumor an arrest might be coming, but he needed to confirm, and well, the secretaries knew everything.

The seats in the gallery were like wooden church pews to keep anyone from being comfortable and to invoke the idea of authority as they did in church. There was a balcony with seats also over the gallery. Those were leftovers from the days of segregation and were only used when the lower gallery was full and overflowing.

Everyone knew the terms "the bar" and "the well." The bar designated the separation between the area on the business side of the "bar," called the "well," and where those observing the proceedings sat, called the "gallery." The "bench" was the large, elevated desk where Judge Throwbridge sat. Traditionally, witnesses were required to stand next to the bench while testifying, usually surrounded by a railing against which they could lean and raise above the ground to aid in voice projection, from which to do so. However, in the fifties, like most courts, Pear Valley added a seat for the witness, though they continued to call it a "witness stand."

Judge Throwbridge's chambers consisted of his offices and a small conference room where a hearing could occur. If one read a notice that says a matter will be heard "in chambers," that simply meant the judge would not be using his courtroom but instead a smaller hearing room. Similarly, if someone was asked to see the judge in their chambers, that referred to his private office.

When Jack arrived, the jury box was full, and he reluctantly sat in the gallery. He checked his watch, convinced he had gotten there early enough, but something was amiss. Everyone from the jury box to the gallery was talking rapidly. Finally, Jack turned to a white-haired gentleman sitting next to him. "What's happening?"

In his long Southern drawl, the man looked up with tired eyes and said, "They done arrested the woman."

Jack looked around. "What woman?"

Annoyed, the man shifted in his seat to face Jack. "Mrs. Allgood was arrested this mornin' by Sheriff Jones. She's done charged with murder. We all knew it was a matter of time."

"You think she's guilty?"

The man scoffed. "Oh, she's guilty, but of what, I can't say for sure. I mean should it be a crime to kill the wretched?"

Jack sat back without responding.

The bailiff bolted through a side door and belted, "All rise. Oyez. Oyez. Oyez. The Superior Court of Callahan County is now in session, the Honorable Chief Judge Emmitt Stonewall Throwbridge presiding." Judge Throwbridge busted through the side door from his chambers and stepped up to the raised bench. He authoritatively seated himself and then said, "Everyone, be seated."

Sitting at a desk below the judge's bench was Don Simone. Don had been the judge's court clerk for almost thirty years and his friend since childhood. He was five years younger than the judge. Simone was tall, about six feet tall, and 160 pounds; he resembled a bean pole. He had slicked-back, dark hair on which he used too much Dapper Dan hair crème, but no one would tell him so.

Even his pencil-thin mustache had been greased into place. If one visualized Rhett Butler from Margret Mitchell's novel *Gone with the Wind*, Don would be his doppelganger. But even with that, what stood out with Don was that he wore a black velvet waistcoat at all court sessions, making him come across as one who put on airs. Don had never been married and was never known to date in town. Rumor had it he would travel to Albany or Atlanta on the weekend and enjoy the company of other men.

In his younger days in school, Don had been bullied. Judge Throwbridge, whose mother was a friend of Don's mother, stood up for him on many occasions. It was partly because it offended his sense of what was right but mostly because his mother told him to. Even as a young man, the judge was formidable. No one messed with Emmitt Stonewall Throwbridge. Some would say it had been apropos since his mother named him after Stonewall Jackson, famous for his steely determination when up against a challenge.

The friendship between these two unlikely men continued as Don, having worked as an investigator in Throwbridge's private practice law office, joined Emmett in court after he was appointed to the bench. The only person in that room with more power than the judge or the sheriff was Don Simone; it was well-known that he had the ear of both men. Everyone wanted to be on Don's good side if they could help it. Therefore, thoughts or comments on his lifestyle or how he dressed were kept very hush-hush.

The courthouse was about ninety-seven degrees with 90 percent humidity due to the lack of air-conditioning. There were ceiling fans in the thirty-foot-high ceilings, but they did little good. Everyone was sweating, which lent to an unappealing smell that lingered about. The windows were open to let the breeze in, but the only thing that came in were armies of flies and gnats.

Judge Throwbridge looked down at his clerk and asked, "What is the first business of the day, Mr. Don?" The court would take up the bench trial matters first. Some would say it was to have the folks who were there to be able to get in and out quickly. The truth is it was to entertain the crowd and let folks see the lawyers work. It was their best advertisement.

Sitting straight and narrow, Don stated, "Up first, Your Honor, is the case of Earl Brown, represented by Ignatius Gilbert, versus Calron, Nancy, and Elizabeth Brown, represented by Conger Simpson, in a caveat to the will of their father, Isaiah Brown."

Conger Simpson was a round man with a wrinkled and sloppy blue and white seersucker suit. He was from Banbridge, Georgia, and was representing the Brown estate. Simpson dabbed his sweaty head with a dirty handkerchief as he herded his clients, Calron, Nancy, and Elizabeth, inside the swinging wooden door on the bar that separated the business part of the courtroom from the spectators. They took the table inside the bar, away from the jury box.

Ignatius Gilbert was just the opposite of Conger Simpson. Gilbert was tall, thin, and dressed in a brown poplin suit with a red paisley bow tie. Not a hair was out of place, and he looked as cool as a polar bear on an ice float. He and his client, Earl, who was contesting his father's will, took the table nearest the jury box. Judge Throwbridge said, "Mr. Gilbert, you represent the caveator to the will?"

"Yes, sir, Your Honor."

"What is the issue here, Mr. Gilbert?"

"Your Honor, we contend that the alleged testator was non compos mentis without mental faculties when he issued and signed the will."

"I know that, Ignatius. I want to know your specific grounds for contending that he was non compos mentis."

Gilbert grew quiet and leaned down to his client Earl, who whispered in his ear. Then he rose to his full height and said, "Your Honor, Mr. Brown walked around with his zipper down." The courtroom broke out in laughter. The judge banged his gavel and yelled, "Quiet in the court! Quiet!"

As order returned, Judge Throwbridge leaned forward, slid his spectacles down his nose, and peered over them, looking straight at the slightly trembling Mr. Gilbert. "Anything else?"

Mr. Gilbert nonchalantly bent down to his client, who whispered in his ear again. Standing up, though this time not quite as tall or confident, Mr. Gilbert cleared his throat and said, "Your Honor, it seems the late Mr. Brown routinely urinated in the yard—"

Immediately Conger threw his pencil in the air and loudly proclaimed, "There goes my will!" The crowd in the gallery erupted again with laughter and catcalls.

The judge shouted, "Order in the court! Order in the court, or I will lock you all up!"

Even with the judge's pleas, the entire courtroom continued the laughter for what seemed like an eternity but was just a few moments. Judge Throwbridge patiently allowed the laughter to subside until it was deathly quiet. Then he pointed his gavel at an unfazed Mr. Gilbert. The judge looked him squarely in the eye and, with his booming voice, asked, "Front yard or backyard?"

Cautiously and with the first sign of trepidation, Mr. Gilbert leaned back to his client Earl, who seemed utterly ignorant that his case was not going well. Earl again whispered in Mr. Gilbert's ear. Gilbert raised back up, swallowed hard, and said, "Backyard, Your Honor."

Judge Throwbridge instantly responded by banging his gavel and loudly proclaiming, "This matter is summarily dismissed; in Callahan County, urinating in your backyard ain't no grounds for a caveat to a will."

As Simpson, Gilbert, and their clients departed, Judge Throwbridge banged his gavel and said, "Call the next case, Mr. Don." He looked over at Sheriff Jones and said, "Sheriff, better check your fly; you could invalidate your will." The gallery and everyone in the courtroom, including Sheriff Jones, laughed.

After the jocularity, several other cases were heard. Then just as it was time to call the criminal matters, the judge's secretary, Miss Wanda Purvis, came in a blue sundress from his chambers. She was a sight to behold. Not a single debutante in Atlanta could hold a candle to her.

She passed a note to the judge and walked out in a Marilyn Monroe saunter. The judge and all, including Don, could not help but stare until she disappeared back into the chamber door.

The judge read the note and announced, "Mr. District Attorney is involved in a significant matter with the grand jury. With the court's permission, he will not be able to attend the arraignment and assignment calendar today on the general docket. Therefore, we will continue the rest of the calendar on Thursday."

"I want the State versus Cook matter attorneys to wait here; all other attorneys waiting on the assignment calendar can come back Thursday morning. You are free to go. All except Attorney Sutton. Please wait for the courtroom to clear after this criminal matter."

Jack did a double take at his name, turning around and watching all eyes on him—or at least it felt that way. Finally, the other lawyers were dismissed and rose accordingly to leave the courtroom. Jack sat back and figured that, given the rumors, the "significant matter" the DA was working on had to be the indictment of Mrs. Allgood.

But as far as the judge was concerned, Jack had done his homework. He had thoroughly researched Judge Throwbridge, who had won his first trial, a murder case some forty years before, and almost every case after that. Judge Throwbridge was a legend. Had he been born a hundred years before and made his way to the bench, he certainly would have been known as a hanging judge. But instead, he was known to be strict by the book. He had grown up in one of the more affluent families in southwest Georgia and always knew he would study and defend the rule of law.

Early in the US, lawyers became lawyers by apprenticing with other lawyers. However, in Judge Throwbridge's youth, law schools had just started to develop. In fact, by the time he was in school, the Georgia Legal Bar required him to attend at least one year of law school before sitting for the bar exam. You had to pass the bar exam to practice. Law school was a three-year endeavor, and most students waited to take the bar in the third year and then graduated. Judge Throwbridge had taken the bar exam just before the second year began.

It took several months for the exams to be graded, and by mid-October, Emmitt Throwbridge was in the first semester of his second year. Then finally, one day in October, the list of those who had passed was released. A copy of it was being passed clandestinely around the evidence class at Mercer Law School in Macon, where Emmitt was a student. He reviewed it and passed the list on. But by the middle of the lecture, he stood up and began packing his books. Professor James Marshall, who had been mayor of Macon and a US congressman from the district and was known to strike fear into students, incredulously exclaimed, *"Mr. Throwbridge, what do you think you're doing?"*

Emmitt Stonewall Throwbridge stood tall and said, "Sir, having passed the bar exam, I'm now an attorney. So instead of listening to you talk about others practicing law, I am going to Callahan County to start practicing it myself. Good day, sir!" The class started clapping as he made his way out of the gallery and left for Callahan County. He was a legend indeed, and he lived up to his given name each and every day.

Jack played all potential scenarios in his head as he waited patiently; if this had any connection to the Allgood murder, Jack knew it wasn't to retain him as counsel but perhaps to have him deliver a message to Truitt himself. Jack smirked, thinking about his ignoring Mr. Truitt's suggestion to cut his hair and trim the sideburns he had grown into lamb chops. Since he and

Ruby were now living in the sticks of South Georgia away from cosmopolitan Atlanta, Jack at least promised Ruby he would dress the part of a metropolitan—holding onto their roots. And on his first assignment day, Jack had put on the suit he purchased just for the purpose of wearing it in court as an attorney for the first time. Jack conscientiously chose to stand out against the traditional local country lawyers with their poplin or seersucker suits or some dark, drab suits with pinstripes and thin ties. He was in Pear Valley to make a name for himself, not to conform and exist.

In fact, Jack wore a brand-new red, white, and blue suit. It was white linen with pale blue and red windowpane stripes. Under the jacket, he had bell-bottom britches. He had a vest and a cobalt blue shirt with seven-button cuffs. The lapels were several inches wide, reaching out to his shoulders. His tie was three inches wide and had red, white, and blue diagonal stripes. It ended just below his chest. His shoes were blue and tan stacked heel laceups to top off the ensemble.

Ruby, once seeing the suit on him, had changed her initial opinion and advised him against wearing it, noting it might be a little too rock and roll for good ole Pear Valley. But Jack had shrugged her advice off, planning to make an impression and a statement.

The judge then spent some time with the defense lawyer and DA in the Cook/catfish case.

Bobby Lee Chambliss was one of the most famous criminal defense lawyers in the state of Georgia. He had been hired by Dan Cook to represent him. The district attorney from Cook County was Bill Willis. He was one of the most respected prosecuting attorneys in those parts. Yet the two attorneys were like oil and water.

Judge Throwbridge had them discuss some of the logistics of the case being tried in Callahan County instead of Cook. The venue had been moved because of how well-known the defendants were. They included the deceased Cook County's Sheriff Cain, who was an alleged coconspirator, and Mr. Cook, who was one of the most successful farmers in the area. Chambliss attempted to display his usual theatrics, but the judge cut it off, made his announcements and rulings, and sent them out of the courtroom.

As the courtroom emptied to only Callahan County Sheriff Jones, Mr. Don, the bailiff, and Jack, Judge Throwbridge looked up from some paperwork he was finishing. Then in a not-so-friendly voice, Judge Throwbridge said, *"Boy,* come up here in front of the bench!"

Jack looked around and suddenly realized everyone else had gone. He shoved his paperwork in his briefcase and slowly walked toward the bench.

"What's your name, boy?"

"Jackson Lee Sutton, sir."

The judge released a puff of air as Jack recoiled a bit. "I told that crazy Frank Truitt not to bring a city slicker like you down here. But the stubborn old man wouldn't listen. Being in the legislature and sitting under that gold dome in Atlanta has gone to his head." As the words flowed out, Jack began to feel himself shrink. He fought hard to look at the judge, and he noted the sheriff's stare appeared just as disapproving. Only a slightly empathetic look from Mr. Don kept Jack from shrinking into a mass of Jell-O.

Judge Throwbridge continued. *"Boy,* don't you ever come to my courtroom or any legal proceeding in this county again wearing that stupid-looking clown suit. If you dare to come back to my courtroom on Thursday looking for an assignment, you had better be dressed like a lawyer, or I will have Sheriff Jones lock your ass up in jail for contempt and throw away the key. Do you understand me, *boy?"*

Jack meekly managed a "Yes, sir."

Judge Throwbridge instructed with his index finger, "Now get out of my courtroom!" But as Jack turned to leave, Judge

Throwbridge added, "And by Thursday, you better get a haircut or start wearing a dress!"

As Jack walked out, he passed the reporter he had mentioned to Ruby. He had been hanging around hoping to get more information on the murder. As Jack all but ran by, Brad stood up and stuck his hand out as he kept the pace next to him. "Mr. Sutton, I'm Brad Lavender with the *Observer*." Jack slowed, not wanting to be rude, and stuck his hand out. Before he could say anything, Brad nodded toward the courtroom. "Well, that was unfair in there," he said with a half laugh to try to help ease Jack's embarrassment.

Jack gave the nod and continued to walk at a slower pace as Brad followed.

"Look. I arrived in town not too long before you. And one thing I've noticed is that these folks are still living in the nineteenth century. Not to mention they're not too keen on outsiders. Hey, I'm grabbing a coffee. You interested?"

Jack was not any less embarrassed but sincerely appreciated Lavender's obvious effort to make him feel better. He knew the press was always after something, but at least they had a starting point Jack could build on. *Keep your friends close and your enemies closer,* he thought.

Jack gave a forced half smile. "Yeah, I should have known better. Hindsight is twenty-twenty, as they say." Then looking down at his suit and making a gesture up and down, he said, "I'd join you, but I'm going to need a rain check. I think changing may be the best part of valor here."

Brad agreed. They parted ways thinking to themselves that the other might be helpful and seemed like a decent guy to boot.

EIGHT
Reality Comes Knocking

The midday sun beamed down on the elderly gentlemen lined up on the front porch of the local country store. They enjoyed Miss Maddie's famous sweet tea while chewing tobacco, conjuring up the recent gossip about the murder.

"Rumor has it she done took out his genitals after finding him in bed with another woman."

"I worked on Allgood's farm for years; he was a cold son of a bitch. But he ain't brought no woman home, 'cept his wife. The bastard did his cheatin' in town."

"Anyone we know?"

"He was as discreet as a cat giving birth. Pretty sure he paid for the sex. He had issues with women. Didn't like 'em much."

"His daddy was a good man, but his momma died young. Maybe that affected his head."

"Either way, I don't much blame his wife for killin' him. He probably pushed her around. Did you ever see anything?"

"Not that I saw. He did say his hands were for the hired help. Treated us like dirt, and we worked for peanuts—cheap bastard."

The men stopped talking as Doc Furman, a longtime friend

of the Allgood family, walked closer, his gait slowing down with each passing year.

"Hey, Doc," the group said collectively.

"What you boys conjuring up today?" Doc asked, wiping his brow of sweat from the hot summer heat.

"You hear? Sandra Allgood's been arrested?"

Doc stood still, almost as if the heat had gotten to him and he would pass out.

"Doc, you all right?"

"Yeah, just a little surprised is all. Wade and I went way back. He was a good man."

"You think she's guilty?"

Doc continued climbing the stairs to the store's front door. "Boys, I don't know what to think anymore. This world has gone to hell in a handbasket. But I can't lie. I didn't much care for the departed." Doc opened the screen door and let it slam behind him. The others raised their eyebrow and continued their speculation.

Sandra Allgood sat in the holding cell, staring at the gray cement blocks in front of her. She wondered where it had gone terribly wrong and if this was the universe's way of punishing her for marrying a man for reasons other than true love. How one minute she had convinced herself that Bill was her night and shining armor only to end up at the hands of his brutality. Some thought he slapped her around, and part of her wished that was all he had done. That would have made her reality livable in comparison. But instead, his cruelty toward her, possessiveness, and the captivity she lived in were beyond unspeakable in contrast.

"Mrs. Allgood?"

"Yes?" Sandra stood and went to the steel bars that separated her and the sheriff.

"You have an attorney yet?"

She shook her head. "Sheriff, Mr. Allgood took care of everything legally. He had an attorney, and I called him, but the man cut the line as soon as I said my name."

The sheriff tipped his hat. "OK, ma'am."

As the sheriff retreated, she said, "Wait! What happens now?"

"The court will appoint one for you. Do you recall the rights being read to you?" The sheriff suddenly started to panic.

"Sir, I've been taken to jail, accused of killing my husband. Anything that anyone said to me is a blur."

The sheriff softened. "You will be provided representation, ma'am. Don't you worry."

Sandra sat back down and cried for what felt like a century. She heard footsteps and immediately wiped her face and sat up. Doc Furman stood next to a new deputy. "Ma'am, you have a visitor."

Sandra stood and walked to the bars. "Thanks, Doc, for coming."

"You OK? Do you need anything?"

"An attorney. I'll talk to Truitt and see if he's willing."

"No. I can't afford a big-time lawyer. Besides, I haven't got a shot in Pear Valley." Sandra sullenly shuffled back to her bunk.

Doc Furman shook his head. "Wade was my good friend, but that didn't mean I felt the same for his son." Doc watched Sandra pick her head up and nod her head. He gave her a half smile and retreated, leaving her alone.

Frank Truitt was in Atlanta for a committee meeting and some face time with the governor. He also planned to spend a few stolen moments with the little red-headed senate clerk that had become his current Atlanta regular side squeeze. He strolled into the Knickerbocker Tavern on Peachtree Street and went over to a group of gentlemen in the back. He paused and lit up his old stogie as he sat with the usual suspects at the same table. "Boys."

"Well, Senator, what's happening in your town? Looks like you got a murder."

"Yeah, well, if you ask me, the sorry bastard deserved it!" Calvin Macon said. Macon was a state representative for the Callahan County district and a longtime family friend of the Truitt family. He had ten years on Frank, but they had been thick as thieves growing up. They lost touch over the years, but when they both wrote the laws instead of defending them, they reunited and never missed their weekly lunch at the club.

"Gentleman, can I get you anything to drink?" the curvaceous waitress asked.

"Double bourbon, sugar," Samuel Scott instructed as he eyed the beauty standing to his right. Scott was a Georgia Supreme Court justice respected more for his familial lineage than his legal mind or faithfulness to his wife of thirty years.

"Two fingers of Blanton's," Frank said before turning to George. "Have you had any dealings with Allgood?"

"No, but our constituents have. He was in dispute with one of his neighbors, a local pig farmer named Bunch. You know him? Allgood supposedly siphoned water from the pig farmers' property but threatened Bunch."

Frank took a long puff from his stogie. "Indeed I do. But Bunch is a pussy cat; he'd never go after Allgood. In fact, Bunch never told Sheriff Jones nor me."

"Said he didn't want others in town to know. Said Allgood was a bastard who had connections. Feared his retaliation." Calvin stretched out the last word as he watched the waitress serve Sam his drink, along with a lot of cleavage on display inches from Sam's face. *She's working for her tip*, he thought.

Frank shook his head and took a long swig. "Allgood may have had connections, but they weren't with the right people."

Sam raised his drink toward Frank once the waitress departed. "Guess that means Allgood wasn't smart enough to have you in his pocket?"

"You got that right," Frank replied, downing the rest of his drink.

"You could represent Mrs. Allgood?" Sam stated, half kidding.

"No one's asked. And I ain't no ambulance chaser," Truitt said, raising his glass to ask for another.

Calvin put his head down and then side-eyed Truitt. Through the rumor mill, he had heard Doc Furman had already approached him. But Calvin knew Truitt only turned down cases for two reasons: One, he couldn't win. And two, because there was no money. Calvin suspected this case met both criteria.

As Jack walked into the Truitt offices, he saw Thelma Cole, Mr. Truitt's secretary of twenty-five years. Thelma was a rather plump, grandmotherly woman who had stuck by Truitt through lean times, and rumor had it that Frank Truitt took care of her expenses when her husband passed away several years ago. Their loyalty to one another did not go unnoticed, but Thelma was no snitch either. Like any good maternal figure, she protected all the men in that firm.

Thelma looked at Jack for a long time, drawing out her visual assessment to drive home her words. "Oh my goodness, sugar. Please tell me you did not go dressed like that to Judge Throwbridge's courtroom."

Jack nodded defeatedly, knowing he didn't have to fill in the details.

"Well, honey, it'll be all right," Thelma said, patting Jack's back like a little kid. "That old judge can get his panties in a wad, but he'll get over it. Just remember things in life are either a good time or a good story. And well, I believe you got yourself a doozy to tell."

Thelma laughed out loud and headed to her desk.

Feeling like he could breathe again, Jack shook his head and smiled.

"Now sweetheart, you better go to Lazarus Department Store. They have nice conservative men's suits. I suggest you pick some up for court. Also, get a good ole Southern blue and white seersucker one for Fridays and political barbeques. A bow tie won't hurt with it either."

Jack smiled. "Yes, ma'am."

"Oh, and sug? Stop by Mr. Moon's barbershop and get that haircut and that fuzz on your face shaved," she grinned at him and followed it with a wink.

"Yes, ma'am." Jack strolled back to his office to see if he could be productive for at least some of the day. His office, if you could call it such, was in the back of the Truitt Law Firm building. The building was a 1920s bungalow that had been converted into an office in the 1950s. During those years, the area, a mere block away from the courthouse, started to have business spill over to those streets.

Because the place had initially been a private residence, the sleeping porch had a slanted roof with its sides enclosed with screens to keep the mosquitoes and gnats out while letting a breeze in to fight the heat and humidity. For Jack's arrival, the porch had been enclosed with actual walls and windows and a ceiling fan to help keep it cool. However, it kept its "sleep porch" name and its feel. He had an old desk, a chair, and a small table that barely fit in the space, forcing him to squeeze between the wall and table to make his way to the desk.

He sat behind his desk, trying to focus on financial data from a divorce case Mr. Truitt had assigned to him. It was hard to look at the bank accounts and purchases to develop a plan for asset distribution among folks who could barely afford to pay their lawyers. He had found that people would rather spend their time fighting with each other and wasting their assets than move to an equitable split.

After a few hours, he looked up to find Mosely Brown in the doorway. Mosely had been in the district attorney's office for twenty-five years and then went into private practice with Truitt in the early sixties. He knew Mosely and the whole town had heard of this debacle, and Jack braced himself for the inevitable lecture. Mosely, in his late sixties, about five feet, seven inches tall with the build of a schoolboy, stood hunched over at his midback with speckled gray hair, wearing an exuberant smile.

Upon eye contact, Mosely maneuvered around the table to a side chair where he sat, stretched his arms over his head in a dramatic fashion, clasped his hands behind his head, and glanced toward the rough wood ceiling. "Jack, my boy, do not let that court thing bother you. Most people 'round these parts have short memories."

Jack gave a half smile for Mosely's getting right to the point. "Yes, sir."

"Besides, when we have something embarrassing happen to us, we think we are the center of everyone's attention or thought. But truthfully, most people are so focused on the good and bad in their own lives they have little time to worry about you. None of us are as important or centered in other people's thoughts as we believe."

Jack sheepishly gave a head nod.

Mosely shared, "When I moved from the DA's office to private practice, I was brash and full of thinking I would be God's gift to law. I thought I was the cat's meow." Mosely rubbed his chin in contemplation as he recalled the early years. "There had been a raid at a club called the Plantation Club. Most counties were dry back then, but Baker County wasn't. Gambling, drinking, naked women dancing and stripping, all kinds of shit went on there."

Mosely leaned back and looked around. "You got any bourbon hidden anywhere?"

Jack shook his head no. He had enough issues, and there would be no need to compound his errors with alcohol.

"Anyway, I knew this girl named Betty Sue Cagle Simmons—she wore tight blue jeans and her hair propped up on top of her head like a soft-serve cone—who had been married to one of the deputies at the time. But word on the street was that she got around. Well, one day, she came to see me over a petition for a change of custody. It seemed her ex-husband, from two marriages before her current one, had filed the petition alleging issues with the safety of her children. He claimed she spent her nights partying at the Plantation Club. I asked her about it. To which she replied, 'It's lies, Mosely. I'd been living at the foot of the cross.'"

Jack turned his head in contemplation. "At the foot of the cross?"

"Well, she claimed to be praying day and night. The problem being I trusted her." Mosely looked up to the sky and let out a long breath. "So we go to court, and she gets called up by the plaintiff, her former husband, for cross-examination. She goes up there, gets sworn in, and sits down. And before her ass even touched the seat, the plaintiff asked, 'Betty Sue Simmons, wasn't that you dancin' naked on the table at the Plantation Club in Baker County, Georgia, on October 27, 1961?' She responded, 'What was that date again?' Well, the whole court busted out laughing. I had my ass handed to me in front of the courtroom."

Jack couldn't help but laugh. He shook his head in understanding. "Point taken, sir."

"I quickly found out that life moves on." Mosely placed his hands on his knees and slowly rose. "It is not what you did yesterday; it's what you do today and tomorrow that counts." Contrary to sarcastic smile, Mosely's expression represented wisdom ᵐth without judgment.

Jack stood. "Thank you. I appreciate you sharing that story."

"Hell, Jack, we all need a friend sometimes. Tell you what. I'm going fishing with this professor from Abraham Baldwin Agricultural College, ABAC as we call it. He is searching for the lost Confederate gold and wants to come down to my place on Lake Seminole, fish with me, and explore for the clues he thinks he has. How about you join us on Saturday?"

Jack protested for a moment but then agreed. Lake Seminole was supposed to be beautiful, and Mosely and the professor would be good company.

Mosely exited, then reappeared. "And Jack, get yourself some bourbon. A good Southern lawyer has some at the ready when there is a friend in need, a client needs comfort, or the pastor sneaks by for a sip." He gave a wink and left.

Jack grinned, nodded, and said to his empty office, "Yes, I'll do that."

—⁂—

Ruby Sutton had a much better day than her husband. At the Fourth of July celebration, she and Denise Walker had decided to meet for lunch that following Monday. They had had a little too much of the local moonshine during the singing and dance that closed out the evening, and Ruby was sure stories would be flowing at Lunch.

Ruby had met Denise by accident at the local Piggly Wiggly when she and Jack first moved to Pear Valley. As independent, attractive, and cosmopolitan women, Denise and Ruby took to each other like fish to water. Having moved into town a year before the Suttons after a messy divorce, Denise felt like an outsider until Ruby. Pear Valley was still, wall-to-wall, a typical small-town conservative place where divorced women were looked down upon no matter the particulars. And they were watched closely to be sure they did not steal a "good woman's" husband. Men did not receive the same admonishment.

Denise had started a job as a cartoonist and political satirist at the *Pear Valley Observer*. It was the county's only newspaper so its owners did well with ad revenue. Many would say that they were printing papers and printing money. Especially during elections. Whether state, federal, or local, the paper raked it in on political ads. The politicians weren't above spending as much or more money than their opponents to gain support and recognition. So with its success, the paper could afford a talented staff, including a cartoonist and political satirist like Denise.

"Ruby!" Denise waved Ruby over as she crossed the street.

"Hey, Denise. Sorry, did I keep you waiting?"

"Oh no. I just got here myself. And I ordered us sweet teas if that's OK?"

"Long as it's not moonshine!"

The two laughed and continued talking about the Fourth's happenings before moving on to more exciting topics. Ruby almost felt giddy at the prospect of spending time with another woman more like herself. Fitting in with the wives of Pear Valley had proven difficult. The other ladies, although on the surface nice enough, had never left Pearl Valley and didn't have as much in common with Ruby.

Stabbing her salad with a fork, Ruby asked, "How do you like working at the paper? I swear your cartoons are amazing!"

"Thank you! Well, I love it. Although my latest cartoon with Truitt's boy in the senate seat did not go over well."

"What do you mean?"

"Truitt is a big name around here and has more control than anyone thinks. I bet your husband's seen it."

Ruby shook her head. "Jack is just thankful to be working. But I'm not a fan." Ruby rolled her eyes.

"Trust that intuition." Denise put her fork down and leaned in slightly. "Speaking of working, didn't you tell me that you were a journalism major? From Wesleyan?"

Ruby smiled and cocked her head to the side. "Yes, I guess I must have. I don't recall much after the third drink other than Leroy Sample arguing with another woman about the moon or something."

Denise let out a laugh. "Yes! He got so mad that he threw his drink down, and she freaked out."

"Yes!" Ruby said a little too loudly as others stopped to stare. She covered her mouth for a split second and then revealed her sweet Georgia smile to the other tables.

Denise shielded her face from the other patrons at the restaurant and shared a dramatic eye roll before asking, "Well, have you ever thought of working at the paper?"

Ruby sat back, grasping her full stomach. "I guess, maybe. I mean what else do I have to do once I finish unpacking?" Ruby thought about Jack's expectations for a family, and they worried her. She knew she would never be like Jack's momma. She loved her mother-in-law; she was the sweetest. But Mrs. Sutton lived to cook, clean, and raise her child. Ruby struggled to make a sandwich, her laundry skills were questionable, and despite daydreaming about their future family with Jack, lately especially, she had been pondering her readiness to have a baby.

Denise could see the wheels turning inside Ruby's head, so she moved forward to cut it off. "I actually am close to one of the featured writers who cover the city beat, and he says he likes writing for them."

Ruby leaned in, gave a smirk, and raised an eyebrow. "Are you talking about Brad Lavender?"

"You know him?"

"No. But Jack pointed him out the other day. He's been writing about the Allgood murder." Ruby looked down at her hands and then leaned in closer to Denise. "I have to admit, my interest in the case is unnaturally peaked."

Denise smiled. "Ah, well, Brad is certainly in the know on that case or trying to be."

Ruby cocked her head to one side, and she watched Denise's face. "Your face just went from pale to rosy pink when mentioning him, and it's not from this heat."

Deflecting, she said, "See, you're a natural! Always looking for a story, and Brad has one."

"So spit it out already!"

Denise pushed her plate aside as her stomach was, unexplainably, too in knots to finish. "Well, he was from Alabama but had written for a big paper in Miami before coming here. He's a nice guy. Very into his work."

Ruby wasn't going to let her off that easy. "Not the story I was looking for."

Denise put up her hands. "Nothing to tell here, ma'am. Just a nice guy from work."

"Well, first, never tell a guy he's nice. Guys hate it when you call them nice."

"Well, if I ever meet another potential husband, nice is first on my list of important qualities. But I am so not there."

Ruby could see it in her face and her body movements. She was infatuated with Brad. He would be lucky to get her. She clearly was the catch of Pear Valley single women. "I know you're not interested, but if you are," observed Ruby, "this is the seventies; you can ask him out."

"Not interested," Denise replied. "Besides, men 'round these parts don't like forward *divorced* women." Denise took a long drink from her iced tea and looked around at all the ladies having lunch, then leaned in. "The men here want their women to be quiet and demur and oooh and aaaah at their every move. Once they get you, they plan to strap you to a stove and take care of them. That's not me."

Ruby gave a nervous laugh aloud. "Well, I think it's time to bring this 1950s town up to the modern day."

"All right, I have a confession," Denise said.

"You're changing the subject, aren't you?"

Denise cocked her head to the side, ignoring Ruby's last remark. "I already talked to the editor about you, and he has an opening for you. So you'll be a shoo-in."

Ruby's smile faded, and she sat back in her chair.

"What's wrong? Thought you wanted to shake the town up."

"It's not that. I hadn't thought about getting back to work. I've been so consumed with the wedding and moving." Ruby looked out at the almost empty street. She missed the hustle of Atlanta more than she realized, and she feared becoming too invested in a town she had no intention of staying in for the long term. Turning back to Denise with a smile, she said, "Let me think about it."

At the end of the lunch, Ruby mentioned to Denise, "You know Jack and I would love to have you for dinner, and you can bring your friend. Brad is it?"

"That's sweet. But I don't know. Can I let you know later?"

"Of course, it's an open invite!"

Ruby felt the perspiration beading on her forehead as she walked to her car after lunch. She could feel the gnats around her mouth and nose buzzing in and out of her ears. She swatted them away, almost picking up the pace to get inside.

Contending with the humidity was part of life in Georgia from the north to the south. Ruby had been used to that. However, the Georgia gnat line was unique to the southern part of the state where Ruby had not grown up. It generally ran from Columbus to Macon into Augusta. The Georgians below the gnat line learned to live with constant sweat and pests surrounding their face, mouths, and ears, along with the constant buzzing in their heads. South Georgia children were even taught to blow puffs of air to keep the gnats out of their mouths and noses. And the funeral home fans you see in most churches or outdoor events were as essential for maintaining the gnats off your face as they were for battling the heat.

Ruby's saunter turned to a quick pace for her car when she heard a scraggly voice behind her. "These gnats are part of life down in these parts. Bet you city folk isn't used to them!"

Ruby glanced back at an unshaven man in jeans, a T-shirt, and a giant cowboy hat standing behind her, chewing on a toothpick. She forced a coy smile and got in the car. Her father always told her it's not rude to be abrupt if you feel unsafe. When she left for college, her father sat Ruby down and said, "Gal baby, we brought you up well. But manners don't matter when you deal with others you don't matter to."

NINE

The Invites You Can't Decline

Tuesday morning, Jack focused on the best new conservative suit he had bought from old man Lazarus and his wife, Bunny, who altered it on the spot for him. Still sore from the previous day's fiasco, Jack also stopped by Mr. Moon's barbershop to get the haircut Judge Throwbridge had suggested. He didn't fear Throwbridge would be true to his word and put him in a dress. Jack did, however, worry his punishment would be far worse. His fledgling career would never survive the blow. So he walked into the shop, ready to rid himself of the hair that could end his career before it began.

Mr. Fuller Moon had been a barber in Pear Valley for forty years, the first thirty of those with his father before he died. The senior Mr. Moon had been the only barber in town for the thirty years. So yes, he had heard the "full moon" jokes but did not appreciate them or understand why so many thought they were hysterical. So it was well-known, at that point, that if you were getting your hair cut or about to, you did not want to mention his name unless you wanted a nick, cut, or ugly haircut.

His mother's maiden name was Fuller. He sometimes wondered

if his parents really meant to do that to him. But being immigrants, Fuller knew his parents had no idea at the time.

The barber chairs were burgundy leather, white marble, and stainless steel. True classics. The floor was art deco white and blue with a pie tin ceiling above it. The walls were covered with posters of the local teams and other events and a few dog barber cartoon paintings. There was also a large portrait of Moon's dad, one to which Fuller gave a respectful bow upon opening and closing each day.

The barbershop was always a gathering place for farmers and businessmen to share humor and political opinions and waste time. It was not unlike the front porch of the country store, except Moon's had air-conditioning, a luxury he had committed to for his customers. And given that word traveled fast in Pear Valley, the men in the barbershop had all heard the story of the literal dressing down Jack had gotten from Judge Throwbridge the prior morning.

Bill Jackson, who was in the chair having his haircut with Mr. Moon, looked and announced to the room, "Lookie here, y'all. We have that fancy lawyer from Atlanta. Well, Mr. Sutton, how do you like Judge Throwbridge's hospitality?"

The room all laughed, and though embarrassed, Jack knew it was time to join in. "Well, they didn't have any sundresses over at Lazarus, so I thought I'd better come to get a trim."

The whole room busted out laughing. His ability to take some ribbing was the mark of character these loitering men could appreciate. A new day and some new appreciation were a move in the right direction for the city boy turned country lawyer. From that point, Jack was accepted and joined in the banter while awaiting his turn for Mr. Moon to "lower his ears."

Jack immediately recognized Moon's shop as the melting pot of rumors and stories. He noticed two men, one in a suit and the other a clerk from Mr. Doyle Carlton's hardware store named Tiny Johnson, playing checkers with bottle caps from the six-ounce

Cokes he sold in the shop. But of course, Tiny was anything but. He was as big as Stone Mountain.

Jack sat back in the wood chair, waiting his turn, and thought, *He's the largest thing I ever saw without a motor.* Tiny tightly packed his four hundred pounds into his rough denim khaki pants and yellow vest from the hardware lumberyard. The top was stretched far across his back; it looked like a tick about to pop. Folds of skin stuck out from his hard hat. But when he spoke, out came the shrill-pitched voice of a member of the Vienna Boys Choir. Jack jerked back in shock. It was not what he expected, but since moving to Pear Valley, nothing was as he anticipated.

While playing checkers, Tiny directed his attention toward Jack. "Mr. Sutton, I remember the first time I met Mr. Truitt. A sixty-two-ton dump truck ran over a tractor, cutting the side of the road, and then went off a bridge and crashed into Attapulgus Creek. The truck was loaded with Fuller's earth." He paused for a second and thought he'd better add more. "That's a fine white powder from a local mine."

Jack put down his magazine and leaned forward; his interest was piqued.

"Mr. Truitt showed up in his big yellow Cadillac. Walked right up to my supervisor and said, 'I am an attorney, Frank Truitt, and I will be handling the legal matters regarding the wreck on behalf of the state. I need to talk to anyone involved or who witnessed the accident.' So the boss man sent him to Mr. Johnny. Mr. Johnny drove the tractor. Mr. Truitt asked and asked Mr. Johnny questions. But after each of their answers, Mr. Truitt would say, 'Oh my Lord,' and shake his head."

Tiny moved one of his bottle tops and then turned back to Jack. "Mr. Truitt then asked me, 'What's your name?' 'Tiny Johnson.' 'What did you see?'

"So I told him I had a little constipation, so I walked down to the creek, undid my britches, and squatted down by the water. I was just starting to strain when, all of a sudden, I heard this tremendous commotion! The white powder comes down like a cloud into the creek and onto my rear end! Then this damn dump truck crashes through the guard rail and falls, landing in the water about ten feet from where I would be doing my business. It caused a wave of water to come at me." Tiny started acting out the scene and throwing his arms around. "Stuff was flying everywhere, I tell you. The driver in the truck is wide-eyed and just rocking back and forth, you know."

Jack was completely drawn in by Tiny's storytelling skills, as was the rest of the shop. "Well, what did you do next?" Jack asked.

"Nothing." Tiny turned back to the checkerboard before adding, "But I didn't have problems with my bowels no more." Tiny let out a high-pitched laugh, and the whole room exploded with laughter.

When Jack returned to the office, he dreaded seeing Frank Truitt after the debacle with Judge Throwbridge on Monday. So when he walked by Thelma, he mouthed so as not to be heard, "Is he here?"

She nodded and pointed at the open door to his office. Jack thought about sneaking out and going in through the back exit of his sleeping-porch office, but he knew he would have to face the music sooner or later. So he took a deep breath and walked over to Truitt's open door.

"Boy, come in here," Truitt bellowed.

Jack walked in with his conservative suit and tight haircut. Truitt looked him up and down, pausing for dramatic effect. "Well, at least you choose well. You don't have the legs to pull off a dress." He took a puff of his cigar. Jack smirked for a second before catching himself.

Truitt held up his hand. "Don't worry, boy. I ain't going to fire you. Yet. I got the Ole Emmitt Throwbridge call and took the shit he dished out. I smoothed it over. He owed me. But now you owe me. You understand, boy?"

"Yes, sir."

Truitt stood and walked to his side credenza, where a decanter of brown liquor sat half-empty. Jack had been introduced to discussions over a brown liquor drink from his first meeting with Truitt. He poured himself more than two fingers' worth and sat behind his desk as Jack waited, knowing more was to come. "So as it goes, I also received an invite."

Jack and his boss exchanged glances, but Jack had no idea what Truitt was referring to.

Annoyed he had to explain, Frank Truitt placed his drink down firmly and raised his voice. "Lady Daisy's party for you and your missus on July 20."

"Oh yes," Jack acknowledged with vague recollection.

"Well, be prepared to catch shit. Just like you did today at Moon's. I expect you to handle it as well too. When those people are under the influence of her garden, liquor, and that gorgeous young Leva, well, shit will fly."

Jack nodded, having no idea who Truitt was referring to and more than slightly questioning how information flowed in that town. Nothing went unnoticed by anyone, and everyone knew everything almost before it happened, especially Truitt.

Jack and Truitt stared at each other for a second, silent, and then Truitt said, "Now get back to your office and get to work! You need to start making us some money. And be prepared for assignment day. He may give you an abused shoat case."

Jack didn't wait for a second to retreat out of there. Being in Truitt's presence reminded him of how his mother described purgatory to him after Sunday school when Jack was a young, inquisitive twelve. Although Jack didn't feel as much an absolution from Truitt as an extended sentence to remain indefinitely in suspension.

Jack walked by David John's office, who called after him.

Jack paused and pivoted. "Hi," he said, knowing that John had avoided him since he started and this was just an opportunity to flex some muscle.

"Well, well. Almost didn't recognize you," David said, leaning back in his chair and placing his hands together in steeple formation. "You look like a respectable Southerner now. Good choice, Sutton."

Jack continued to take his arrows gallantly but took the opportunity to test how much his fellow lawyer knew. Jack closed the office door and took a seat before it was offered. "What's a shoat?"

"Why are you asking?" David picked up a file and started to open it once the fun of ridicule failed to present.

Jack restated Truitt's words.

David looked up and laughed. "The old man loves to tell the story of his shoat case. A shoat is a young pig that has just been weaned." David leaned back in his chair. "So the story goes, this lady worked at a hog parlor—where young pigs(shoats) are raised in pens and fed to get them ready for market. She called the sheriff and said, 'One of my hands is down in the hog parlor butt naked, and we're scared.' So the police show up and find this guy naked in the parlor with all these sows running around. So one of the officers yelled, 'What the hell are you doing?' 'Fuckin' these sows,'" David said, lowering his voice like a middle-schooler trying to hide the foul language he proudly knew.

Jack couldn't help but chuckle.

"So the guy had said it so honestly and brutally that the officer didn't know what to say. So he brought him in on bestiality charges. Truitt was appointed to defend him on the criminal charges of bestiality. But Truitt was known for being creative or, as some would say, a smart-ass. He still is." David gave an exaggerated eye roll. "Anyway, the hearing comes up, and the sheriff gets on the stand. He starts to tell how the hand had made the statement.

Truitt questioned the sheriff, 'Did you identify the violated pig in question and have them go to the Mitchell County Hospital for a rape test kit?'"

David shook his head and continued. "'No,' the sheriff answers. Then Truitt asks, 'Given the mix of pigs, did you verify if it was a sow or boar he was alleged to have sex with?' Sheriff says, 'No.' Then Truitt follows it with a 'Did you get a statement from any of these sows or boars?' Again, the sheriff said, 'No.' Truitt then argues to the judge that under the law, a statement by the accused in proximity to where the crime occurred is insufficient to bind a defendant over to the grand jury."

Jack shook his head and gave an earnest laugh.

David continued. "'Come on, Emmitt,' the sheriff protested. But because of Truitt's genuinely smart, if not smart-ass approach, the judge threw out the bestiality charge and sent the boy to Southwest Georgia Institute to test his mental health."

"Interesting," Jack said with a smirk.

David opened the file in front of him then glanced up as he rested his hands on the desk. "Well, Throwbridge is notorious for handing out the bad cases to lawyers who piss him off. So you're in for it," David snarked while shooting the "Get out of my office look" toward Jack, who got the hint.

Thursday morning, the office of District Attorney Rush Layton buzzed with activity, phones ringing, typewriters clicking away, and Sheriff Jones pacing by the desk of Layton's secretary, Linda.

"How long will he be on the phone?" Jones asked.

Linda stopped typing and looked over her half glasses. "I don't know." She resumed her typing as Jones rolled his eyes. He and Linda had a well-established love-hate relationship.

Jones and Layton, however, maintained a healthy professional respect for one another but never socialized outside of work. For the most part, Layton was a workaholic and protected his personal life like Fort Knox, which only fueled the town's need for more details. And finding his backstory, they did.

When Layton was eleven, he had been playing football at a family picnic with his dad and other relatives. The family had gathered off Highway 82 on the banks of the TyTy Creek in a picnic area. His dad always carried a police radio with him. There had been a call for all officers to report to an ongoing hostage situation at the Rose's Department store in Tifton, where his father was a cop. His dad kissed him goodbye and said he would return in time for the ice cream that his mom and aunts were churning.

When his father got on the scene of what turned out to be an armed hostage situation, one police officer had been shot and a store clerk and some shoppers were being held at gunpoint. The plan came for some officers to sneak in the back door and surprise the gunman while others distracted him with negotiations in the front.

Layton's dad was first in. The man was at the front of the store with a handgun. When he walked slightly away from the hostages to yell at the officers out front for not meeting his demands soon enough, Layton's dad saw his chance. His dad came out, aimed his gun at the man, and yelled, "Police! Drop it!"

The man, who later proved high on opium, turned and fired. At the same time, Layton's dad shot off a round. Both bullets found their mark. Layton's dad struck the man squarely in the chest, exploding his heart. The man's shot hit Layton's dad an inch above his left eyebrow, tearing the top of his head off.

Layton's dad was honored as a hero, but it left an indelible scar on his young son's heart. Rush learned that the perpetrator who killed his father had just been released on bail for drug use days before killing his dad. The family attorney told Rush and his mother that the prosecutor was soft on crime and this act could have been prevented.

So by his senior year in high school, Rush decided to become a prosecutor to fight crime and uphold the law. He went to Mercer Law School and got his degree. He then joined the DA's office in Callahan County as an assistant, where he developed a solid reputation for being fearless in his pursuit of justice.

By his midthirties, Rush got elected district attorney. Layton made a name for himself in prosecuting violent crimes and drug dealers. He had secured several notable convictions and a well-regarded reputation across the state.

Layton had actually been brought in as a special prosecutor to investigate the arrests of Martin Luther King Jr. and Herb Phipps in Albany. Rush oversaw their freedom and prosecuted several police officers who killed two of the young men protesting in cold blood. When he was attorney general for the Johnson administration, Robert Kennedy presented him with a distinguished service award for his actions.

The door to Layton's office flung open. "Sheriff?"

"Layton. Any news before we head in there today?"

Layton looked up at the sheriff, who twirled his hat in his hands. "You have doubts?"

The sheriff cleared his throat. "Ah, no, just don't want any surprises in front of Throwbridge."

"What you produced is conclusive, according to the lab. You have anything else you aren't telling me?" Layton asked, his head down, reviewing a file in his hands.

"Nope."

"Did everything by the book?" Layton looked up.

The sheriff shook his head yes.

Layton responded in kind and closed his file. "OK, good. I'll see you in court." The sheriff placed his hat back on and tipped his hat to Linda, who paid no attention as she went back to typing.

When the sheriff was just out of earshot, Linda turned to Layton. "I don't like him."

Layton shook his head. "Maybe not, but he is our town law enforcement, and it's his ass on the line out there. So having an ounce of compassion and some respect might be in order." Layton started to head into his office.

"Did the gold digger get herself an attorney?"

Layton stopped and turned back to his secretary. "How judgmental, even for you. Did your husband make you drink decaf again this morning?"

Linda didn't crack even a smirk. "I hear things. She's no innocent."

"Gossip and conspiracy theories from your weekly luncheon with the town ladies do not equal facts," Layton scolded. "The defendant will be represented. Although I'm just not sure it will do her any good."

"Who's the poor sucker who has to defend her? I want to know who I'm going to have to deal with."

Layton pointed to the stack of files on her desk and raised an eyebrow. "Make sure those get filed. I'm off to court." Rush appreciated Linda's dogged approach to her job. She reminded him of his mother in many ways, but her prickliness got under his skin.

She glared up at him, annoyed, and gave him a smirk. He returned the gesture.

Thursday morning, Daisy sat on her porch overlooking her gardens and contemplated her next move. Lady Daisy, as she was known around town, did not work, had never been married, and had no family anyone knew of. Rumors were that she had a trust account or personal wealth from somewhere, but no one in Callahan County knew where. Although her checks were from First Atlanta Bank, causing speculation and dissatisfaction from the local financial community.

Some who did business on land dealings with her learned Daisy was her name of choice, but her legal name was Rebecca Sarah Steinberg. That revelation led to speculation, humor, and animosity based on stereotypes associated with the name. Callaghan County was predominantly Protestant, with only one group of Catholics having immigrated from Ireland. Jewish faith and culture were not evidenced there. No one knew where she came from or her age. Everyone knew she had been in the county for over forty years, leaving her probable age between fifty and eighty.

However, most of the talk about Lady Daisy centered around her psychic and mystical skills, both professed by her and pronounced by others on the receiving end. A few years back, a local high school basketball star, Steven Meders, was burned in an accident at his part-time job. His parents believed in healers and had called Lady Daisy to his hospital bed. Steven had severe burns on his arms, chest, and back. The doctors said it would take months to heal with scar revision and surgeries; even then, he would have scars.

As Meders lay in the hospital writhing in pain, his parents crying in the corner, Lady Daisy whispered over his burned areas and, as she left, placed the charm in his mother's hand for her to place under Meders's mattress. Four weeks later, Steven's burns had healed with no need for surgery and little evidence of scarring. It was still discussed today as a miracle, though no one knew what kind.

Some say that's when Lady Daisy's phone started ringing off the hook. She received requests to help others with emotional or physical conditions, some on their deathbeds and others needing a reprieve from their ailments. Many folks swore by her, others scoffed, and several just reserved ruling.

On any given day, Lady Daisy could be found tending to her beautiful garden in the back of her house, shaded by live oaks and pines. She was equally known for her garden parties. Recently, she started to think now would be a good time for another shortly after meeting Ruby and Jack Sutton, *the splendid young couple who had just moved in a few blocks down*. It had been about three months since she had thrown her last celebration to welcome the new pastor coming to the Pear Valley Baptist Church, Pastor Roberts.

And just as Lady Daisy meticulously planned out her garden, she applied the same effort to her parties. Of course, delicious, homemade treats would be prepared by the bakery and café in town, the Upside-Down Cupcake. But her signature unique and colorful cocktails would be prepared by Leva Barkas, Lady Daisy's choice for bartender. Leva was a tall, slender woman with long blonde hair that made a Southern man and some Southern women weak in the knees. Of course, it didn't hurt that Leva dressed provocatively and flirted with reckless regard when she worked the bar. Daisy attributed it to the alcohol she consumed on the job, but the women in town were not convinced. Rumor had it Leva never left a party without a gorgeous young man or woman or an underworld spy. But Lady Daisy scoffed at those rumors, as most emanated from the mouths of jealous wives.

In her living room stood an antique grandfather clock, a gift from her grandfather, that chimed every hour, and the rings reverberated through the house with an ominous, deep, muddled sound that made most shudder. Some reported they felt an odd chill. And when Lady Daisy greeted her guests, she warned them that when the clock chimed eleven, everyone must stop and leave. "If you dally, you will not be invited back!"

Lady Daisy was eccentric beyond measure. There was no dispute on that fact. Yet everyone wanted and waited for an invitation to a Lady Daisy party. If one didn't arrive, the uninvited would look for a way to get one. And her next party for the Suttons would be no exception. However, the first invitee after Jack and Ruby was the newly widowed Sandra Allgood before she got taken away in handcuffs. Lady Daisy should have regretted sending the invitation out so soon, but she was not one to shy away from controversy. She rather liked inviting it whenever possible. It added a little spice to any gathering.

Jack all but ran to the courthouse that morning and headed straight to Judge Throwbridge's chambers. Don, Wanda, and Sheriff Jones were seated around the table and drinking coffee. Jack stood in the doorway. His attire and grooming expressed his respect for the words of the esteemed, albeit cranky, judge. Before anyone noticed him, he heard Miss Wanda and Mr. Don chatting about the Allgood case. It had been the talk of the town since the DA had filed charges against the widow, Sandra, on Monday.

They looked up, and Wanda welcomed Jack with a cool "Well, Mr. Sutton, it sure is good to see you, and that sure is a nice suit." She, Jack, and Don smiled. Even Sheriff Jones's frown all but turned upside down a little.

Mr. Don added, "You got to ride the horse that throws you, even if it is Judge Throwbridge."

Miss Wanda told him the judge was in and to go into his private office. Jack nodded and proceeded forward.

Judge Throwbridge was six feet, four, and known to more than occasionally interrupt lawyers when he thought they were wasting his time. He did not suffer fools or lawyer's bullshit lightly. It was also rumored, and the rumor was true, that he carried a .45 caliber pistol beneath his robe. Once, when an irate defender charged the bench, Judge Throwbridge conked him on the head with the butt of his gun. When asked why he didn't just shoot the defendant, Throwbridge said, "Didn't want to waste a bullet on the sorry bastard."

Jack knocked and waited for the judge to give the OK before

he walked in. Jack immediately issued his best sincere and earnest apology and accepted it with a nod of dismissal.

"Remember where you are, boy. Show respect, and you'll receive it."

Jack nodded. "Yes, sir."

"I'll see you in the courtroom for assignments."

Jack felt relieved yet still unsettled as he entered the courtroom for the arraignment. And despite the cool cordiality, Jack suspected that both Truitt and the judge would hold this over him for some time. As Jack sat, he noted several other lawyers looking in his direction. They probably had experienced Judge Throwbridge or other judges scolding and lived through it. As reassurance, they all appeared to give him a "stand tall" nod, which he returned.

The first case involved the son of a prominent African American priestess of the Holiness black church in Camilla, well-known for all the great blessings she gave to the community. She hired a lawyer to defend her son, who was charged with the theft of pecans. Now in South Georgia, nobody steals pecans. It would be like stealing oranges from the groves in Florida.

South Georgia was one of the world's top harvesters of pecans. Pecans, pronounced *pee*-can," in Georgia were sold everywhere, and stores paid a premium to get them. Jack recalled calling them "pa-conns" the first week in Callahan County. He was in Ellenton at the country store delivering a will that Mr. Truitt had drafted to the store owner, a lady everyone called Granny Wright. Jack was starving and had purchased a homemade brownie with nuts and asked, "Are those 'pa-conns' in the brownie?"

Granny Wright went about setting him straight. "Now, now, son. That won't do. Say it with me: *pee*-cans."

Jack had dropped off legal papers, but he was the one schooled that day as Granny continued. "Words and their pronunciations matter south of the Mason-Dixon line. Now if you were in Virginia driving south, the signs on the side of the road would say, "Facilities." Once you cross into North Carolina, they would say, "Restrooms." Once you got into South Carolina, they would display, "Toilets." Once you get into Georgia, the signs say, 'Pee-can,' which is how you say it."

Granny and a couple of farmers at the store broke out in laughter, and Jack joined in. He had been taught.

Jack said, "Well, ma'am, I'll never forget that one. The brownies with *pee*-cans are delicious."

Jack listened as the case facts unfolded. There had been a big corn festival where soy, corn, and pecans were sold. A guy who owned a hardware store, and you could sell your harvested pecans to him, and he would sell them in the store. This is where the son of the priestess stole pecans from.

Judge Throwbridge took the bench. A local deputy was called as the first witness.

"Your Honor, I was on duty the night of—."

"Lord Jesus, God, Jesus, save that child! Save my baby!" Sitting in the front row, the priestess and mother screamed in the courtroom. "God, Jesus, Lord!"

Judge Throwbridge, irritated, said to the defense attorney, Coppedge Dodson, "You think you can control your people?"

Coppedge tried to calm her. "Ma'am, ma'am, please." She breathed heavily; her eyes were closed as she clutched the raggedy Bible to her chest. Then as Coppedge whispered in her ear, she stopped screaming for the Lord but continued to rock back and forth in prayer.

Judge Throwbridge told the witness to continue, and he started his testimony again. "This young man was in the bushes when—."

"Oh, Lord Jesus, God Almighty, save my child!"

"Calm her down, Mr. Dodson," Throwbridge snapped. The judge then stood up and leaned over the bench with his brow furrowed in irritation as he spoke to the lady. "Ma'am, this is a preliminary hearing, but if you can't control yourself, I will have my bailiff remove you. Do you understand?"

Her eyes sprang open, and she nodded a yes.

The judge sat down and directed the witness to continue.

"I saw this unusual conduct, and I decided to keep him under surveillance because I felt like something was about to happen. So I parked my patrol car and watched him. He was peering through the fence."

"What did you see?"

"Well, he peered through, and then he jumped the fence to where the pecans are stashed at the hardware store and snatched a bag—."

"Oh God in heaven, have mercy on my child! Spare him for his trespasses! Save him! Save him!"

Judge Throwbridge shouted to the bailiff, "Get that mother out of here!"

The bailiff went to the defense table and grabbed the defendant's accused son. He started taking him out of the courtroom. The mother was screaming, and Judge Throwbridge yelled to the bailiff, "Not him! I am talking about the other mother!"

The low murmurs of chuckles and snickers could be heard as the witness continued.

By the time Don, the clerk, announced, "Next on the docket is the state versus Sandra Allgood on the charge of first-degree murder," Jack had assumed he would leave empty-handed that day. "On the second day of July this year, Mrs. Allgood is accused of intentionally shooting her husband, William J. Allgood, seven times, causing death—murder in the first degree." Jack thought, *I need another cup of coffee,* as he fought his midmorning slump.

Throwbridge looked questioningly at the district attorney, George Layton, a slender man with thick, gold, aviator-shaped eyeglasses and longish hair he slicked back.

"Six bullets not enough?" the judge asked.

"Not according to the police report, Your Honor," Layton answered. "In addition, while there was a suicide note, the state is prepared to prove Mr. Allgood was not the author."

The judge cocked his head to one side. "Well, how dumb would a man have to be to shoot himself seven times when committing suicide?"

Layton shifted his weight and cleared his throat, seeing the agitation rise in the judge. "Well, Your Honor, we think it was a plan that went haywire when—"

The judge cut him off. "That was a rhetorical question, Mr. Layton. And from what I know and heard about Mr. Allgood, nobody will miss him much," the judge continued. "Which means there will be a long list of suspects, I presume. Unless your presence today indicates you have conclusive and surefire evidence against the defendant."

"The state believes so, sir," Layton answered definitively. Layton expected unusual questions from Judge Throwbridge, so he was prepared for this one.

"You better do more than just *be-lie-ve*, Mr. Layton," the judge commented emphatically before turning to the part-time public defender, Clem Dawkins.

"Mr. Dawkins, how does the defense plea?"

"Not guilty, Your Honor. Mrs. Allgood has lived in this community all her life with not so much as a speeding ticket. Therefore, we do request reasonable bail."

"Mr. Layton?"

"Objection, Your Honor. Defendants who are charged with murder do not get bail."

"Well, generally, that's true, but the judge does have something to say about it," Throwbridge retorted. He neither liked nor disliked Layton. For the judge, the jury was still out on the esteemed prosecutor.

"Your Honor, the community is in no danger from the

defendant," Dawkins said. "And before this, she has never been in trouble with the law."

"You can say that about any number of murderers, Your Honor. Most wives who kill their husbands don't have previous prison records," said Layton.

Sutton glanced over at the defendant. She stood beside her lawyer at an average height of around five feet five, 110 pounds, and had gorgeous raven-colored hair. She turned and looked around but didn't smile, which Jack thought was understandable. But then her eyes caught another person's in the gallery, and her flatlined look broke into the slightest upturn.

Jack followed her gaze and noticed Doc Furman seated among a few of the old-timers in town.

Judge Throwbridge skimmed through some papers that Jack assumed listed the background of Sandra Allgood. Then the judge looked at the defendant. "Mrs. Allgood, your trial has been set for a month. Plan on killing anyone during the next four weeks?"

Jack gasped and coughed at the question, as did most of the courtroom. It was a distinct breach of judicial protocol. Layton rolled his eyes and slapped the paper in his hands against the table.

"No, no, Your Honor," she stuttered, barely audible to anyone in the gallery.

"I don't see Mrs. Allgood fleeing the county. I'll set bail at a hundred dollars," Throwbridge said.

Layton would have protested, but he knew once Judge Throwbridge had made up his mind, the chances of changing it were the same a snowball melting in Siberia.

"There is another issue I need to bring before the court, Your Honor," Dawkins said. "There's been an abundance of cases my office is handling. I'm involved as local counsel for the defense in the catfish case, and right now, I don't have time to prepare for a murder trial. So I would request another attorney be appointed in this case."

"Doesn't the defendant have the resources to hire her own attorney?"

"No, Your Honor, and that's the second issue I wanted to discuss. Her deceased husband handled the accounts of the family, and the way he legally set them up, Mrs. Allgood is barred from obtaining any money without her husband's signature."

"Sounds like him," the judge said. "Bring me the legal papers requesting those restrictions be lifted, and I will sign them. As for a new lawyer—" He looked over the courtroom, and his eyes stopped on Jack.

"Mr. Sutton?" he said.

Jack looked around in disbelief before he stood up. But the second he stood and looked at the judge, he felt like he was about to lose his breakfast.

"I had planned to appoint you to assist Mr. Dawkins, but now we need a lead lawyer, and you seem to be dressed like one today. I'm appointing you as the lead defense attorney in this case."

"Er ... Judge ... Your Honor ... er ... I've never tried a murder case ... I've never tried a case at all, for that matter."

"Didn't they teach you criminal law at that university you attended?"

With caution, Jack, in his deepest Southern drawl, responded, "Yes sir, Your Honor."

"And you passed the Georgia Bar exam?"

"Yes, sir, Your Honor."

"Always a first time." The judge paused and looked over his half glasses at a now white-as-a-sheet Jack Sutton. "And I'm sure you will do a good job for Mrs. Allgood. She will be available to discuss the case since I granted her bail. Are there any other matters that need to come before this court?"

Jack sat, and although he wanted to raise another objection, his mouth didn't seem to be working, and what little wits he had left advised him against it.

"OK then, the court is adjourned."

Judge Throwbridge banged his gavel. Jack raised his eyes to heaven and muttered under his breath, "Good Lord, save me from myself!"

Jack turned and caught the eye of Brad Lavender, who was sitting in the back of the courtroom. As they walked out together, Brad offered, "I'm going to make you more famous than Billy the Kid."

"Jesus, Brad, he was an outlaw."

"Yeah, but the dime store novel writers made him into a legend, and I plan to do the same with you, my friend."

Jack raised his eyes to heaven again and this time said out loud, "Good Lord, save me from myself!"

Brad slapped him on the back, laughing, and turned toward the newspaper office.

The Winthrop aircraft was rugged and reliable and evolved into a high-wing monoplane taildragger with a welded steel tube truss fuselage, metal spar wing, short take-off landing (STOL) characteristics, good range, and speed. The fast-cruising aircraft was being produced in a small company factory in Ohio. But the company had decided to look south due in large part to good flying weather and lower labor costs. When Bill Allgood had learned of this craft to aid in his businesses, or so he claimed, he helped recruit the company to Callahan County.

Horace Brumlow, the president of the Pear Valley Chamber of Commerce, paced back and forth in the "press room." He had been waiting for this day for almost six months. It would be the biggest thing to happen in the town since the chamber opened, and surprisingly, he had Bill Allgood to thank for it. But what started with Allgood was finished by Brumlow and others. There had been scores of meetings and letters and phone calls and conferences, and there had been a time when they thought the deal might fall through. Brumlow credited the Reverend Richard Mitchell of the First Methodist Church for standing up at the last meeting to declare, "God loves Pear Valley, and He's going to bless us." Brumlow doubted but hoped the pastor did possess some pull with the Lord.

The chamber's small room for press announcements had been set up with microphones, a desk, and a podium. In front of the podium were three dozen chairs in anticipation of the day's big unveiling. Horace, County Commission Chairman Elton Elder, Mayor Dutton, and the two executives of the Winthrop Aircraft Company, Ben Maule and Dalton Hamilton, would occupy the seats at the front of the room, facing the attendees, many of whom were from the press.

The five men filed in and took their places as about twenty people, including the media representatives, had already sat down. Craig Wolf, the owner of the small radio station in the town, had badgered Brumlow for two weeks about the announcement, but Brumlow refused to say anything. He told Wolf, "I get this may mean more advertising for you. But you'll have to attend the press conference to see what the announcement is." Wolf had shot back, "If it doesn't get postponed because of Allgood."

When Brumlow took his seat, he saw not only Wolf but a reporter from Brunswick, Georgia as well. The reporter was a tall, skinny man with a balding head and curiosity in his gaze. He took a seat in the front row and nodded to Brumlow. Brumlow smiled, thinking, *The announcement might even make the Brunswick paper.*

Brad Lavender rushed in at about the last second. In theory, Brad was on features and investigative reporting, but at the *Pear Valley Observer,* you did what you had to do. And despite being surprised by this assignment, Brad's initial irritation shifted. He started to rethink the story from a different angle, a potential melting of Allgood's untimely death and his recent push for Winthrop to make Pear Valley its home. *Perspective,* he thought as he took his seat.

Brumlow had been looking for a local paper reporter and started worrying. Once he saw Lavender, Brumlow walked to the podium and didn't waste any time.

"Ladies and gentlemen, thank you for coming. This is truly a tremendous day for Pear Valley. There are two gentlemen here at the table that you probably don't know, so please allow me to introduce them: Mr. Ben Maule and Dalton Hamilton, the president and vice president of the Winthrop Aircraft Company. They build single-engine airplanes, and they have chosen Pear Valley as the site of their new manufacturing facility. The Winthrop aircraft has one of the industry's shortest takeoff and landing requirements. And I would be remiss if I didn't acknowledge the efforts of the late Bill Allgood to have introduced our wonderful town to this great company!"

Brad perked up as he contemplated Allgood's motives.

The chamber chair went on. "The building will commence next month. It will be a small plant at first, employing approximately 150 men. It will be a shot in the arm for the local economy. These are well-paying jobs and will give a great boost to the financial sector of Pear Valley and Callahan County. It will take about four months to construct the plant, but we hope to have people working in the brand-new plant within six months."

Applause broke out, provoking a proud smile to creep across Brumlow's weathered face.

He continued. "As I said, the two executives will now give you details about the matter, and the chamber does have packets about what this new company will mean for the community. You are welcome to pick up a packet as you leave and breeze through it while you are here. This is truly a new and fantastic day for our city and county. This move will have strong financial ripples throughout the community."

Brad's hand shot up.

"Yes?"

"You stated Mr. Allgood was involved in bringing Winthrop here. What was his motive as a farmer?"

Brumlow gave a muddled laugh before standing straight and clearing his throat. "I don't know that we can answer that. Unlike many things Mr. Allgood did, he took his reasoning to the grave."

"But do you have a suspicion?"

Brumlow grew visibly more uncomfortable. "Mr. Allgood was a farmer, but he was also a businessman. Having smaller planes made here would mean more jobs for the community he loved, and the more Pear Valley prospered, the better he would do. Plus these aircraft can be used for crop-dusting."

"And one more question—"

"I'm sorry. Let's move to Aaron?" Brumlow cut Lavender off and moved the questioning for a few more minutes before ending it.

TEN

The News

Robin paid the bail and expected her friend to emerge straight away. Instead, the officer told her to wait in the plastic seats next to the potted plant. She shook her head, thinking with all Sandy had, how was it she wound up being the one who needed saving?

After Sandy and Bill married, Robin and Sandy only spoke a handful of times. Robin sensed that Bill wanted to ensure his new wife cut all ties from her trailer park past, and Robin was a casualty. She recalled showing up at the plantation house one day when the maid had come to the door. "Can I help you?" the maid snapped with the fierce judgment of the hired help. The maid told her to wait on the porch as she went back inside.

Robin sat in a long line of white wicker rockers and waited over twenty minutes. When a red-faced Bill emerged, he snapped, "Sandra's out shopping."

Robin stood up from the rocker. "Oh, um, well, she had called and asked me to come over."

Robin, who was tall, slender, and blonde, could feel Bill watching and even undressing her with his stare. Bill's tone softened as he moved in closer. "You must be mistaken. I'll let her know you came by." And after brushing his hand against her shoulder, Bill retreated, slinking back into the house.

The maid came to the porch and watched Robin get in her green AMC Gremlin. Robin kept an eye on her rearview mirror as she drove down the long driveway back to the road. As she looked back, Robin could have sworn she saw her friend in the upstairs window with her hands pressed against the glass.

But over the last year, so much had changed. She hated herself for what she had done, and she cringed to think how Sandra would react if she knew.

"Ma'am, your friend is on her way down!" the officer at the front desk yelled over, snapping Robin out of her thoughts.

Sandra burst through the door to Robin's left and ran into her friend's arms. They hugged for a good minute and left without saying a word to one another.

As Robin pulled up to Sandra's home, she asked, "You want me to come in with you?"

Sandra turned to look at her friend. Silence lingered as they looked at one another. Robin, feeling uncomfortable, diverted her eyes. Sandra grabbed for the door handle. "I'm good. But thank you." Sandra reached over and touched Robin's arm, gave a soft squeeze, and got out of the car.

As she drove out of the private road onto the local road back toward town, Robin's mind raced from one thought to the next, and she failed to notice the car following her. Suddenly, a car pulled out of the side road ahead of her, causing her to slam on her brakes. "What the hell!" she screamed.

The car, a black Mercury four-door, took off and then slowed. Robin glanced in her rearview to see the exact same type of Mercury behind her and approaching her at a fast speed. She stomped on the gas to gain distance but then hit her brakes when the car in front came to a complete stop. Bookended by these two black sedans,

Robin panicked. She threw her car in park and made a run for it toward the wooded area on either side of the road.

Before her feet left the road, two hands grabbed her from either side and pulled her, twisting and screaming, back toward one of the sedans. The men forcibly threw her into one of the back seats and slammed the door behind her.

—◆—

Jack parked the car and stared at the law firm's old building. He sat, hands on the steering wheel, thinking, *David or Mosely should be handling the Allgood case*, and he more than feared Truitt's reaction. But then Jack thought, *No, David wouldn't be the answer either.* The general understanding was that Truitt pushed David hard and got little back in the way of cash coming into the firm. Thus, the need to bring on someone young and hungry, like Jack, to take over the practice when Mr. Truitt retired. Or at least that is what Brown told him. But after being dressed down by the powers that be and handed a case he wasn't ready for, Jack started questioning his abilities.

When Jack walked up the pathway toward the front door, every step felt labored as if he would melt on the bricks. His hand finally reached for the doorknob, but the door flew open, and Jack jumped back.

"What the hell took you so long?"

"Sir."

"Come into my office, boy," Truitt said, turning and walking toward his office. He looked neither pleased nor displeased. On the contrary, the former senator was as stoic as a champion poker player. Jack knew he could turn on a dime in his short but few dealings with Truitt.

Mosely Brown came down the hall as Jack stepped into the foyer, closing the front door behind him. Brown gave him a nod toward Truitt's office, and they went in together. The office was originally the living room. There was a center fireplace with a tufted oxblood leather couch directly in front of it. Truitt's desk backed up to the window, which he mostly kept covered with closed plantation shudders.

Jack and Mosely walked in as Mr. Truitt started to look over legal papers. Truitt slammed the folder shut as Jack and Mosely sat before the vast partner-style double desk. Silence. Frank then leaned forward, spit into the spittoon, and wiped the corner of his mouth and bottom lip with a stained white handkerchief. He leaned back and zoned in on Jack with his cold, dark eyes. Jack steadied himself to remind the old man that his legal time had been co-opted by the local judge.

"OK, out with it, boy."

Jack fidgeted in his chair and gave a glance toward Brown. "This came completely unexpected this morning. I did what you instructed. I went to the courthouse and Judge Throwbridge's chambers and apologized. He accepted and told me to get in the court," explained Jack without taking a breath.

"And?"

Jack choked and coughed. "After hearings and assignment calendar, that's when he assigned me to Sandra Allgood."

"The fuck you say?" Truitt bellowed as he leaned forward again.

Jack assumed he already knew. He turned to Brown, who looked equally surprised by Jack's announcement. *Why else would Truitt be at the door when I got here?* Confused but somewhat emboldened, Jack said, "Apparently, she didn't have any money—"

Truitt stood up. "No shit, boy! How the fuck did this happen?" Brown shook his head and shrugged his shoulders when Truitt looked over at him. "You were supposed to be assigned to the nut case!"

"Pecan theft," Brown interrupted. Truitt didn't respond angrily, which spoke more about his respect for Brown than any patience he might have had. Instead, Brown, taking note of Truitt's expression, got up and excused himself.

Truitt continued. "So you're telling me the judge just assigned you this case out of the blue? You were just sitting there and he just *gave* it to you? Do you know how many other more qualified litigators could have taken this case?" He stared straight through Jack.

"I tried to explain that, sir."

"You tried to explain that you are grossly underqualified?" His tone rose a few octaves in complete disbelief. After what seemed like hours of silence between the two, Truitt raised his hand, leaned across his desk, knitted his brow, and spat, "Judge Throwbridge saw you, banged his gavel, and said, 'Welcome to Pear Valley.' You damn well better be ready to be worthy of his hospitality."

Jack nodded.

Truitt, in true form, went from zero to one hundred and back again in less than a second. He almost chuckled as he shook his head. "I guess he is giving you enough rope to hang yourself. That old bastard got me."

Jack smiled nervously.

Truitt shot his associate's balloon before it inflated. "Boy, Throwbridge and I have a history. This is more about him and me than you. You are highly unqualified. But you damn well better come up to speed with the name of this firm riding shotgun. You hear me?"

"Yes, sir. Loud and clear." Then Jack stood and walked to the door before he mustered up enough courage to make a plea. "I doubt I can do much else while preparing for the trial the next three weeks," he explained, feeling he had nothing left to lose at this point.

A calmer Truitt looked at his young apprentice. "Yes, we can't have you doing minor real estate matters when you have a murder trial on your plate. So just ignore everything you are working on now. If there's a deadline involved, hand it over to David. And if you have any questions about the trial, ask Mosely. He had handled several murder cases before he retired from criminal law."

Jack began to walk out when Truitt called after him, "When are you speaking to your client?"

Jack turned and only partially stepped back into the office. "I spoke to her briefly after court. She is set to be released from jail later today. We arranged for her to come to the office tomorrow at 10 a.m."

"They released her?" Brown asked, coming up behind Jack.

Truitt shook his head. "Something about this smells wrong. On so many levels." Turning to a slowly retreating Jack, he said, "Look. Take her to the conference room, not your office, when she comes in. Mosely, I want you present. She can discuss her case with both of you."

He spat the tobacco out of his mouth into the spittoon and eased back into his chair. He flipped open a cigar box on his desk and pulled out a long, thick Cohiba Cigar. He loved his cigars; this was a Cuban Cohiba, given to him by a lobbyist at the state capitol. He picked up a silver lighter, flipped it open, and moved the flame to the tobacco. "I admit our district attorney, Layton, is a man I don't particularly like. But he is handling this, isn't he?"

"Yes, sir. I spoke to the public defender briefly, and he said Rush Layton would be prosecuting."

"Layton only takes cases with three rock-solid eyewitnesses and a signed confession. He's a rule player, a career climber, and he plays to win." Truitt sat back, tented his fingers, shook his head, and let out a breath. "Well, Mr. Sutton, welcome to the hot seat."

Jack nodded and started to leave again, but Truitt wasn't done.

As he stood up and started to pace, Truitt continued. "Many people knew Bill Allgood, but not many liked him. That will be a point in your favor. Of course, you can't put anyone on the jury who knew the defendant, but you may have a chance to get a few folks who knew what a sorry bastard he was. Plus that wife is a pretty young thing, and the men on the jury will like her. Accentuate the cleavage, boy. You're going to need all the help you can get."

"I'll remember that, sir," Jack said.

"Well, stop standing around. Get the hell out of here and start building your case."

Jack nodded and all but ran to his office.

Life in Pear Valley was a molasses lifestyle. One of the first people Ruby met upon moving in had commented, "There are two settings around these parts: slow and slower." So when Darlene Calhoun asked Ruby to join her book club a few weeks later, Ruby gave it a second thought; her choices were limited, to say the least. Jack also nudged her to accept the invitation.

"Why am I doing this?" Ruby whispered sharply to herself as she left her house.

In her head, she heard Jack's voice coming back with "Because being neighborly is the Southern way."

"Jack Sutton, this is your doing!" Ruby shouted to no one in particular.

Ruby decided to walk to Darlene's house that day since it was so close. But she instantly regretted it when an annoying group of well-dressed women and men holding Bibles came her way. This, she had learned, was the main staple of small-town Georgia, where groups of religious zealots would greet you on the street and ask, "Have you found Jesus?" The phrase made it sound like the Savior himself was hiding behind a tree.

Ruby, a Methodist and well-versed in the biography of John Wesley, a remarkable man and founder of Methodism, found these groups insufferable. They reminded her of John Wesley's wife, who would have driven most ministers to atheism.

Ruby smiled sweetly at the group and continued without responding, swatting gnats as she made her way to Darlene's. Lately, all she could think about was the possibility of working at the local paper. She longed to be back writing again. But for now, she knew Jack was right about settling in and creating a life in small-town Pear Valley. Besides, Darlene owned and operated the Upside-Down Cupcake, a local café and bakery that even Ruby had to admit rivaled Atlanta's finest.

She waved as Darlene opened the screen door. "Oh, I'm so glad you made it," Darlene said.

"Thank you for the invite. I couldn't look at another box to unpack," Ruby replied with her sweet Southern smile. Although she had been unpacked for some time, feigning being overwhelmed was the hallmark of the genteel Southern woman. *Mama taught me well*, she thought. And for a brief minute, Ruby felt the recurring pang of homesickness.

Darlene waved Ruby in to sit on the back porch with the other ladies. As Ruby moved through Darlene's foyer, she could see this woman was all in Callahan County. Ruby stopped at her wall of pictures. "Was this you?" Most were black and white, but the one that caught her eye had Darlene in a baby blue dress and long blonde hair, compared to the short salt and pepper she had now.

"Yes. Me and Judge Throwbridge and Frank Truitt; you wouldn't know the rest."

"You went to school with them?"

"High school, yes. My late husband and I both did. There was no place we'd rather live and raise a family than here in Pear Valley."

"How wonderful," Ruby said with a smile as the two continued onto the porch. She wondered if she would ever feel that way anywhere other than Atlanta.

"Ruby, honey, I'm so glad you could come. We love you and

that adorable husband of yours," Darlene said as she held the door open to the back porch.

"Thank you. I heard the book club is one of the highlights of Pear Valley. I'm so glad y'all invited me," Ruby said in her practiced reply. She made sure to emphasize her Southern drawl.

As she entered the porch, she saw that the other three club members had arrived. Barbara Rivers, the wife of the president of the Pear Valley Bank, sat on a green sofa with Gretchen Diamond, who owned a small dress shop in the town. Seated in a rocking chair was Annie Shirley, on the local school board and a first-rate singer in the choir at the local Baptist church, occasionally having a solo.

The book club usually reads the classics of English literature. Still, Gretchen had encouraged them to branch out and include mysteries in their reading list, so this week, members had read Agatha Christie's *And Then There Were None.* However, as Ruby entered, the conversation had nothing to do with the book. The talk centered on the Sandra Allgood arrest and pending trial.

"Ruby!" the ladies exclaimed in unison.

Ruby smiled. "Hi, ladies. Thank you for letting me crash y'all's book club."

"Well, we wouldn't have it any other way," Annie said, holding her tall glass of what appeared to be iced tea up to toast the new member. The others followed with their glasses.

"Ruby, sit down," Darlene instructed, pointing to the loveseat opposite the sofa. And help yourself to a treat. I'll grab your drink."

Barbara leaned in when Darlene left. "You've never had an Arnold Palmer until you've had one of Darlene's. She adds a little vodka to the tea and lemonade."

Ruby looked at all the smiling faces staring back at her. "Well, I guess I'll find out." Ruby glanced at the tray of goodies on the coffee table. "Oh my, are these from the Upside-Down Cupcake?"

"Dig in, darlin'. You can afford it," Barbara said with a hearty chuckle, "unlike us more senior ladies."

"Speak for yourself!" Annie snapped, wearing a wide smile.

Ruby shook her head and shared the laughter with these old friends. They were her mother's age, and it oddly felt like home. When her mother and her friends would pull Ruby into a conversation, it would always take an off-color, if not embarrassing, turn.

Barbara stuck to her agenda, and today it was Allgood's murder. "You know, Bill Allgood banked with us, but no one was happy when he walked in the door. He always looked like a sourpuss and acted like it too. I don't know if he ever said a kind word to anyone," Barbara said. "I could not imagine what being married to him was like. And I wouldn't want to."

"I don't know if they can get a jury in Pear Valley," Annie said. "This is a small town. Almost everyone knew William. But few knew Sandra. We all just seemed to know *of her*. So where do you get an impartial jury, especially when everyone hated William?"

"If I killed my husband, that's the type of jury I would want—full of people who hated him," Ruby said, taking a bite of a coconut confection.

The ladies all went silent and stared at their newcomer. Ruby instantly regretted speaking and covered her mouth as she savored the sweet treat.

"I wonder if the judge will move the trial," Gretchen all but whispered, breaking the awkward silence. Ruby wondered how she sold anything by being so shy.

"There is no telling what Emmitt Throwbridge will do," Barbara said. "Don't get me wrong. He is a first-rate judge. I don't think there's anyone in the state who knows the law better than Emmitt Stonewall Throwbridge," she went on, intentionally drawing out the judge's name even longer than she usually did. "He is so flamboyant, which doesn't come close enough to describe his behavior in the courtroom. He's handling that catfish trial from Cook County also. I don't see how he can do both."

"Is that the one where the late Cook County sheriff, Warren Cain, and Dan Cook, who owned about half the county, were accused of growing marijuana?" Gretchen asked and then dropped her head to look at the napkin in her lap as if she were embarrassed to say the word.

Barbara answered, "Yes. They arrested them while the four were catfishing at night in a pond in the middle of a pot field. The deputy over there, Tom Armond, his mother, Peggy, and I are friends. Tom said their plan was to harvest the crop the next day, and they wanted to get the fishing in after inspecting the crop."

"As y'all have heard, the sheriff died in the line of duty. He ran his car into a bridge rail at seventy miles an hour the day before he was arrested. Everyone knows he had gotten tipped off!" Darlene yelled from the kitchen.

Barbara went on. "Peggy said that there was another partner only Sheriff Cain knew about, and he had not been identified or arrested. Cook seems to be going to stand trial on his own."

"Well, then, Cook could accuse anyone of getting the light off him, right?" Ruby said, grabbing for a petite four.

Darlene walked in and handed Ruby a drink as she sat next to her. "Warren had been a childhood friend of ours. Frank and me, that is. We all went to high school together before Warren's family moved to Cook County. His father had taken a job managing the farm for Dan Cook's daddy.

"I heard Frankie was quite the ladies' man. He had all the girls after him. Some girls had little pet names for him. Mira's was Big Frank, if you know what I mean," Gretchen added as the ladies snickered, which sparked her blushing and fanning herself.

Ruby made a note to herself to privately follow up on that tidbit. Although given the free-flowing Arnold Palmers spiked with vodka, one could ask, "Was it information or misinformation?"

But Ruby knew within each piece of gossip sat, at least, some truth. *And it might be helpful to have a little dirt on Jack's boss; this book club might be fruitful after all.*

Darlene returned to the kitchen and yelled, "Y'all, remember Frank is Ruby's husband's boss!" Darlene reappeared. "Ruby, Frank, and Warren called themselves the dynamic duo, and as I said, they liked to have nicknames for their paramours. Warren called me Dari and called me often," she added a wink and a blush as she entered the porch.

The other ladies chuckled.

Darlene sat and then quickly moved to the business at hand. "Well, how many y'all liked the book?"

All five hands went up.

"Whenever I read a whodunit, I can never figure out who really did it, and it was the same with this book. I kept thinking, *You're running out of suspects,* so the ending came as a surprise. But it didn't cheat the reader. So then I thought, *Well, I should have seen that,*" said Annie.

"Christie is a master at giving clues without really appearing to give clues. She's brilliant. If there were a Pulitzer Prize for mystery books, she should have gotten it," Barbara said.

Ruby sipped the vodka-spiked Arnold Palmer, and it was excellent with just enough vodka to make the day better. "I had read the book some years ago, but I reread it this past weekend. I admire Christie's style, where she slips in vital clues without the reader noticing. And I think the plots, like this one, are very well constructed. But I don't think she's great at characterization. Most of her characters are—" Ruby looked up toward the ceiling and then back at the ladies. "I'd say one-dimensional. On the other hand, her strength is definitely in her plots. I can barely figure out who the murderer is, but it's fun trying."

"I agree," Darlene said. "It's fun trying, and I didn't figure out this one either. And then, like Annie, I said, 'Well, yes, of course,' at the end of the book. And I thought her prose, while not exceptional, was more than adequate for the novel. It was fine, and I thought the pace was good too."

"I must admit I've always had a weakness for mysteries. Some people look down their literary noses at them, but I have always enjoyed them. Reading a mystery is a great way to spend an afternoon," Ruby said. She took another sip of the lemonade. "And in my mind, two of the greatest mystery writers today both have the same last name. John D. and Ross MacDonald. They are excellent storytellers, but they write very different types of mysteries."

Barbara laughed loudly. "The Allgood case would not have made a good Christie novel. She just killed her no-good, crude husband. As far as I am concerned, she should have shot him long ago."

"Barbara!" Gretchen gasped, followed by a little chuckle she tried to hide with her delicate hand.

Barbara laughed. "There's an old story about a Baptist preacher who tried never to say anything bad about people. So when a true scoundrel died, the minister went to the funeral. People were whispering, 'What could he possibly say good about this guy?' So the minister goes up, stares at the man for a few minutes, and says, 'Well, he sure had good teeth.'"

The ladies laughed.

"I'm not sure Bill Allgood even had good teeth. Didn't he have some gaps in his mouth?" Annie asked. "Ruby, your husband doesn't have anything to do with the trial?"

"No, thank goodness. Jack is the low man at Mr. Truitt's office. I think he mostly does minor real estate matters and things like that."

"You know, I'm a little surprised that Allgood had been the one who got shot," Annie said. "Not that I'm a gossip, but Carol Daniels has been carrying on with Bob Hoffman for a few months, and both are married but not to each other. Carol's husband is known for his temper, and Bob's wife, Charlotte, knows how to use a .38 special."

This was the one thing Ruby didn't like about small towns and loved simultaneously. The gossip.

"That's always been his reputation," Darlene said. "And Charlotte knew that when she married him. He's just like his father, Bob Hoffman; he was the same way. Back some years ago, some buckshot peppered his backside. They took the lead out of him at the ER."

"OK, let's pass on to a more enlightening conversation. We have a new lady in town. Let's not give Ruby a wrong impression about our citizenry. She'll want to go back to Atlanta," Gretchen added softly.

"No," Ruby said, shaking her head. "There's a few ERs in Atlanta have done the same buckshot-from-the-buttocks medical removal procedure on a few folks. Except up there, sometimes the shooters use more than buckshot."

"OK, let's have dessert," Darlene said. "And let's leave buckshot and bad teeth out of the conversations."

ELEVEN

No Good Deed

The unshaven man walked out of the courthouse, around the square, and returned to the red Ford pickup. His partner, still inside the truck, said, "What did you find out?"

"Nothin'. They let the wife go and put some young yahoo in to defend her."

"What do we do now?"

Shifting in his seat, the man placed his hands on the wheel and rang them tightly. "We wait for instructions." He started the truck, and the two rumbled down through the town center, heading out toward the lake.

The passenger mumbled as he chewed on a toothpick and looked out the window. "I don't like waitin'."

Stepping on the gas, the driver spat back, "What does it matter? We gettin' paid, ain't we?"

"That's nothin' if cops be blamin' us for the killin'!"

"Shut it! We didn't kill nobody!"

"Yeah, but we—"

The truck skidded to a stop as a car honked and drove around.

The driver lunged toward his passenger, finger in his face. "You shut it. You got that? We don't know shit!"

—⚬—

Louis clicked the receiver down on the pay phone before heading back into the diner to update Diego.

"So what did you find out?" Diego asked.

"Let the wife go. Seems like the law doesn't have a case."

Diego shook his head and got up from the booth. Luis followed behind as usual. Diego walked over to the waitress and stuffed a five between her exposed cleavage. "Keep the change," he said with a wink before heading out the door. Once his boots hit the dirt parking lot, he turned to Luis.

"Guess we got lucky," Luis said, passing his cousin and heading to the van.

Diego stuck his foot out, and Luis lost his balance as his body hit their van. Diego got in his face and gripped Luis's shirt as his knuckles dug into Luis's collarbone. "No such thing as luck happening to you. You have to make your own. Get the boys to follow Tanner. I want to know his every move. You understand?"

"Yes, boss."

—⚬—

Ruby smiled as she left the book club. To her surprise, she genuinely enjoyed this part of Pear Valley culture. As Ruby passed by where Lydia Meyers lived, she slowed to take in the picturesque gardens. Lydia was middle-aged and had more than a green thumb. Ruby thought, *This woman might have a green forefinger and pinkie.* Almost all of Lydia's large lawn was covered in azaleas, camellias, and gardenias spread out among southern pines and an occasional magnolia tree. She also had a row of camellias she planted along the back of the property.

A dirty red Ford pickup sputtered down the street at a curiously slow speed. Ruby turned to watch. Two sun-soaked faces inside the vehicle gave her a nod as they passed. Ruby kept a watchful eye on the truck, which appeared to speed up and make a left at the end of the street.

"Ruby, you're looking pretty as a peach today."

Ruby jumped back and nearly lost her footing. "Hello, Lydia. Sorry, you startled me. I was at Darlene's book review club. I'm on my way home, but I had to take another look at your yard. It is so stunning and lovely."

A few years past the midcentury mark, Lydia had a few gray hairs among the red. While Lydia's fascination might be considered odd, if not a fixation, she did have a beautiful yard. In fact, the chamber of commerce had recently listed Lydia's house in their tourist pamphlet given to newcomers and visitors. Her house was a unique feature of Pear Valley. "Thank you, dear. It sure does take a lot of care. I wonder how long I can keep it in such good shape."

"I hope it's a long time," Ruby said. An awkward silence settled in as Lydia started pruning her camellias. "Well, I better keep walking. Nice to see you again," Ruby said before she took a step.

No reply. Ruby wondered whether the older woman had heard her. But as Ruby took a step backward, Lydia stopped and turned toward her. "Excuse me for being so blunt, but how is your husband getting along with Frank Truitt? Frank can be difficult."

Ruby took a step forward cautiously, closing the distance between them. "He is a little tough. But Jack's handling it."

Lydia walked up to the white fence between them and held onto it. "Honey, they get old and forget they were young once. I remember a story from years ago when Frank was just starting out. There was this giant drug raid in south Georgia with the GBI. Much to the chagrin of the local pastors, lawyers all over town were getting cases and cashing in on the money. They could charge $500 for a retainer. Frank got a call from an American gothic-looking family, members of the Church of God. Their son had been arrested for possession of marijuana in an attempt to distribute it. Most of the lawyers in town were already retained for others, and Frank, being young and inexperienced, was available. So they went to his office."

After a deep breath, Lydia continued. "They gave him a rundown of the case, and he was acting like hot stuff. He leaned back in his nice suit, drinking coffee as this poor farming family begged him to defend their child. Acting all-important, he said, 'Given the circumstances, the retainer will be a thousand dollars.' He leaned back against his chair, the back of the chair broke off, and he hit the ground. His coffee mug flew into the air—utter silence. When he got up and looked at the poor family, black coffee covered their faces. Thankfully, it wasn't that hot. But in a panicked voice, the father said, 'Thank you, Mr. Truitt. I think we will go elsewhere.'"

Ruby laughed and said, "Oh my!"

Linda laughed also. "He was just a brash young man who could tell those stories before he became stiff and full of himself. So don't let him get you or that fine young husband of yours down."

"What was Truitt's wife like? I mean I saw him with his grandchildren at the pig race, and he seemed like a genuine grandfatherly type with them."

Lydia shook her head. "Oh, she was as sweet as a pecan pie! Sad how she died so unexpectedly. It was an aneurysm. Took her in her sleep. Frank just grew mean as a rabid dog afterward."

"Oh wow, I had no idea."

"There's a reason Thelma has stayed on so long. But on a happier note, how are you adjusting to the rest of your life in Pear Valley? After living in the big city, I know it must be challenging."

Ruby wanted to learn more about Truitt but answered Lydia's question so as not to be rude. "I miss Atlanta, but I'm getting used to it here. While I hate the gnats, we certainly never had anything as beautiful as your garden in Atlanta." *A little lie never hurt anyone*, she thought. But she added, "We just had asphalt freeways with cars rushing by."

"Well, thank you, darlin'. You're as sweet as honey."

Jack went in early Friday morning to ensure the conference room was presentable. Truitt and Mosely both had a habit of leaving books out after reviewing them for legal research and their empty coffee cups and full ashtrays. Jack couldn't deny his stomach was in knots. Not only did his senior partner think he was about to fall on his face, but he could tell Ruby had doubts last night when he told her he had been appointed. "Wow, this will be a big case for you, Jack. Are you ready for it?" Ruby had questioned.

Jack knew it wasn't her words so much as her facial expression that had him feeling a little depleted. And hell, he doubted everything too. She had tried to explain what the ladies at the book club said, but he stopped listening after her initial comment.

Jack took about ten more minutes to polish the conference table, dust the chairs, lamps, and framed pistol Mr. Truitt had from a German colonel in World War II, and hastily run a vacuum cleaner over the rug before his client arrived. Finally, he shoved coffee into the percolator and added water.

Jack returned to the conference room and saw a smudge on the table he had missed.

"You can scrub that until the cows come home, but it won't make your case any stronger," Mosely said as he dropped his legal pad on the shiny table.

"Sorry I have to bring you into this, Mosely, but Judge Throwbridge totally surprised me yesterday."

Mosely laughed. "Shucks, boy. You're not the first person Judge Throwbridge has thrown in a raging river without a life vest. I dare say you won't be the last either. He has a justified reputation in this part of the state for his distinctive judicial style—more myth than legend. He gets away with a lot because of it. But beyond the hoopla, he is an excellent judge. The court of appeals overruled one of his decisions a couple of years ago, but the supreme court overruled them. The ruling sort of cemented his reputation for knowing the law."

"Well, Truitt even thinks he's an idiot for picking me."

Mosely laughed. "Truitt has his panties in a twist because he probably thought Throwbridge would ask him. It's part ego and just part how Truitt is about everything."

Jack cocked his head to one side as if questioning Brown's declaration.

"Let's start with you giving me a brief summation of this case." Mosely changed the subject as he slid into one of the oxblood, leather, highbacked chairs and leaned on the freshly polished table, tented his hands to his lips, and raised his eyebrows in anticipation.

"Yes, sir," Jack started to pace next to the table. "The prosecution claims Sandra Allgood shot her husband seven times the night of July 2 of this year. The state says that the late Bill Allgood and his wife Sandra were the only two people in the house that night when she pulled out the gun and started shooting. Allgood was shot seven times."

"Seven shots? Did the shooter miss once or twice?"

"She hit him with every shot, according to the police report."

Brown nodded. "Be careful with that 'she,'" Mosely jokingly scolded.

Jack actually gasped at his faux pas and cleared his throat, trying to regroup.

"Just joking, boy. I know what you meant, and well, people in the South usually know how to shoot."

"But there was, apparently, a suicide note, which the police have, along with the six-shot revolver."

Brown chuckled. Then he shook his head. "Well, that's a bit unusual. Why would the shooter, even if it was Sandra Allgood, leave a note and then shoot her husband seven times. Or even shoot him, then leave a note? By virtue of the seven shots, no rational person would think they could cover that up as a suicide." Brown stopped speaking and thought before saying, "All right, so they will probably use a local person to do the handwriting analysis. Be there when it is collected, and also ask it to be sent to the GBI lab. They're better. You're up on their Brady requirements, right?"

"Yes, sir," Jack quickly said. He had reviewed criminal procedures since he got the case less than twenty-four hours ago.

"I remember some story details in the *Pear Valley Observer*. I skimmed the story. But I thought I heard the final shot hit his genitals. Was that right? I hate to think I misread a fact such as that. It shows I might be going senile."

"No, that wasn't in the story. It was revealed in court though."

"Well, that shows a crime of passion, or at least someone trying to make it look that way. Was the husband seeing another woman? Or was our defendant doing anything nefarious? We need to be sure she is clean too. The note, if she wrote it, could indicate premeditation as well."

"How so?"

"Well, this is just speculation. But if she did shoot him seven times, she logically wouldn't think she could pass it off as a suicide. Yet the state might argue that she initially only intended to stage it as suicide, but things got out of hand when she started the killing. And then she forgot about the note. Emotions are the cause of much sloppiness with a killing like this."

Jack stopped moving and leaned against the high-back chair across from Brown. "I haven't spoken to her yet. This morning will be the first time. But from *his* reputation around town, I'm guessing he probably had some honey on the side, which could support the crime of passion theory and potentially premeditation."

Thelma knocked on the door and walked in. "A Sandra Allgood is here to see you," she said.

"Please bring her in, Thelma," Brown said before turning to a now ghost-white Jack. "Don't get ahead of yourself. Let the facts unfold."

When Sandra Allgood walked in, Jack and Mosely stopped like deer in headlights. Sandra Allgood, up close and in person, stunned. Her flowing, dark, wavy hair, piercing green eyes, and curves to rival any backroad left even the most faithful men gasping for a breath. Jack caught himself. "Mrs. Allgood, please come in." He escorted her to the chair at the head of the table, and he promptly took the seat across from Mosely.

Despite her incarceration, Sandra looked refreshed. She wore a white linen vest, matching bell-bottom pants, a brown and yellow paisley puffy-sleeved shirt, and a matching headband. Her makeup looked expertly applied as her raven hair flowed to her shoulders. Looking back and forth between the men, she said, "Hello, I'm Sandra Callahan Allgood."

She had added the maiden name to show she was no stranger to Callahan County. While the Callahan clan had been a founding family in the county, all of their influence and family wealth had been depleted by the time Sandra was born. They were still treated well, but everyone knew they lived hand to mouth.

"Good to meet you," Jack said. "I will be handling your case. This is my partner, Mosely Brown. He's got the experience. I just supply the good looks to the team."

She smiled quickly and then grew serious as she stood next to the chair Jack had pulled out for her. "I didn't do it. I didn't kill my husband."

Jack put his hand out to tell her to relax and sit down. "Mrs. Allgood, we'll get to all that. We are here to guide you through it. Remember we're on your side."

Sandra sat as her eyes shot to the ceiling and back at Jack. She near his last comments. "But I won't lie, I didn't love him er."

Jack could sense her growing anxiety. Her reaction to the meeting and obvious trepidation were promising signs from where he sat, and he made a note. "OK. Let's back up and start from the beginning. Can you tell us what happened the night of the murder?" Jack asked.

"I can certainly tell you what I remember of it."

"What do you mean?" Jack asked.

Sandra shifted in her seat and inhaled deeply. "Bill usually comes and goes at his leisure. Sorry, I should use the past tense now, I guess." She flashed a forced a smile as she fidgeted with her hands on her lap. "Bill came and went as he pleased. That night, I asked him what he wanted for dinner. He said nothing because he said he couldn't stay, that he had business elsewhere. There was nothing odd about that. I spent most nights alone. But then he asked if I wanted to have a drink with him. I said yes because he seemed in a decent mood."

"Decent mood?"

"At home, Bill usually drank heavily and alone. Straight bourbon or whiskey, mostly. But he poured us both a whiskey. I sipped it, and he gulped his down. But like I said, he was in a decent mood, and we talked like we did when we were first married."

Mosely interjected, "You didn't normally get along?"

Sandra ignored his question and continued. "He asked if I wanted another, and I said no. But he poured me another glass anyway. We even sat next to each other, and he put his arm around me just like he did in the beginning, before—"

She caught the emotion in her throat and took a second to regain her train of thought. "I finished the second glass and felt dizzy. But I hadn't eaten much that day, and I think the liquor got to me. He suggested I go lie down and that he had to run an errand.

He told me to take a nap and said he'd probably be back by the time I woke. I said OK, so I went up to my bedroom."

"And did you wake up before the morning?"

"I can't really answer that. Initially, I couldn't recall anything. But I've started to remember more and more."

Jack put his hand up. "So you recall more than you told the sheriff?"

Sandra didn't answer Jack's question directly. "When I woke, I was shaky. The room spun, and my head killed me. I remember hearing sounds like a loud banging, but everything seemed muffled in my head. I got up but couldn't really stand. And I couldn't see too clearly. I realized I was still in my clothes from the night before. I held onto the wall for support and got as far as the hallway when I heard it again, but that time it sounded more like a shot, along with people yelling. Then nothing. I don't remember anything after that."

"What time was that?" Mosely asked.

Sandra shook her head no. She fidgeted in her seat and kept looking down at her hands. Her explanation wasn't a lie. It just wasn't the whole truth. Bill had come home in a mood, just not a good one. The two had shared two drinks, but he *forced* her to drink. And when the drinks relaxed Sandra enough, she spewed venom at him, accusing her husband of killing her beloved horse. The two had exchanged vicious expletives and accusations—most of which could be used against her. After all, this was the South, and the good ole boys' network would look to hang her, and she knew it.

Jack interrupted her thoughts. "So you now recall waking up and hearing the gunshots? What happened next?"

"I don't know. That's all I remember." Sandra started to cry. "You have to believe me! I just don't remember."

Jack sat back and shared a knowing look with Mosely, who got up to retrieve some coffee. "Take your time. We are on your side here, OK?" Jack said. He could tell by her darting eye movement and fidgeting Sandra was withholding information, but he wasn't sure how far to push her. She had a fragility that he couldn't put his finger on, contrasted by a seemingly repressed spirit. Sandra was the type of woman to command a room but at the same time fall to tears with one negative comment.

Mosely reentered with a tray of coffee, followed by Thelma, who brought a platter of assorted Danishes. They placed the items and gave Sandra some coffee and a fresh box of Kleenex. Mosely took his seat, coffee in hand. "So you're sure you only had two drinks that night?"

"Yes, positive," Sandra muttered as she picked up her coffee and took a sip. "I missed this the most in jail."

Jack cleared his throat, noting Sandra's slight change in demeanor. "So let's go back to when the sheriff's department showed up."

Sandra waited a minute and then started. "They were very nice. I had to lie down again; I was a bit overwhelmed. There was a young deputy there and the sheriff and some other people. But again, people were coming in and out so fast that I couldn't keep up. Finally, the deputy told me he would be sure everything was locked up when they left. He asked if I wanted to call anyone to be with me. He said they would leave a car out front and I shouldn't be worried. He was very kind. Franklin was his name, I think."

Mosely put a hand up. "That was it? No questions?"

"Maybe, I'm not sure. It's all just a blur."

Jack and Mosely shared a look, and then Jack continued. "I understand it's hard, but I need you to focus. Take your time."

"Well, the Monday after my husband's funeral, they came to the house, the sheriff and that nice young deputy. They read me my rights and put me in the car. Sheriff Jones told the deputy it wouldn't be necessary to handcuff me. I thanked him, and that was it."

"Was that the first time they read you your rights?"

"Yes, I think so."

"What was the reason they gave for the arrest?"

"I was being charged with Bill's murder."

"And what did you say?"

Sandra looked out the window and then back to Jack. "I didn't say anything."

Jack and Mosely looked at each other before Jack turned back to Sandra. "Let's back up. The morning you found your husband, Mrs. Allgood, did the officers ever call in a doctor to check on you, bring EMTs, or take you to the hospital?"

She shook her head. "No, they didn't. An ambulance must have come for Bill to take him out because I saw his body left on a stretcher. But no one checked me out."

"They didn't take him in the ambulance; he was picked up by the coroner, ma'am. And at that time, they didn't ask you any questions?"

"Nothing other than what happened." Sandra started to cry again. Dabbing her face, she said, "All I know was when I woke up, my husband was dead."

Jack didn't see any tears, and he was looking this time. He recalled what Ruby had said about Sandra not using her handkerchief at the funeral. So he pushed a little more. "So at the time of questioning, you hadn't recalled the shots or the sound of someone running?"

With dry eyes and a controlled tone, she said, "Yes, that's right."

Jack sat back and said, "Mrs. Allgood, how much did you have to drink that night?"

"Just the two glasses. I told you."

Jack rubbed his forehead. "The prosecution will have a field day with this testimony."

Silence. Then Mosely interjected, "When they read you your

rights at the time of the arrest, did they ask you if you had killed your husband?"

"Yes, but I said, 'I didn't kill him. I didn't kill him.'"

Jack started to lose his patience. "Wait. You just told us you didn't say anything when they arrested you. Which is it?"

Brown gave a "calm down" hand gesture to Jack.

Sandra remained silent.

Mosely interjected to alleviate the tension in the air. "And at any point did the police search the house?"

"Yes, I remember them going all through the house. I assume that was a search. I had to sign a paper saying they took some items."

A calmer, controlled Jack asked, "Do you know what they took?"

She shook her head. "I really don't know. I didn't really pay attention to the comings and goings, as I said." She looked back and forth at both men and could sense they weren't buying what she was selling. "Look. Do you know what it's like to find your spouse murdered and then get arrested? It's not like anyone is prepared for this," Sandra said, dropping her head and staring at her hands.

Mosely softened. "We understand. We are just trying to be prepared for the prosecution."

"Do you remember if you were slurring your words with the officers, Mrs. Allgood?" Jack asked.

"I don't remember."

"And they never called a doctor or an ambulance for you, correct?" Brown said.

"No, I don't think they did. If they did, no one showed up. I never saw a doctor."

"Did they ever show you what was supposed to be a suicide note?" Jack asked.

"No, I didn't know one was found at the house until sometime later. But then they had it the next day and never showed it to me. So I don't even know what it said."

"You didn't ask?" Jack asked, incredulous as to why anyone wouldn't want to know their loved one's last words.

"I told you all that I know, Mr. Sutton. I can't explain my actions. I know you're trying to read into them, but I can tell you there's nothing behind them but confusion and fear." Sandra started to cry—or whimper—but still no tears.

Mosely shot a look at Jack, and he softened. "As Mr. Brown said, we are just trying to build a defense that will overtake the prosecution's case. Our questioning must be tough to prepare you for what will happen in court."

Jack had wondered if the EMTs had given Sandra a mild sedative; he could only assume they were there per protocol. He made a note to check the reports. After all, it would be understandable since a woman whose husband had been killed and charged with his murder would probably be anxious. And the drugs could account for her poor recall of what happened afterward.

"The prosecution has to show us that letter," Brown said. "And I will be extremely interested to see it. Also, we can find out what else they took from the house."

"Mrs. Allgood, are you sure the police didn't ask if they could call a doctor for you?" Jack perseverated on this issue, even though he wasn't sure why.

As if filling in the blanks for Jack, she said, "Do you think something was in those drinks Bill made for me?"

"That wasn't my question. But now that you mention it, why do you think Bill might have slipped you something? Had he done it before?"

"How would I know?" she replied as her eyes grew cold and angry. Sandra waited for them to move on with the questioning. She didn't want to broach the subject of drugs. Many times in the past, she had woken up bleeding, her clothes ripped and her body bruised—so many she had lost count. Bill had a habit of slipping things in her drink, but it would just be her word, and she feared no one would believe her.

"Is there anybody you can think of who would want to kill your husband?" Jack fought his mounting frustration.

Still somewhat snarky, she said, "You don't have enough paper on that pad for all the people who hated him. Bill could be an asshole." She blushed, and her mood shifted, admonishing herself for letting that slip. "I'm sorry. It's just been a lot." She shook her head. "I knew almost nothing about Bill's business. He didn't talk about his work with me and made it clear he didn't want to, so I never brought the subject up. I know times had been very hard for a few years, but he seemed to act like things were getting better in the last year or two. He bought new vehicles, farm equipment, and some neighboring land. He took hunting trips up north and to Mexico with Jerry Roberts, who managed the farm for him and some friends."

Jack perked up. "What friends did he have, Mrs. Allgood? We're going to need to talk with them."

"Well, Jerry Roberts and Tony Tanner were two of his consistent people around him. But maybe I misspoke. The term *friends* should be used loosely. Jerry managed our farm, and Tony worked on Dan Cook's farm. Jerry's getting along with Bill was to preserve his job, and Tony was that classic hanger-on guy. He had gone to college with Bill for a short time and, in fact, was the best man at our wedding. He was always around here and there. He would occasionally do some work for Bill. If Bill called, Tony stood at attention like a dog waiting for crumbs to fall."

Changing the subject, he said, "Did you and Bill go on any vacations? Did you go along on any of those other trips with Jerry and Tony?"

"Two years ago, I went with him on a trip to Miami. He had a business meeting and had asked me." Sandra failed but wanted to say that she and Bill got into a huge argument because he wanted her to go to a nude beach and she refused.

"Do you recall seeing anyone else at your house the night of the murder besides you and your husband?"

"When I first came out of the bedroom after dozing off, I went toward the top of the stairs, where it opens up to the foyer, and I thought I saw a shadow on the floor below. But then my vision was cloudy, and it seemed like a dream. It didn't feel real. So I can't be sure."

"Back up, Mrs. Allgood. Was this seeing something at the same time you heard the banging and yelling?" Jack asked.

Startled, caught off guard, Sandra quickly answered, "Yes, I think so. Maybe."

Jack took a deep breath, but before he could go at her with another question, Mosely asked, "What kind of businesses did your husband have?"

"He had several. He had the farm, which was the biggest one. I really don't know how large it is, but I think Bill bragged that he owned over a thousand acres inherited from his father. He rented some of it out for people to farm, and Jerry managed the rest. Bill wasn't big on working with his hands. He was also obsessed last year with some airplane company. Said it was going to be a gold mine. He never talked about the other businesses with me, but he would meet with partners in those businesses. At least that's what he told me."

Jack asked, "Did you know your father-in-law well?"

"No."

"Did Bill ever mention how he and his dad got along?" Jack asked.

Sandra swallowed hard and thought some before speaking. "I heard Wade was a sweet and decent man. He worked around the clock, according to Doc Furman and Jerry Roberts. It was only during the final month of his life that he slowed down."

Jack quieted his tone. "Tell us about your marriage."

"Not much to tell. Normal marriage, I guess." Looking down at her hands, Sandra fought the tears. "You know it's possible to have disagreements and still love that person simultaneously, Mr. Sutton. It's also possible to not be in love but not want that person dead. I didn't kill him."

Brown smiled. "If we are to believe gossip, we will suspect you had more than just disagreements. The prosecution will get into it. We need to be prepared. His personality may actually be a plus for our case."

Jack checked his watch. "Mrs. Allgood—"

"Please call me Sandra. I plan from this day on to return to my maiden name, Callahan. Sandra Callahan."

"Sandra, it is. This case came as a surprise, and Mosely had scheduled an early afternoon appointment today. But we do need to ask you more questions. If you could return at three o'clock, we'd like to continue. If that's inconvenient—"

"No, no. I can come back. I'm glad, Mr. Sutton, you were the one they chose this morning." She shot both men a forced smile and walked out.

Mosely gathered his things and looked at Jack. "Thoughts?"

"Who gets arrested if they are innocent and doesn't say anything? And what's up with her moods? One minute she's 'crying'"—Jack made air quotes—"and the next, she's ready to take my head off."

"How long have you been married, Jack?"

"A little over two months."

"You won't ask that question a year from now. And no, I've had clients accept the arrest and wait on the information for later; that's common."

"Well, if I was arrested for something I didn't do, I'd shout it from the rooftops!" Jack said, gathering his stuff.

"You think she's guilty?"

Jack stopped and looked at Mosely. "Not my job."

"Good answer. But look at it this way: it may make the rest of the summer a little more interesting than we thought," Brown said. "To be honest, before this happened, I thought life had gotten dull around here."

Jack walked out of the room, saying over his shoulder, "It's not dull anymore."

—— ·——

When Jack arrived home that night, Ruby was in the backyard watering the little garden they had planted. Everyone in Pear Valley was expected to grow their own vegetable garden, or at least that's what the book club ladies told her. And a bored Ruby decided to give it a try, her "when in Rome" moment.

Jack walked around the side of the house and went straight for a kiss from Ruby. He playfully put his hand in front of the water streaming from the hose, splashing some of it back on Ruby. Ruby squealed. Jack smiled and then turned serious, drawing Ruby closer. "Babe, let's sit down for a moment."

He went and turned off the hose and led Ruby over to the swing in the backyard under the grape arbor. This was one of his favorite spots in the "house Grandma bought." It was a large area, twenty feet by thirty feet. Large posts were on each side with trusses topped with a metal cow gate fence. Growing on top and forming a dense roof that resulted in shade from the sun were muscadine and concord grapes. The floor was covered in grass, and the sides were open. A wooden bench swing was on the back side, looking out over the garden.

Jack and Ruby playfully settled in the swing. Ruby, seeing the look on Jack's face, asked, "What is it, Jack?"

"Mosely and I interviewed Sandra Allgood today," Jack rubbed his newly cut hair, still not used to it being that short.

"And?"

"If you were arrested on charges for my murder, how would you react?" Jack questioned.

"I would scream, 'I didn't do it!' and demand my lawyer right away."

"Exactly. But let's say, for argument's sake, you did kill me. What would you say?"

"I'd probably keep my mouth shut because I'd be afraid to say anything. Why?"

Jack raised his eyes to the sky. "That's what I thought," he muttered, dropping his head in his hands.

Ruby put her head on his shoulders. "Jack, what's wrong?"

Jack sprang back upward, pulled Ruby in, and kissed her. "Nothing, just checking my instincts. When's dinner?" Jack asked, standing up and holding his hand out for his wife.

Ruby took his hand but remained seated. She looked up at Jack. "Your instincts have always been spot-on. Don't doubt yourself now."

Jack pulled Ruby up, hugged her, and thought how lucky he was to have her, even if he sensed she was giving him the standard pep talk.

Later that evening, Jack was on the front porch swing. "Baby, you hardly ate any dinner," Ruby said, walking out onto the front porch where Jack sat with the Allgood file on his lap and a plate of food on the coffee table going cold.

Jack looked at his beautiful bride. "Yes, I'm sorry. I've been researching legal precedents and reviewing the evidence."

"For what?"

"Trying to come up with a solid defense." Jack threw his head back and stared up at the porch ceiling. "Just not having any damn luck."

"Maybe you need to leave it. You know what happens when you overthink things."

Jack took Ruby's hand and pulled her beside him for a kiss. "I married a smart woman."

Ruby pulled back and placed her hand on his chest. "Look. I want to talk to you about an opportunity." But the words had no sooner left her mouth when Jack had pulled her in for another long, deep kiss.

—⚶—

The following week at the office, Jack found himself running to the small bathroom in the hallway because of explosive bowel movements. It was a condition lawyers get when they have a stressful case, and the anxiety works its magic on the gastrointestinal system. Mr. Truitt told Jack a story about it in the interview he had with him for the job.

"Boy, what we do is serious business. People put their lives and livelihood into our hands. Of course, that affects you mentally, but stress can also cause you to be incontinent of your bowel and bladder. When that happens, it means you are taking the client seriously and putting yourself on the line for them. Of course, you must learn to control it as you get older, but it will hit you hard when your dick is in the vise the first time. When that happens, you will be running to shit water."

Jack started to see exactly what the old man meant. Between his visits to the hallway bathroom and the spraying of air fresheners in the bathroom, he reviewed legal precedents and identified witnesses he needed to follow up with. It was a busy week. They received follow-up details from their client, and Jack went from a feeling of total incompetence and insecurity to a manic ego and confidence with his best John Wayne strut. He and Mosely wanted to interview all of the officers and personnel who had gone to Mrs. Allgood's home. He also wanted to find out the forensic evidence gathered and any results from this. Their list, or "proof development," as Brown called it, grew and changed all week. Most of all, he needed to see the suicide note. Layton's office was at the top of his list.

—m—

By the time Saturday came around, Jack wanted to get out of fishing with Mosely. He had more work to do on the case. But when Jack hinted on Friday afternoon that they should work instead of fish, he knew Brown wasn't taking the bait. "Boy, you ever heard that all work and no play makes Jack a dull boy?" Jack smirked as Brown continued. "Well, this case will depend on you not being a dull boy. And I intend to help with that. Be at my house at 5 a.m. We're going fishing."

So slightly before the crack of dawn, Jack leaned over and gently kissed a sleeping Ruby. She looked so peaceful. They hadn't had much time together that week, which only added to his guilt for going fishing.

Mosely, Jack, and Jim Abney, a history professor from Abraham Baldwin Agriculture College, were to meet that morning at Mosely's family fishing cabin on Lake Seminole, built in 1957. His father had constructed it on farmland that had been in the family for a hundred years. Before then, in 1946, Congress authorized the Flint River and the Chattahoochee River damming. So they joined and formed the Apalachicola River in the southwest corner of Georgia along its border with Florida. The Brown family's farmland flooded, and Woodruff Dam was built. Almost overnight, the fields where they used to grow corn and cotton became waterfront property. The lake filled in 1957, and the cabin was built. The lake was, therefore, full of cypress trees and knots, making it a haven for fish—full of largemouth bass, perch, and catfish. It also had its fair share of alligators and snakes.

Jack and Mosely rode down together and had some time to

talk on the way. Mosely shared his wisdom as always in his quiet, thoughtful demeanor. "Focus on the evidence. Who gathered it, how it was gathered, how it was stored, who processed it, and how it was processed. Then question it all. And then, question it again."

Jack nodded, appreciating the 180-degree contrast between Mosely's mentorship and Truitt's abrasive, fear-inducing approach. "Yes, sir. We need to focus on the suicide note and if we can prove Allgood tried to drug his wife. Pretty sure our officers bundled the investigation too."

"Yes," said Mosely, "but don't fixate on just those last two pieces. The drugging will be hard to prove since it doesn't appear she had been tested. And going after the sheriff's office won't win you any medals. My dear mother would say, 'You win more bees with honey than vinegar.' And let me tell you, down here in the southernmost part of Georgia, you better be all honey if you want to survive. People don't take kindly to anyone who upsets the norm."

Jack only half listened to Mosely as his mind raced with the ever-changing information. "They released the scene too early. That would never fly in Atlanta. We could've gotten the wine glass and tested it."

"Look. We don't have a lot of murders around here. I agree they messed up a lot, but that's done. So look at everything. Analyze all of their evidence but look for evidence in other sources also. Following the money or need for money usually leads to answers. Again, no matter what, avoid pointing fingers. You're the new guy on the block; you won't win if you get her off but make a whole lot of enemies around here."

Jack shook his head and wondered if he and Ruby would have been better off in Atlanta. At least he wouldn't have to worry about protecting egos. "Did you read the article yesterday? The press is calling it the 'suicide-note murder.'"

"Yeah, that Lavender is trying to make a name for himself on this case. The beauty of being a reporter is that you can manipulate things to fit your byline. Just don't be the one to tip them off on anything. Unless, of course, it works in your favor."

Jack, still only half listening, changed the subject. "I did some research and found a woman named Annie Masterson, an investigator from Macon. I was very impressed with her credentials. She specializes in criminal cases, and I'd like her to dig into Allgood's activities. I want to pull the trigger on hiring her. What do you think Truitt will say?"

"Truitt will say no to anything that costs money, especially when there's doubt on the client's ability to pay. So let *me* ask him." The two rode in silence for ten minutes before Brown asked, "Do you still have doubts about Sandra?"

Jack shook his head no and then yes. "I think it's possible Allgood drugged her at the beginning of the evening. But I don't know why. Of course, there's no way to prove she was or wasn't drugged, thanks to the sheriff. All we have is what she's telling us, which isn't much, and she's all over the place."

"You think he might have been thinking of killing *her?* Maybe she killed him in self-defense?"

"That crossed my mind, but I'm not sure. I mean if it was self-defense, why not say so and this whole thing could be wrapped up right away?"

"I once read about a case where a woman killed her lover in self-defense but fearing no one would believe her staged it to look like a suicide."

"What happened in the end?"

"She did time for lying to authorities."

Jack rubbed his forehead. "I'm not sure about anyone or anything in this case. Not exactly a typical case study I encountered in school. We would have said, 'Oh, something like that would never happen in real life.'"

Mosely grinned and replied, "And I would tell them, 'Hey, you want real life. You come to southern Georgia, and I'll show you real life." Mosely grew quiet and added, "In all seriousness, don't make assumptions this early. It could be the nail in your coffin and hers."

Jack shook his head yes, and then stared out the passenger window. "Something seems off with her."

"Yeah, I felt it too. But being off doesn't equate to guilt."

Mosely pulled down the dirt road toward the cabin. When they emerged from the tree-lined drive, they saw Jim Abney's brown Dodge Dart parked by the front entrance. Abney was originally from Enigma, Georgia, where his mother ran Big Jim's restaurant. To all in the know, it was the most refined cooking between Tifton and Brunswick on Highway 82, except for their mamas, of course. Mrs. Abney had amazing fried chicken, fried okra, and anything else you could think of to fry. Her lima beans, squash, and collards were also mouthwateringly good. Her cornbread had jalapeno peppers and was a meal in itself, especially if you dipped it in buttermilk.

Abney was in his late thirties, seeming old to Jack. He was about six feet tall, skinny, and prematurely balding brown hair. He had a protruding Adam's apple and a slight hunch on his back. He reminded Jack of Ichabod Crane from the Washington Irving novel.

After exchanging pleasantries, they individually checked their gear and headed to the dock below the cabin. It sat among water oaks and cypress trees on the shoreline with moss hanging off them. The water appeared black with a brown tinge on the outlining areas. There was an occasional lily pad with a white flower growing out of it. Jack was sure he saw a pair of alligator eyes peering at him. Without bothering to glance up, Jack asked Mosely if it was an alligator, and Mosely gave a dry reply. "Could be."

The trio got in a johnboat that seemed small and unstable to Jack. They pushed off and paddled along the shoreline and spots that Brown seemed to have predestined in his mind. Fortunately, the cool water and the trees on the banks, along with the cypress groves in the water, created a cooler environment than those in the hay fields or tobacco patches were feeling.

When they arrived at one of Mosley's favorite spots, they stopped to drop their lines until Brown declared it was time to move on. As the three watched their bobbers, Abney began telling the story of the lost Confederate gold. He vividly brought them back to the 1860s and the turmoil as the Civil War ended. He noted, depending on your perspective, it was either the War of Northern Aggression or the Great Rebellion.

He then told them the story of the lost Confederate gold on the shores of Flint River near the lake. "Along the banks of the Flint as it flows into the Apalachicola River was Fort Scott, built in 1816. The intent was to protect what was then the southern border of the United States (the border between Georgia and Florida), subject to various types of invaders operating through or out of Spanish territory. The fort was abandoned after Florida became a US territory in 1821. However, the Confederates occupied it for training briefly during the Civil War.

When Jefferson Davis was escaping Richmond, an advance troop party went out ahead of him, and rumors were that they had the Confederate treasure. When Davis was eventually captured in Irwin County, Georgia, seventy miles north of Fort Scott, rumors are the advance troop buried the gold and planned to come back after everything settled down. However, on their way to turn themselves in to a Union garrison, they were attacked near Omega Township and killed by bandits wanting the gold. Rumor is the gold is still at the old Fort Scott today."

Mosely laughed. "I've been hearing that tall tale all my life and ain't seen no gold yet."

Abney agreed. "But I appreciate you letting me stay in your cabin this week and search for it."

Mosely turned to Jack. "Jim here is writing a book about rumors of where the lost Confederate gold may be."

"You're writing a book?" Jack asked. "Wow, that's amazing and too much work!"

Jim cast his line. "From what I hear, you're the one with a full plate."

"A full plate of information that has no pattern."

"You know what old Mosely here and I have learned over the years. If you just step back and listen, the connection will reveal itself. Sometimes, it's not the effort you put in to figure things out but your ability to listen for the whispers among the screams. That's the sweet spot for getting to the truth. It's why I come here."

"Yeah, I can see how the solitude can help."

"No, it's more than just being quiet. It's about uncluttering your head and giving space for the answer to go. Fresh air, nature, and disconnection from our crazy lives let our creativity flow."

Jack nodded and suddenly realized that this trip was, in Mosely's mind, a necessary effort in the process of forming a solid defense.

TWELVE
An Unfolding Story

The following morning, Jack slept in. The Saturday fishing trip had, at least temporarily, relieved his bowel issue. When he got up, he found Ruby already in the living room watching Oral Roberts preaching on television. Oral Roberts was in the middle of saying that if all his zealous followers around the country contributed a million dollars that morning, he could build the Oral Roberts University, and God would come and take him to heaven. *Good riddance*, Jack thought.

In southern Georgia, unlike Atlanta, you had two choices for television. One was channel WALB out of Albany, the NBC station, and the other was WTAL out of Tallahassee, the CBS station. The up-and-coming ABC network did not have affiliates in south Georgia, and you could not watch those shows. You could watch *All in the Family* and *Sanford and Son* but not *S.W.A.T* or *Kojak*.

As Jack poured himself some coffee, Ruby shouted from the living room, "Get your butt upstairs and get dressed! I told the pastor of the Pear Valley Methodist Church that we would be at services this morning. There's Sunday school at ten and preaching at eleven. We will then have a picnic lunch with everyone on the church grounds by the cemetery. Get dressed so we won't be late."

"You did what?"

"Honey, may I remind you again that this is a small, Southern, Bible-toting town, and *you said*, 'It's important to be seen in the community.' Prospective jurors for your case will be there and prospective clients. Remember the same reason we stayed for the Fourth and went to some man's funeral we didn't even know at the time. Besides, Lady Daisy will be there!"

"Will she be giving the sermon?"

Ruby laughed, rising from the couch to join Jack in the kitchen. "No, but if she did, it would probably be good. Reverend Richard Mitchell is young and friendly. He is not the hellfire and brimstone type like Reverend Williams from the Pear Valley Baptist Church we heard a few weeks back. I'm sure he'll be very interesting. You may really like the service."

"OK," he sighed and nodded. "I'll admit you have a point. I'd rather not be in the rumor mill this week for *not* attending services! I do, however, have to go to the office this afternoon. I am meeting with the DA this week and need to be prepared. From what I hear, he's tough."

Ruby nodded understandingly. "How is Sandra doing?"

Jack sipped his coffee. "I don't know. She's a hard one to read. One minute I think she was railroaded, and the next, I feel like she knows more than she's letting on."

"She's probably scared to death. I know I would be."

Jack put his half-empty cup in the sink and pulled Ruby in for a hug. "Well, thankfully, I won't give you a reason to shoot me."

"Yet," Ruby said with a smirk as she started laughing. Jack hugged her tighter, and the two shared a kiss. Afterward, Ruby leaned back. "Have you asked her if she did it?"

"You never ask the question you don't already know the answer to; that's one of the first things they teach you in law school."

"Well, if she did it, and the rumors about her husband are true, it was probably self-defense."

"I'm done talking about this. I think we have time for a little fun before we shower," Jack said as he swooped his bride in his arms and headed back to bed.

—∞—

After a good sermon by Reverend Richard Mitchell, Jack and Ruby walked around the neighborhood for some fresh air and exercise. Ruby had been impressed by the reverend's knowledge of the Bible. He didn't make anyone think they were worthless and did not insinuate giving money would help stop your slide to hell. He used the wisdom of the scriptures that were insightful. In her days at Wesleyan, Ruby had been surprised by how many William Shakespeare quotes came from the Bible. *Regardless of someone's religious belief, there is a lot of wisdom in that book,* she thought.

In the sermon that morning, when the scriptures mentioned "death" or "darkness," they referred to one's spiritual demise more than physical death. The reverend had said, "When the scriptures mention 'death' or 'walking in darkness' or 'walking in death,' they are not speaking of physical death or the cessation of existence because man is a spiritual creature. He is a spirit, has a soul, and lives in a body. One day, all of us will leave the body. If you don't believe that, go to the cemetery and look at the tombstones. These are people who have left the body. But they still exist. They are in heaven, or they're in hell. Believe me: heaven is better. But neither group has ceased to exist. So when the Bible says 'walking in darkness' or 'walking in death,' it means you are walking without the light of God in your life. And if you continue to walk in death in this life, you must go to the place of death when you leave the body. Believe me: that's not where you want to spend eternity."

The reverend laughed occasionally and smiled when he preached, placing the entire congregation at ease and open to his words.

"So did you enjoy the service?" she asked Jack.

"Yes, surprisingly." He shot Ruby a smirk, and she gave an eye roll in return. "He was a very good speaker. I liked how he used 'now listen' and 'believe me' to introduce ideas he wanted you to focus on, moving you from the morass of words and showing that something special and important was coming. Impressive. I may even incorporate that into my style when I make legal arguments, especially to a jury. And ultimately, that is what a congregation is: a jury deciding if they will accept or believe your evidence. How was that for my paying attention?" Jack asked, a little smirk plastered across his face.

Ruby looked at him and rolled her eyes again. "My, my, Mr. Sutton, I don't know nothing about no jury arguments," she said in her thickest Miss Mamie *Gone with the Wind* accent. Jack playfully put his arm around her and squeezed her.

They walked to the park a few blocks from their house. The park was an entire block long with massive oak trees and wide-open grassy areas, with several picnic tables and wood coverings. There were playground toys for younger children and a sandbox for toddlers. It also included two tennis courts and two basketball courts on the other side of the park. As they looked around, they saw several people walking their dogs. Another two men batted a yellow tennis ball back and forth. Ruby pointed toward a walker with a black dog. "I would like a golden about that size," she said, pointing at the dog.

"He's a beautiful dog," Ruby said as the lady walked up to them.

"Thank you," the lady said. "This is Carter. He's very friendly."

The black lab had started sniffing their hands, and Jack petted him.

"How long have you had him?"

"Almost five years. We got him from the pound after someone threw him out of a car and onto the highway. I couldn't imagine someone not loving a dog this nice. I grabbed him up. Both my husband and I love him. We have a fair-sized backyard, but Carter loves walking too, so we try to take him to the park three or four times a day. It's good exercise for us as well."

Carter held his head high while looking at the couple he had just met.

"Wish I had some treats," Ruby said.

"That's OK. Believe me: he gets plenty. My husband goes overboard with treats. Whenever Carter enters the kitchen and looks at my husband with those big, wide eyes, Don can't resist. And Carter gets a treat."

"I would be that way too," Jack said.

"Come on, Carter. Let's go," she said. Carter gave one joyous bark and followed his owner.

"It would be nice to have a dog," Jack said. "They're a lot of work though."

Ruby ignored the last comment. "I'll start my search for a retriever tomorrow."

They strolled down the block back toward their house. The two tennis players were now playing a set on the courts in the Robert E. Lee Memorial Park. "That's two to one," he said, holding a tennis ball. "My serve." His opponent nodded.

Jack and Ruby started down the road that bordered the park. Jack offered, "Learned something yesterday from Mr. Truitt," he said. "A rather distressing story about the town."

"It's been such a lovely day. I would say don't tell me, but my curiosity would get to me, so go ahead."

Jack laughed. "OK. It may be distressing, but it does tell you something about the South. This happened about fifty, maybe sixty years ago. Since the town didn't want any blacks in it, the town elders thought they would create a different town for the blacks. If you drive about five miles east on this road, you will run into the town of Gifford, which is all black. They forcibly moved them from the part of town called the Quarters. The area now happens to be the headquarters of Roberts Gin, Seed, and Trailer Park.

The thing is the elected officials don't really have any taxing power. They have to go to the county commission to get anything done. The guy who named it Gifford was Alexander Roberts, one of the town's wealthiest men who wielded a lot of influence. He was on the city council and got the other council members to name the Negro community Gifford. That was because he hated a man called Ben Gifford, who also lived in Pear Valley at that time. The two men carried on a feud for forty years. Roberts thought it would be a great joke to name a Negro town after a man he hated."

Ruby looked shocked. "Really? I can't. I mean I can't put a response to that in words. For the first time ever, I'm speechless."

"It was said later that Ben Gifford didn't mind it and was proud of it. Roberts died about twenty years ago, but Gifford is still alive, although he's about eighty."

"I guess all towns and the people in them have their secrets," Ruby said. "Well, thankfully, racists like Roberts will continue to die. Lord knows the world will be better for it. I long for the day when Reverend King's dream of all people being judged by 'the quality of their character and not the color of their skin.'"

"Great thoughts, but they got him killed. Hopefully, brave people will 'stand in the gap,' to use a biblical phrase, as your Reverend Mitchell would," Jack said, proud he had gotten in the biblical quote.

"Ah, you *were* listening," Ruby chided before changing the subject. "Speaking of judging people, do you think Sandra Allgood will be judged fairly by a jury? Some don't agree with the 'mean husband deserving his fate' theory and see her as a gold-digging opportunist."

Jack stopped and let go of Ruby's hand. "Who told you that?"

"I overheard these women talking at the church picnic today."

Jack rubbed his forehead. "The damn gossip in this town is stifling."

"So you're thinking she didn't do it? I'm confused based on our talk this morning."

"I don't know if she did or didn't!" Jack caught his escalating tone and curbed it when he saw others look their way. He and Ruby continued to walk a bit before he said quietly, "Sandra Allgood deserves a fair trial either way. It's what our judicial system is founded on: assumed innocent until proven guilty. But with the gossipmongers, I don't know if she will get an impartial jury, and *that* bothers me."

"Can't you get the trial moved then?"

"Yes, I could try. But then what if the majority of the rumors are in our favor? It's too early to judge. I need a damn defense strategy first!"

That Sunday afternoon, Jack returned to the law library to be sure he knew all the obligations the prosecution had under the new laws.

Earl Warren served as the fourteenth chief justice of the US Supreme Court from 1953 to 1969. The Warren court presided over a significant shift in American constitutional jurisprudence, which has been recognized by many as a "Constitutional Revolution" in the liberal direction, with Warren writing the majority opinions in landmark cases such as *Brown v. Board of Education* (1954), *Reynolds v. Sims* (1964), *Miranda v. Arizona* (1966), and *Loving v. Virginia* (1967). *Miranda v. Arizona* was a landmark decision in which the court ruled that the Fifth Amendment to the US Constitution restricts prosecutors from using a person's statements made in response to interrogation in police custody as evidence at their trial unless they can show that the person was informed of the right to consult with a lawyer before and during questioning and of the privilege against self-incrimination before police questioning and that the defendant not only understood these rights but voluntarily waived them.

Brady's rights came from the US Supreme Court case *Brady v. Maryland* in 1970. The case ruled that the government must turn over all evidence, precisely any evidence that might exonerate the accused. As one of the most critical cases in the area of criminal procedure, this decision helps ensure that criminal trials are fair.

Ironically, the change came after Warren left the court and Warren Earl Burger, a Warren critic, was appointed in 1969 by President Richard Nixon. Although Burger was perceived as a conservative and the Burger court delivered some conservative decisions, the Burger court also had some liberal decisions regarding abortion, capital punishment, religious establishment, school desegregation, and criminal rights with the Brady decision during his tenure. Miranda and Brady were viewed by many as a radical change in American criminal law.

Jack spent his afternoon and evening and most of the next day reading case after case to prepare for his meeting with Layton. He felt an intense pressure to prove himself, but even more to protect Mrs. Allgood and her rights, even if she was guilty. The coin of innocence versus guilt was still flipping in the air, and there was no way, at this point, to know how it would land. Jack had arranged another meeting with Sandra that week, but he was starting to believe she would muddy the waters even more for him.

Brad, wearing his straw Stetson Ranger hat he had adopted as his headgear of choice since coming to Pear Valley, walked up two of the three steps to the porch of Ida Florence, an older woman who smiled and rocked in an old rocking chair daily. Miss Ida, as she was affectionately called, was a spinster. She had never married. Rumor had it she had been jilted by a lover in her youth and never found anyone else.

Most people in the town knew Ida spent most of her day outside rocking when she wasn't gardening her roses in the backyard. She was a former schoolteacher who had retired several years before. Ida seemed to enjoy spending the day on the front porch watching the people go by. If anyone dropped by to talk, she was even happier.

During baseball season though, her porch was empty during some afternoons. Although she hadn't cared about baseball during her career as a teacher, she had picked up a considerable fondness for the game during her retirement. So when there was an Atlanta Braves game, she usually sat in her living room listening to the Braves. She even had a Braves pennant hanging on her wall.

"Well, it's Mr. Lavender. How are you doing, Brad?"

He tipped the Stetson.

"Getting better every day, Ida. How are you, ma'am?"

"Enjoying the sunshine. Did you come to talk a spell, Brad? If so, I can pour you some lemonade."

"If you poured about half a glass, I'd appreciate it," he said, sitting next to the charming woman.

"And why would the brilliant reporter from the *Pear Valley Observer* want to talk to me?"

"Because, as many people have assured me, Miss Ida Florence knows everything about everybody in this town. They tell me, quote, 'It's amazing. Miss Ida knows the secrets of the town and most people in it. She makes the FBI look like pikers when it comes to getting information. So help me, she knew Reg Davis had committed to Florida State before his parents did. And she knew Rob Shaw was making hooch out in the county long before he was hauled off by the ATF.'"

Ida snickered as she sipped her tea. "Sounds like you want to know something."

"I sure do. Just for curiosity's sake and because I'm covering the Allgood trial for the paper, I wanted to get a little background on William Allgood. I've heard rumors he wasn't a model citizen. But I also want facts, not gossip; it's why I came to you."

Ida laughed with an unladylike snort and caught herself. She then sipped some more lemonade. "Well, thank you for not meshing me with the Pear Valley gossipers." Ida tilted her head for a second and stared at Brad. "You're not a country boy, are you, Brad?"

"No, ma'am. I grew up in Birmingham."

"So how did you get to south Georgia?"

"Long story. And I promise to tell you if you spill the beans on Allgood."

Ida took a long sip of her drink and then set it down. "Deal."

Brad uncapped his pen and opened his pad. "I'm curious. I've heard Allgood wasn't a great loss for the town."

Ida lowered her voice. "No, it wasn't. Bill Allgood was a bad seed. He was the mean mutt in the litter of one. His father, however, was a fine man. Wade Allgood worked hard every day and was in church on Sunday. But something went wrong with the son. If Bill had had a brother, it would have been a Cain and Able situation, with Bill being Cain. He was always a shallow, selfish individual and a lazy mutt. Sometimes with successful, strong men, all the vibrant genes seem to be with the father, but the son is lackluster, not as energetic, and seems to have much less talent. So the father has all the good genes, and the son is left with the mediocre," Ida rambled. "It proved true, to some degree, with the Allgood family."

"Did the father and son get along?" Brad asked, writing in his notebook as fast as Ida could talk.

"Somewhat, I guess. Never saw them together much. Wade Allgood was always working and left Bill with the housekeeper most of the time. But Wade's diligent, hardworking, friendly, and dyed-in-the-wool attitude never permeated his son's skull. Father and son were as different as night and day. If you want my opinion, he deserved to be shot. Sandra should have done it a lot sooner."

Brad chuckled at the woman's frankness, then thought for a moment. "Would the late Mr. Allgood have been involved in illegal activities?"

Ida gave Brad a wink. "Well, who knows? But I did hear about the local marijuana smuggling. That seems to be big nowadays. And since you mentioned it, Bill was friends with Dan Cook in his younger days, who is one of the people in the marijuana case. And before that, Bill had been in financial difficulty. But I heard from a reliable source he was starting to get his feet back under him, and money seemed to be flowing his way, but not because of the farm."

"Who told you that?"

"Now Mr. Lavender, you should know I won't reveal my source." Ida smiled at Brad before she continued. "Bill also lobbied for that new company with the airplanes to come here, and some folks thought he might have a financial interest in the whole thing. Which makes sense since Bill wasn't much of a lobbyist prior."

Ida stopped for a drink and gave Brad a minute to catch up with his notes. "Keep going. I'm good."

"Yes, whatever Bill was involved in, it wasn't decent or honorable. I'll tell you that. Once in a while, Wade would stop by after church on Sunday to say hello and have a little lemonade with me."

"Bet he told you a lot too," Brad suggested with a smile.

Ida knew better than to take the bait. "If he did, that was between him and me. It's your turn. Tell me about an Alabama boy and why he came to Pear Valley, Georgia. Don't have many Tide fans in this part of the country."

"How do you know I went to the University of Alabama?"

She pointed toward the street. "Do my failing eyes deceive me, or is that an old University of Alabama sticker on your back windshield?"

Brad smiled and nodded. "You have sharp eyes, Ida."

"So how come you're up here? How long have you been with the paper? Seems like about six months."

Closing his pad and capping his pen, Brad answered, "It's been just over a year. Time does fly." Reflecting, he noted, "I was working over in Miami on the *Dade County Floridian*, and I fell in love. She was about two years older than me, and life seemed perfect." Brad took a sip of lemonade, stalling to think of how to let as little out as possible while making Ida think she got the scoop. "Well, back then, I figured I could move to a more extensive paper within the media organization that owned the *Floridian* and get more money for us. Shari had separated from her husband, and both filed for divorce. It was in the works but not yet final. They had two children and owned a little café on the outskirts of town. It was a good location, and they were making reasonably good money. I must admit I thought the husband was a fool to split with Shari."

He paused for a moment.

"So what happened?" Ida asked.

"A few days before the divorce was final, the husband returned and asked Shari if they could rethink the whole matter. He said he still loved her and the children and was sorry. He said he had made a few mistakes but wanted to make it up to her. That he loved her and wanted to continue the marriage." Brad dropped his gaze. "So after thinking about it for a while, she agreed. With two children, she wanted to keep the marriage. And the last I heard, they were making a go of it."

"But you didn't want to stay there, not with the woman you loved being married to another man?"

Brad nodded. "That's about it. So I looked around, and the *Pear Valley Observer* needed a reporter, and I figured in a smaller, slower environment, I could gain some space and pursue other interests. So I'm here to report and hopefully write a novel."

She smiled. "I've heard it said every reporter has a novel on him. What type of novel?"

"Science fiction. I'm a sci-fi fan. I am trying my hand at short stories now. Submitted one recently to a publisher in New York but haven't heard back."

"I hope you sell it, dear," Ida said, reaching out and giving Brad's arm a pat. "Miami's loss is our gain."

"I appreciate that." Brad drained his lemonade glass and stood. "Thank you very much, Ida. By the way, I have to ask. Do you think Sandra Allgood killed her husband?"

She sniffed as if a bad smell had wafted by. "If any smart woman saw a rat scurrying across the floor, she would shoot it."

Lavender nodded. "I'll take that as a yes."

"That is a commentary on the rat, not the shooter," Ida said. "But you shouldn't prejudge these law cases. You never know what a jury will do. I served as a juror once. Emmitt Throwbridge was the defense attorney."

Perking up, Brad asked, "Judge Throwbridge?"

"Yes," said Miss Ida. "It was before he was a judge and just a bright young lawyer many in town said was skilled. This was a civil case where Emmitt's client was Culpepper Shirley Jackson III, and he clearly rear-ended the driver in front of him. Emmitt stood up in his closing argument and said, 'If a car suddenly stops in front of you, what are you supposed to do? What did you expect Mr. Culpepper Shirley Jackson to do? He was driving an automobile. He was not driving a submarine. He could not have plunged into the concrete depths and gone underneath the driver. He was not piloting an airplane. He could not have pulled back on the wheel and flown over the vehicle in front of him. So what was he supposed to do besides brace for impact out of the utter recklessness of the driver stopping suddenly in front of him?'

"In the end, they found Emmitt's client not guilty. You never know what a jury will do," she said with a smile.

Brad smiled in return and started to head toward the porch stairs.

Ida called after him, "By the way, when will you ask that little Denise Walker out?"

Genuinely surprised, Brad stopped and responded, "What do you mean?"

"Come now, Mr. Lavender. We all know you are sweet about her. Step up; life is short."

"Well, I better go. Thank you for the lemonade; it was delicious."

"Squeezed it myself, like any self-respecting Southerner."

Brad thought for a minute and turned back. "Did you hear anything about the possibility that Allgood drugged his wife before he died?"

Ida smiled. "What makes you think he'd do that?"

"Rumor has it that Sandra has no recollection of what happened. But she says it wasn't her that shot him."

Ida took a long, slow drink and put her glass down as the ice cubes rattled against the glass. "I don't know nothin' about that night specifically."

Brad listened and then had to ask, "That night? Then do you know about other nights he may have drugged her?"

"What goes on in the walls of a home, especially those inhabited by many, don't always stay contained around these parts, Mr. Lavender. I will say that it's not beyond the realm of possibility."

Brad smiled and got the tidbits he'd come for. "Thank you for your time, Ida."

"You're quite welcome."

As he walked from the house, Brad thought about what he so willingly shared with Ida. He hadn't told anyone his real reason for leaving Miami before, not even his closest friends in Florida. He laughed, realizing that Ida had a cunning ability to suck you in and turn the story around. Her sweet and unassuming demeanor made her the spider to the fly, and he wondered how many other people had told her secrets.

THIRTEEN

The Interviews

From his request the week before, Jack had a Monday morning meeting with several deputies who responded to the call on July 2 at the Allgood home. His first interview would be with Rodger Franklin, the deputy who signed off on collecting the evidence. It was Franklin's first official murder investigation, and his nerves showed as he sat down with Jack. After brief but cordial introductions, Jack asked if he could record the conversation, and the deputy agreed.

"Deputy Franklin, how many crime scenes have you worked?"

"The Allgood murder would be the first."

Jack let out a breath of air. "Did you initially think it was suicide because of the note?"

"No, sir. There were seven bullet wounds; we ruled that out pretty quickly. Plus one of the shots took off his private parts. I don't care if you were going to kill yourself. No man would take that shot."

Jack suppressed a smirk. "Deputy, then did you collect the evidence, including the suicide note, because you thought this was a murder?"

"Yes, sir. Either Mr. Allgood had planned to kill himself and someone beat him to it or the killer wrote it to look like a suicide. So we sent it off for a handwriting analysis."

"Why would the killer write a suicide note for a man they shot seven times?"

In his dry tone, Franklin said, "Maybe he's just stupid."

"You said *he*. How come?"

"Force of habit."

"When you were on the scene, did you suspect that Mrs. Allgood could have killed Mr. Allgood?"

Franklin stopped himself for a second and thought about his boss warning him about the words he would use with this attorney from Atlanta. "He will try to trip you up, Franklin!" He sat and thought then answered honestly, "No, sir."

"Why?"

"Because at the time, she seemed out of it, distraught like anyone would be waking up to find someone they loved died."

"So you find the note and think it could be a clue. Did you ask Mrs. Allgood for a writing sample from her and one from Mr. Allgood?"

"Well, we had some papers from Mr. Allgood's desk that had his signature on them so we assumed he wrote them, and I used a receipt Mrs. Allgood filled out to confirm the items I took from the house as a sample for her writing."

"OK, back up. You didn't confirm that the papers on Mr. Allgood's desk were in his handwriting?"

Deputy Franklin squirmed in his metal chair. "Yes, I must have."

Jack shot him a skeptical glare.

"I mean yes. I asked Mrs. Allgood if those were his papers."

Jack released an exasperated breath. "Tell me: did Mrs. Allgood read the receipt to see the items removed from her home?"

"No. I mean I guess. I told her to, but like I said, she was pretty out of it at that time."

Jack shook his head, but at least Franklin's testimony matched his clients. Jack asked, "Did you tell her you would use the note to check her handwriting against the note?"

"Ah, no, sir," Franklin stuttered as if suddenly aware of the problem he had caused for the prosecution.

"OK, let's change gears. Did anyone swab her for gunshot residue?"

The deputy looked blankly at Jack. "She wasn't a suspect at the time."

Jack controlled himself despite wanting to strangle this kid, so he pressed politely. "Did you read her the Miranda warnings?"

"Yes, sir. The day we arrested her, we did."

Jack made a notation on the legal pad in front of him. "Mrs. Allgood said she had a drink served to her by her husband the night before. Did you collect that drinking glass so we can test it to see if she was drugged?"

"Drugged, sir?" the deputy asked. "Why would we think that?"

Jack sat back in his chair. "Son," said Jack, though he was not much older than the deputy. Being a lawyer gave him some authority, and he was going to use every bit of it. "Did you save the glass?"

"Ah, ah, no, sir," he said softly. "There was no reason to."

Jack stood and began to pace the room with his hands on his hips. "You have on your notes that you found an earring near the body. Have you tested it for fingerprints?"

"No, sir. But the sheriff said we didn't need to because Mrs. Allgood was missing one earring, and it was the same one we found."

"How do you know she was missing an earring?"

"She only had one in her ear when we got there."

"Were there any other signs of a struggle on her body? Did you think maybe she lost it in a struggle with the deceased?"

"Her losing it in a struggle? I guess it could've happened. But we didn't see no bruises on her or anythin'."

"Yet you think she could have lost the earring in a struggle?" Jack sat back in the chair. "Deputy, did you test the weapon for fingerprints?"

"Yes, sir."

"And?"

"There weren't none."

Jack sat back down, folded his hands in front of himself, and leaned in. "So basically, you had no real evidence linking Mrs. Allgood to the murder of her husband? And that's why you didn't arrest her that night?"

"Well, we were still investigatin', I suppose."

"So what changed?"

"You'll have to ask the sheriff and the DA. That's not my decision."

"And all you have now is a note, a gun, and a random earring? A note you still have yet to determine the writer, an unregistered gun with no fingerprints, and an earring you think belonged to Mrs. Allgood, found in a home she lives in?"

Franklin shook his head slowly, fearing his boss's explosion over the interview.

"Thank you, Deputy," Jack said with smugness and satisfaction.

When Jack went to work the following day, he was scheduled to meet with Brown and Truitt to update them on the case. When he arrived, Thelma let him know they were already in Mr. Truitt's office.

Brown was sitting in one of Frank Truitt's green, well-cushioned chairs. He was finishing up a story with Truitt. "So Ben takes her out, and they have a good time. Not off the charts or anything, but nice. So he takes her back to her place, says good night, and tries to kiss her. She jumps back and says, 'I don't kiss on a first date.' So Ben says, 'How about the last one?'"

Truitt smiled at the joke and changed his demeanor as he looked over at Jack. "Keeping banking hours, boy. Early bird gets the worm."

"I'll remember, sir" was all Jack could think to respond. Truitt nodded toward the other chair for him to sit down.

Jack took the cue and sat. He proceeded to tell both men about the events the day before with interviews of folks at the scene, especially Deputy Rodger Franklin. He noted he was still waiting for the Brady disclosures and had other discussions.

"Deputy is a damn idiot. Have you confirmed everything with his boss?"

"Not yet, sir. I am talking to Sheriff Jones later today."

Frank Truitt leaned back in his chair and tented his hands. "There was a dope dealer that I represented for a short time. He came in and wanted me to take his case. I usually would have said no, but I was going to charge him $10,000, which was like $100,000 nowadays. So I told him I needed $10,000 cash to do the case. I figured that would scare him off. He said he didn't have ten grand but give him a day or so. I said, 'No, you need to have the money now.'

"So the guy pulled off his watch and handed it to me. That damn thing was so heavy my hand dropped when he put it in my palm. I told him, 'I'm not running a damn pawn shop!' He said, 'Do you have a jeweler in town?' So we took the watch to the jeweler. The watch had a gold inlay with diamonds and all that. The jeweler told us that the watch wasn't worth $10,000. It was worth $40,000. So you bet your sweet ass we put that watch in our safe deposit box, and I represented him."

"Were you able to get him off?"

"Oh yeah. The deputy who arrested him didn't read him his

rights or let him make a call. The law's idiocy got me a big payday, and this kid got off."

Mosely asked, "So did you sell the watch so you could take your fee and run?"

Frank laughed, holding up his wrist. "Still got it."

Frank and Mosely laughed out loud. Both senior partners could tell Southern slice-of-life stories, even if they had little to do with the moment's conversation.

Jack was antsy to get moving. "So there's a reporter from the Macon paper down here now to cover the trial?" Jack had been approached by the reporter. He did not give them anything. He did call Brad and let him know the competition was in town in hopes Lavender would keep tabs on him.

"From Macon?" Truitt asked.

Mosley jumped in to answer, "We may get one or two others too. The suicide note does make this trial unique, not to mention the six-shot revolver. I'd bet my life Atlanta is sending a reporter down here also."

Truitt shook his head but also grinned. "It is unique but clearly not suicide. But out of curiosity, do we know what the suicide note says yet?"

Mosely answered again, "No, we are waiting for it to be produced. But we have to acknowledge that it doesn't mean Allgood wasn't attempting suicide; someone could have just beat him to the deed."

Jack let out a huff. "Deputy Franklin suggested that too, in his interview. But as for the note itself, the prosecution has it and seems to be dawdling a bit in turning it over. Legally, they have to, so I don't know why they are stalling. I will go to the judge and demand it if necessary. They did indicate they were getting the handwritten analysis that we asked for," said Jack.

"What's the update on Mrs. Allgood's finances?" Truitt asked.

"Still waiting on the bank. It should be soon. The deceased

husband, who no one is mourning, had pretty well tied up his wife financially. Almost as if he anticipated his untimely death." Jack waited a split second for a reaction from Truitt, but he didn't deliver. "So the judge appointed a guardian who must OK large purchases until a final legal ruling is made. But spending for legal defense is legitimate and allowed under the temporary new order the judge signed. I'm sure she will get the entire estate, but it will take a while to void what her husband did."

Truitt nodded. *"You* had better figure out a way to get us paid. What's your defense?"

Jack froze. He didn't have an answer to that question yet.

Brown interrupted. "I thought we would try the rarely used tactic of saying, 'The defendant was a no-good SOB who got what he deserved.' If any judge would accept that line of defense, it would be Throwbridge."

"If he did, you'd probably get a directed verdict of not guilty," Truitt said with a deep, hearty laugh.

Jack jumped into the big-man pool but started to doggy-paddle his way through. "Our client says she's not guilty. And we're thinking the drink her husband gave her that night may have been drugged with something and that the original plan was for *her* to die that night. But someone changed the plans. The problem is no one tested Sandra Allgood," Jack said. "Now I'm trying to find out what the deceased was involved in that could get him killed and why he might want to kill his wife."

Truitt didn't let a breath go between Jack's ramblings. "Wild-ass theories don't win cases, boy! With Allgood, the reason could be almost anything. Your job is not to solve the case. If you want to do that, go be a detective. Your job is to create one tiny hole in the prosecution's case!"

Truitt calmed as he shared a glance with Mosely. "Let me know what Layton says after you two talk. And we will figure this out." Truitt added, looking at his partner, "Mosely, stay with him on this."

Brown scratched his chin and took a shot at taking some heat off Jack. "You know the catfish trial is coming up in a few weeks?" He paused and waited for a response, but a wounded Jack and an angry Truitt said nothing. "As you know, Dan Cook's on trial for being a coconspirator with a dead sheriff for no less than running what was basically a marijuana farm, all while having an undercover GBI agent posing as a game warden and acting as a coconspirator with them. That will make headlines too, so we might lose some of the press that could taint the jury."

"It could, but most likely, the jury pool is already tainted. I'm not saying anything because it's probably in our favor if the rumor mill is correct," Jack said.

Mosely continued. "True. But here's another wild theory. Cook County is just next door. Is it possible that Allgood could have been mixed up in that somehow? He started getting financially healthy in the last couple of years and has promoted the short take-off plane manufacturer project with the chamber of commerce. What if he was involved and decided to turn over the state's evidence? Or he planned to steal the crop and cash it in for himself? If the grass growers found out about it, they would want to silence him. And those boys don't use words. Violence is the only language they speak."

Truitt's teeth bit into the cigar. His eyes flashed. The lit end of the cigar flared red. Slowly he lifted the cigar from his lips. "Dan Cook's screwed in that one. I doubt if Allgood had anything dealing with them. Allgood and Cook did not see eye to eye."

Truitt puffed and exhaled a few times as Jack and Mosely waited for him to finish his thought.

"But you are right about those cartel boys. I once represented some boys from New York. They were sons of a Mafia don up there who decided they would import some drugs with a Mexican cartel.

So this huge Continental pulls up in front of the office. This big guy walked in with this pinstriped suit, fedora hat, and gold pinky rings with diamond studs. He asked me to represent the boys in drug cases in Cook County, saying my old friend, the sheriff, had given them my name when they asked for lawyers.

He had an attaché case with him. He opened it and inside it was $50,000. I damn near choked. I blurted out, 'Where did you get the money?' He looked through me and said, 'You concentrate on getting the boys free and don't worry about the money. For your sake, you better be as good as I've heard.'"

Jack sheepishly asked, "Did you win the case?"

Truitt snickered, "Still here, ain't I? Turns out the sheriff had lost some key evidence, and the boys got off."

Brown piped in, "Wonder if your old buddy got a bag of cash for his disorganization?"

"Nah," Truitt quickly interjected, "he was just sloppy. Cain was too stupid to get paid off. I have to say it shocked me when I heard he was in cahoots with Cook and the undercover GBI agent. Anyway, I doubt Allgood had any connection to the late Sherriff Cain or Dan Cook. Like I said, Cook and Allgood didn't appreciate one another."

Brown saw his opening and stepped in. "If Allgood was involved, that might help our defense, even to cast doubt. We could hire an investigator to find out."

"Not worth it. Don't either of you waste your time on a goose chase. Focus on the facts you have. Nothing more. We don't need to do the prosecution's job for them."

Brown raised his eyebrows to Jack to relay the "I tried" message. Jack nodded in return.

Brown followed Jack back to his office, and as Jack squeezed himself behind his desk, he let his anger out. "Now I'm trying to be a detective!" Jack flung a file on his desk onto the floor as he flopped in his chair.

"He's just messing with you. Keep your focus," Brown pointed out. "Let me know what you find out with Layton."

"I thought he wanted you to go with me."

"You don't need a babysitter. And learn to shake him off, or he'll win."

"Win what?"

"In breaking you down to feed his ego. It's happened before." Mosely pointed toward David John's office, their muted but sometimes affable colleague.

FOURTEEN

The Prosecution

Jack met with District Attorney Rush Layton for his Brady disclosure on Tuesday morning. He had a reasonable opinion of Layton and felt he would be straight with him on the revelations if there were any. Layton's reputation for being an aggressive prosecutor was well-established, but he was also known for respecting the law and his obligations under it.

Jack walked into Layton's office, and they shook hands. "Hi, Jack. It's nice to meet you. I've heard a few things about you. Welcome to Pear Valley."

Jack smiled. "Thank you. But don't believe everything you hear."

"Oh, I don't. Have a seat," Rush said, pointing to an empty chair opposite his large, gray, metal desk, unusually tidy for a DA.

Once Jack was seated, Rush spun around in his chair, removed several files from his back credenza, and placed them on his desk. He pulled one and handed it to Jack. Layton cut to the chase of what he saw as the state's smoking gun.

In a patriarchal voice, Layton said, "You're new in town. I want to try to save you from embarrassment. Review this, and I will talk to you about pleading your client out."

Jack's dad had always said to be wary of people "working in your best interest." He flipped the file open and started reading.

An analysis by a local handwriting expert had found a match with the suicide note. To Jack's shock and surprise, the expert's report indicated the note matched the handwriting sample taken for Mrs. Allgood the night of the shooting. The match was devastating evidence. It would show Mrs. Allgood was at least complicit in her husband's murder, if not the murderer herself. But as he read the cryptic message, that didn't make anything clear either.

Layton leaned across his desk. "Got to give her credit; she tried."

Damn, Jack thought, *I'm done*. But Jack put on his best poker face, closed the file, and said, "I'm not sold. But I had the pleasure of interviewing Deputy Franklin yesterday. Given that my client was never notified that she was, in fact, providing a writing sample for this purpose, I want this information excluded from the evidence." Jack followed it with "I would also like to have the sample reviewed and examined by the GBI handwriting expert in Atlanta."

Since his requests followed protocol, Layton had no choice. "Well, there is no way the note is going to be excluded, but you have your right to a second opinion. I'll have my secretary get this over to the GBI lab today."

Layton admitted to himself that this battle had just ramped up a notch, but he didn't worry about the outcome from the GBI. Allgood murdered her husband, and she wrote the note, pure and simple.

Jack left Layton's office and headed down the long stairs toward the front door. With each well-placed step, the reality of how damning the match of her writing to the suicide note drove home the fact that this was a capital murder case, and he had no idea what his argument would be. His legs wavered a bit, and then as his right foot hit the front hall, his intestines groaned. He looked around, spotted the door, and ran to the men's room.

—ɯɯ—

Denise Wagner sat at her drafting table, drawing the day's editorial cartoon for the paper. With her head cocked to one side, the newsroom could see her bright smile as she intently worked on her next creation. Her desk had the perfect view over the entire newsroom, and she could keep track of anything brewing, keeping her on her toes all day. She lifted her eyes to see if Brad was at his desk, but it was still empty, and she felt a twinge of sadness. Denise thought about what Ruby had said and then shook her head, ridding herself of the thought. *Brad and I are just good work friends. That's all.*

She had mentioned Ruby Sutton to her editor, Evan Conover. He was impressed by her resume and the samples Ruby had given her. He told Denise to let her know to come in, and he would finalize the deal. Ruby would be thrilled, and Denise looked forward to having her there to talk to.

Because currently, the paper was primarily men, and Denise being stunningly beautiful made many of them mute in her presence. Denise was tall with brown hair, large eyes, and a figure that had caused several Georgia males to bump into buildings. In fact, upon spotting Denise, one man bumped into the courthouse so bad he knocked himself back to the sidewalk. He suffered a minor concussion, and the poor fellow had to be hospitalized.

She was working on a drawing of Mrs. Allgood leaving the courtroom when her phone rang. As she dabbed the cartoon, she reached for the phone and absentmindedly pulled the phone to her ear.

"Hello, this is Denise."

"Well, hello, Miss Walker."

"Brad?"

"The one and only."

Laughing, she said, "Very funny. Where are you?"

"Just finished an interview. About to grab lunch and thought you might want to join?"

"I can't today. I have an appointment. Rain check?"

"For you, any day you want."

Denise laughed, then hung up the phone and dropped the receiver back on the hook. Her smile widened as she thought about Brad before her brain put her mood back in check, and she shook her head and got back to work. Her marriage had only been a source of misery. Her ex had mocked her drawings and viewed them with disdain. In contrast, Brad applauded her work and encouraged her to do more. But the safety she felt with Brad only caused Denise to keep those growing feelings in check. She feared getting hurt again. Denise placed her pencil down and looked out her office window, recalling the night she and Brad were stuck at work and somehow the conversation never ended.

It had been several weeks prior when Brad had ordered a pizza and showed up at Denise's desk just as she was gathering her stuff to leave.

"Pizza?"

"Yes, if you're sharing!'

"I am."

"Perfect. I just dropped off my copy!"

Brad opened the box, and they both dove in.

Denise started. "I'm trying to get Evan to give Ruby Sutton a chance here. She's got the education and experience."

"Trying to replace me already?" Brad said, feigning a frown.

"No, never, but it would be good to have more females around. We are a little testosterone heavy here. Besides, moving here can't be easy. She came from society in Atlanta so I am sure this is a culture shock." Denise took a bite, and the two ate in silence before she added, "Speaking of adjusting, it's only been a year since you abandoned those questionable beaches in Miami. You regret it yet?"

"No comment on the beaches, but I like it. I'm surprisingly busy all the time, which I like, and I found someone to join me for pizza. What's not to like? Besides, my grandmother used to say you can't be depressed if you don't have the time," Brad laughed.

Denise joined in. "She was a smart lady," she said and then she wiped her mouth and placed her hand over her stomach. "Thank you. I needed the sustenance."

Brad grew serious and leaned in. "Look. I'm an investigative reporter, so it's in my nature to ask probing questions, but why would any man let you go?"

"Well, he didn't. I left on my own." The two shared a quiet stare before Denise added, "I was sick of being his punching bag."

Brad stopped eating and wiped his mouth. "Oh wow. I'm sorry. I didn't think it was anything like that."

"You thought he cheated?"

"I guess."

"Most do. Nope. I'm sorry. I didn't mean to put a downer on our dinner here, which thank you for sharing. I hadn't eaten since last night."

"That's not acceptable."

They laughed and talked for over three hours. Finally, when the night cleaner rolled his bucket and mop as he walked by them, he cleared his throat, and they got the hint and left. As they left the newsroom that night, Denise offered, "You know, that man took everything from me, even my last dime, but I'm slowly getting it all back. Thank you for dinner tonight."

"You got it. One day, I'll take you to a real meal."

Denise looked at him with a noncommittal glance and said, "You know where to find me."

—⟋⟍—

Robin had lost all track of time and orientation. She had told them all she knew, escaping charges and jail, but the Feds were tight-lipped as to the next steps. However, they made it clear that once they had all the information they needed, she would be relocated.

—ɷ—

After his talk with Ida, Brad sat at his desk trying to piece together the facts of the catfish case and what relevance or defense they may provide in his murder case. While Brad dug deeper into both cases, he glanced up toward Denise's desk. He watched her intently work at her drafting table, and he thought about how her divorce had cost her. Ida's words about Denise replayed in his head for a minute before he shook his head and tried to refocus.

—ɷ—

Ruby had been set to meet Denise at Mabel's Place on Ellington Highway for lunch. Mabel's reminded Ruby of the great meals her nanny, Maude, made for her in her childhood. Glancing up from the menu, Ruby saw Denise walking toward her and smiling. "Why are you so happy?"

"No reason. Just a beautiful day."

Ruby laughed. "OK, you know I don't believe you, right?"

Denise took a deep breath. "It really is the reason. Now let's go grab lunch; I'm starving." Denise reached for a menu on the table.

"Me too!" Ruby said. "But I already know what I want."

Denise dropped her menu and looked at Ruby. "So you know my editor, Evan, is interested in hiring you?"

Ruby shifted in her seat. "Yes, and I've been thinking about it."

Denise, not one to mince words, asked, "What's the holdup?"

Ruby waited for the waitress to deliver their water and asked if they wanted another drink. Both ladies ordered sweet teas. After the waitress left, Ruby leaned in. "The truth is it's Jack. I haven't had a chance to discuss it with him. He's been so preoccupied with this trial I don't think I could get his attention if I stripped naked in front of him."

"He's a typical man; that would work for sure. So do it tonight. He seems cool; I doubt he would have a problem with it. It is the age of women's liberation, you know. Even if it doesn't feel like that down here."

Ruby looked down and opened the menu without responding.

"I'll take that as a 'Yes, I'll do it,'" Denise said, returning to her menu.

—※—

Jack had found Tony Tanner's and Jerry Roberts's addresses and mapped out the routes with his Rand McNally the night before. Since Jerry worked on the Allgood farm, he drove to the offices next to the livestock barn and pulled right up to the front door. The dirt road dust flew all around as Jack got out of the car. He made his way to the front door of the offices in a mobile home, knocked, and began brushing off his suit.

No answer.

"Mr. Roberts?" Jack yelled, hoping the man was inside and giving it another knock.

Jerry got up from his desk piled high with papers and opened the door. "Yes, hi. You must be Jack Sutton. Come in, please."

"Yes, thank you for seeing me." Jack sat in a free chair and noted Jerry's tall and thin body. He thought he would look like a zipper if he stuck his tongue out. "I just wanted to ask you a few questions."

"Shoot," Jerry said, sitting behind his desk and clearing a path so he could see Jack.

"How close were you to Bill Allgood?"

"I worked for his dad, and since he passed, I worked for Mr. Allgood, running the farm for him."

"So he trusted you with running the farm?"

"I wouldn't say that."

"Then what would you say?"

"He had me run the farm because I knew how, and he hated farmwork." His face gave no signs of emotion.

"Why keep the farm if he hated it?"

"Because you don't bite the hand that feeds you."

"So it's profitable?"

"Didn't say that."

Jack could see Jerry calculating his words. The mad came across as reticent and downright tricky, so he pushed. "Then what would you say about the finances?"

"We cover our bills."

"And do you cover those bills with farm earnings?"

"Mostly."

"Where does the money come from then besides the farm?"

"I don't ask questions, Mr. Sutton. If we were short, I told my boss, and he supplied the difference. Mr. Sutton, what's the point?" Jerry asked, shifting in his seat and crossing his arms.

Jack changed the subject. "How well did you know Sandra Allgood?"

"I knew her. Just not well."

"She told us you and Bill would go on trips together. He never mentioned his young, beautiful wife."

"What trips?"

"She said you and Mr. Allgood had taken a fishing trip to Mexico."

"I didn't take trips with Bill Allgood. I was told to go along as the help. He had some friends who wanted to do a trip, and I did the toting and cooking and cleaning."

Jack nodded. "How often do you see Mrs. Allgood?"

"Rarely. Other than to ride her horse, she never mingled around the farmhands or the farm itself."

"I see. Do you know Tony Tanner?"

Roberts sat back in his chair and parsed his lips for a second. "I do."

"How do you know him?"

"He helped us on the farm when we needed extra help or he needed a job."

"So he and Mr. Allgood were friends?"

"They knew each other. That's all I can confirm."

Jack couldn't seem to crack him, and his frustration elevated. "Do you know anyone who would want your boss dead, sir?"

Jerry cocked his head to one side and then looked out the window before turning back to Jack, his brows knitted together as he leaned toward Jack. "I don't know anyone who *didn't* want him dead."

"Do you think his wife wanted to kill him? I mean there are plenty of rumors about his other women."

"That's not a question I can answer. If she did do it, well, I'm pretty sure she had a good reason."

Jack cocked his head. "What makes you say that?" Jack looked out the trailer's window and then back at Jerry. "Did you hear them fight? I mean noise travels even for a house that far away. Supposing the screams got loud enough."

Silence filled the space between these two as Jerry stayed mute. Then Jerry stood up and started walking to the door. "Not that I recall. Now I have another appointment I need to make, or the livestock won't get fed."

Jack gathered his notepad and pen and walked to the door. "If you think of anything, let me know. If you want to help her, silence isn't the answer."

"Thank you, counselor."

Jack walked down the two metal steps as Roberts slammed the door behind him.

—⟋⟍—

Jack pulled Cindy into the diner with her 396 purring. He could not resist revving the engine to show all that raw power; he was still just a boy inside. Focusing back on business, he could see a short, dark-haired man seated by the window who fit Tanner's description. Jack entered and slid across from him in the booth. "Tony Tanner?"

"The one and only. You must be Jack Sutton, world-class attorney for the beautiful Sandra."

Jack sat back, shocked at the sheer exuberance Tony displayed. His deep Southern accent made it hard to catch every word, plus he kept a toothpick in the side of his mouth that he played with nonstop. Jack tried not to watch. "So I need you to tell me how you knew the deceased."

Tanner let out a hoot and slammed the table like he was at a comedy show. "Ole Bill and I go back to college. Well, probably not like the college you went to. We did a few months in community college. He was a shitload of trouble even back then!"

"What do you mean?"

Tanner cocked his head to one side and leaned in. "I think it's pretty well-known that Bill liked his fun and helping others have fun too." Tanner followed up with a wink.

"Did you know Sandra well then?"

Tanner sat back and took the toothpick out of his mouth, looked at it, placed it back in, and started moving it around with his tongue, then moved it to the side before he spoke. "From what I could tell, she liked to spend Bill's money real good." Tony leaned in. "And between you and me, he was getting ready to give her the boot, if you know what I mean. I'm sure that's why she killed him."

Jack wanted the floor to open up and swallow him. "Were you aware of Bill mistreating Sandra physically?"

"Bill was a bastard and liked to have his fun, but I ain't never seen him hit no woman. He cheated on her for sure, but there was no hitting." Tony slurped his coffee, then leaned back in. "There was a time when Bill showed up at my place with scratches on his face though. Said Sandra went all sorts of nuts on him when he wouldn't give her money."

"Was Bill having money issues?"

Tony let out a loud laugh. "No way. He was tighter than bark to a tree; that's why he had so much money. Why, his young wife made his life hell. She was expecting more than she got."

"You seem sure Sandra was capable of such murder. Why?"

"Because there ain't nothin' meaner than a woman scorned or kept on a budget." Then Tony offered, "Word of advice, Mr. big-time lawyer. She did it, and you should cut your losses."

"Good to know," Jack said, dropping a few dollars on the table before leaving. As Jack walked back to his car, without noticing the red truck, he thought, *Time to call the investigator. I am way over my head with this. And note to self: don't call Tanner or Roberts to testify.*

When Jack made it home for dinner, he could see Ruby on the porch waiting for him with a glass of white wine. "Hey, babe," Jack said, taking the stairs two by two. He leaned in and gave his bride a lengthy kiss. "I see you poured my wine already."

"You know it. I wanted to talk to you."

"Same, and I think I better go first because I feel you will be angry."

"What's wrong?"

Jack leaned against the railing so he could face Ruby. "I need to hire an investigator on this case to help us track down witnesses to build and create our defense. I think we can free up the funds from Allgood's account to pay for it, but it's going to take time, and I don't have time."

Ruby put her glass down. "Jack?"

"Ruby, listen. I'm overwhelmed with this case. It's only temporary."

"Why doesn't the firm pay?"

Jack swallowed hard and breathed, "Because Truitt said no."

Ruby sat back in her chair, picked up her wine, and took a sip. "Babe?"

Ruby looked at Jack. "I hate that man. But I love you. And Daddy always said his rise up the law ladder didn't happen without him eating some s-h-i-t." Ruby felt if she spelled out a swear, she wasn't really saying it. "It's fine."

Jack pushed off the railing, leaned over his wife, and drew her in for a big kiss. "You're amazing. What did you have to tell me?"

"Well, since we're talking money, I got an offer to work at the *Pear Valley Observer*. And after your news, it sounds like the cash will come in handy."

Jack shook his head and went immediately silent. He never objected to his wife wanting to work; he was not like one of those traditional men who thought she had to stay barefoot and pregnant in the kitchen. But he had hoped that they were at that point to start a family. Her taking a job would delay those plans.

"Jack?"

Jack avoided eye contact and sat in the chair next to Ruby. "Where is this coming from all of a sudden?"

"You aren't on board. Why?"

"I just thought we were thinking of having kids soon. If you start a job and get pregnant immediately, how will that work exactly?"

Ruby grew quiet and stood up. "I guess I'll figure it out," she said before walking inside with the screen door slamming shut behind her. Jack lay back and looked up at the porch ceiling, thinking, *What else?*

Wednesday morning, District Attorney Rush Layton was less than pleased. When Sheriff Jones brought this slam dunk case to him, it all seemed black and white. A woman shoots her husband, finishing with the last shot in his groin, and tries to pass it off with a suicide note. He had all but written his summation in his head:

Sandra Allgood was a young woman married to an older but wealthier man who was a known philanderer. Feeling scorned, Sandra knew the easiest way to gain her husband's fortune was getting rid of him. So she set out to shoot him and make it look like suicide. To make it happen, she would use the element of surprise. So she walked in on him while he was indisposed. Sandra never thought Bill would get up and run. But he did. Bill Allgood ran for his life, and she went after him in a blind rage and kept shooting, one right after the other. And when he finally succumbed to his wounds, she put the final bullet in the one thing he couldn't keep in his pants.

The case would be especially timely for Layton's career. But with everyone enthralled with the transfer of the catfish case to Callahan County and District Attorney Bill Willis from Cook County prosecuting it, Layton could lose the wind from his sails.

Because of the prominence of the late sheriff and the Cook family, the catfish trial had been moved from Cook County to Callahan. So Willis would try it in Layton's backyard, exposing him to local voters and getting a lot of press—the press Layton wanted on his trial.

Layton and Willis were the most likely next appointment to judge if a vacancy came up. The governor had to appoint someone, or if not, they would have to run against each other in an election. So to gain an appointment, good press was essential.

And as such, Rush contemplated the trouble the young defense attorney Sutton was working up. He had reviewed the information that emerged from Sutton's interview with Deputy Franklin, which infuriated him. And he had reamed out Sheriff Jones for over fifteen minutes. "How could you let that boy go talking to the deputies and then raise questions about the way you gathered evidence or failed to gather evidence? What the hell?"

"Look, Rush. I—"

"I don't want to hear any damn excuses. If the only piece of evidence doesn't come back from the crime lab in Atlanta as her handwriting, we're screwed. We have no fingerprints off the weapon, you never tested Mrs. Allgood for gunshot residue, or the glasses left on the counter, and you left the scene without securing it until we've had a chance to send the GBI in. Not to mention you never had her checked out by the EMTs that night!"

Before Walter Jones could answer, Layton's secretary buzzed to tell him that Bill Willis, who was in town, was here to see him. *Oh my God*, thought Layton. *What else can go wrong today?* Layton hung up on Sheriff Jones without a word and stood to greet Willis as he let himself into Rush's office.

"How's your case looking, Bill?" Layton asked when Willis walked in.

Bill chuckled and said, "Better than yours. I heard the cops fucked you up on evidence collecting and then some."

"Jones needs to be on top of his deputies and get his department in shape. They look like the Keystone cops!"

"Especially these days. The criminals have more rights than the victims, and with the accuracy of new testing methods, they missed the boat for sure." Willis sat down, as did Layton. "I was discussing criminal rights with the governor on my recent trip to Atlanta. You know he and I were in the same fraternity at Valdosta State, though he was a few years earlier than me."

Layton thought, *Willis is baiting me.* Rising above the temptation to get in the gutter with Willis and point out that the governor and his family were longtime friends, he decided to stay diplomatic and stay on the issue. "Is that so? Well, as for our defendant, if I get her handwriting on that note, I have her," said Layton, although he knew his evidence, if true, would only be circumstantial. And given the area, Sandra Allgood could still walk. "What about your case?"

"Well, I have Cook dead to rights, and Sheriff Cain is already dead. Some people still believe that line-of-duty crap, but I know he drove into that bridge pillar because we were about to throw his ass in jail. Those secret recordings by that GBI agent Jernigan are pretty damming evidence. Jernigan was quite the guy, he befriended both of them, and they trusted him completely. He got in and secretly recorded most of their conversations. But there is still a loose end."

"Really?" a genuinely surprised Layton responded. As he and Willis sat down, he asked, "What loose end?"

"Well, we know that Cook and Cain were behind the growing. They were childhood friends in Callahan County, where Cain's family was from, and Cook's mother had lived here when estranged from the family. Evidently, a friend of the Cain's and another guy were going to transport the goods to the cartel who had now moved their operations into the states. But supposedly, from listening to the only tape where Cain mentioned this, only he knew who the accomplice and his partner were, and the dead man ain't talking."

"What sort of partner?"

"Well, Cook had the land and grew the stuff. The sheriff and what they thought was the district game warden provided security and protection. But there is reason to believe that Allgood facilitated that connection to a partner or partners who had the connections to the Mexicans and delivered the goods to them. We're thinking Allgood didn't have any real connection; he was just the middleman."

"Cook and Jernigan did not know who the partner or partners were?"

"No, part of the way the cartel works is to limit contact there. The theory was the whole chain won't fall if one gets caught," observed Willis.

No shit! Layton thought. Layton leaned back in his chair, tented his hands to his chin, and asked, "What do you have to figure out who these secret partners are?"

Willis continued. "The evidence comes from one of the tapes from Jernigan. One day as they were nearing harvest and talking about transporting to the cartel, in a meeting with Cook, Jernigan recorded them in the sheriff's office referring to the 'lead' partner.

"Until then, everyone thought Cain was the real mastermind of the deal and had brought on Cook because he had a sizable farm where you could hide the pot fields. They recruited the 'game warden' to be sure he did not find the fields when he was doing flyovers looking for fields baited for doves or deer. Evidently, that is a trend around the country, getting the game wardens involved to prevent detection. That was one of the reasons the GBI planted Jernigan.

"However, on this tape, Sheriff Cain said he and his partner, a guy he referred to as 'Baldy,' developed the plan and that he would deal with harvest and transport. The sheriff bragged about how he had kept everything under wraps, and now it would be up to Baldy to finish it."

Layton nodded. "Why a partner to just harvest and transport? Cook and his boys could do that."

"Well," started Willis, "it was not just harvesting and transporting but also having the relationship with a cartel to sell. They needed someone to connect to the cartel, and according to what the game warden learned, that was the sheriff's secret partner. He had told them, 'You don't need to know anything else. You are better off not dealing directly with the cartel. They can be dangerous.' Cook, being the pussy he was, readily agreed to leave it to others. Not wanting to appear suspicious, Jernigan said he did too. So when the crop was ready, Jernigan and Cook went to Sheriff Cain's office to meet and talk about the harvesting and transport. They got there, and Cain was sitting at his desk with his feet up on it right there in the Cook County Courthouse."

"Well, that takes." Layton cleared his throat. "You know what?"

"Balls! Exactly! So on the tape, Cook says, 'Boys, it won't be long now. The stalks are grown, and we're ready. I've got everything in place for Thursday night's removal and transport.' The game warden can be heard asking, 'Where are you meeting the cartel, and how do we know we will get paid?' He was trying to figure out this accomplice, and Cain put his feet down and responded, 'Rick, I told you Baldy and his men will take care of that. He won't cheat us.' The game warden didn't push after that because he assumed he'd have another shot at the information."

Layton leaned on his desk. "Well, your GBI agent should've known better than assume, don't ya think?"

"Like he had any idea Cain would off himself once they were discovered?"

"Well then, where is there evidence that Allgood helped make the connection? Are you thinking he's Baldy? And either way, you only have a couple choices: turn up the heat on Cook, find someone named Baldy, or link him to Allgood and the guys he hired to harvest and transport the weed. Now tell me about the surveillance tapes. What do I need to know?"

Not amused, Willis leaned back in his chair. "Well, your dead boy Allgood showed up in two tapes. It could have just been the wrong place at the wrong time. He happened to be at a restaurant having lunch with Cook and the chairman of Cook County Commission, Terry Teague, who we know is a standup guy. Seems Allgood had a set lunch to talk with Teague about some plane manufacturing plant he was helping bring into Callahan and that there might be an opportunity for some support business in Cook County."

"Yeah, that would be Winthrop Aviation. Allgood helped get them to relocate here from Ohio. But there's much speculation about Allgood's motivation where that's concerned."

Willis kept going as if Layton hadn't said a word. "It was happenstance that Cook was there, and they had just offered for him to join them. We've found no connection between Allgood to this drug case *yet*. But I've got a call into the Feds on him. The second was an incidental finding where Allgood was at a strip club out on Highway 41, and it just so happened Cook and Jernigan were there also, but they were not together."

"Shit!" exclaimed Layton. "Under this new Brady standard, I'll have to disclose this to the defense too."

Looking genuinely sympathetic, Willis replied, "I know. I hate to give you that information, but if I kept it from you, it would only bite me later."

Layton said, "I appreciate your position. Be prepared for Sutton wanting your files once I tell him."

"By the way, did that fool boy really show up in Emmitt's courtroom in a white poplin suit and a blue shirt?"

They both laughed out loud. "Yep. It was the stupidest move I had seen in a long time. But I wouldn't underestimate him. He recovered well. Old Truitt must have seen something in him."

"Yeah, I need to find time to talk to Truitt. I understand he and Cain clashed over criminal cases in past years. Maybe he can give me some insight into Cain and who this Baldy guy could be."

"Good luck. It's hard to get old Frank's time unless you are paying him as a lawyer or getting votes for his senate seat," Layton said, smiling. He turned and buzzed his secretary for coffee. "You want anything?" he asked Willis.

"Nah, I've got to get back. I can't stay here and help *you* all day. I got my own work to do."

Layton laughed. "Yeah, *your* help is what I need." Willis walked to the door wearing his usual smirk when Layton stopped him. "Wait. I'd do a little more digging into Cain's story."

"Why?"

"Because he wasn't the guy that was in the fast lane. From what I've heard, he was that all-American, rule-following, family man. Did you ever ask yourself why he got involved?"

"Money and greed, my friend, gets 'em every time."

"I guess. Makes me question humanity," Layton said, raising an eyebrow. "And let me know if you find out anything about Allgood. I don't believe in coincidences."

Layton's secretary walked in and set his coffee on his desk. "Are you sure none for you, Mr. Willis?"

Willis shook his head no.

Layton thanked his secretary as she placed the cup on his desk and walked out quickly; Layton looked at Willis and shot him a smirk. "Just look into it. And keep me posted on what you find out."

"Right back at ya," Willis said before he walked out.

Layton grabbed the Allgood file and started to go back over everything.

FIFTEEN
Mounting Evidence

Jack was in his office, pouring through the Brady material the DA had provided through discovery. Going through the financial records, he found that Allgood's financial situation had been improving significantly in the last few years. Supposedly it was from business dealings with bringing the airport manufacturer to Callahan. It seemed the company had been providing Allgood a fee to promote their interest. It seemed to explain some of the extra cash but not all of it.

Stuck in the middle of the materials, he found a reference to Bill Allgood showing up in two surveillance tapes in the catfish case. However, the memo went on to note that there were hundreds of tapes, the appearance in those two was incidental, and the Cook County DA had ruled out any Allgood involvement with the plot. The memo, noted on the back of an unrelated memo, went on to explain that the incidental finding was part of the ongoing investigation in the catfish case and that any information needed to be sought from the Cook DA handling that case, Bill Willis.

This placement of the information concerning Allgood had Jack questioning what the DA might be hiding or attempting to hide from him. Had he not been flipping over every page that he went through meticulously one by one; he could have missed it. *Was that the intent? Could it be possible Bill was involved in the catfish case and the DA didn't want him to know it? It would establish a motive for having him killed by someone other than his client.* He slammed the file shut and grabbed his phone to dial up Bill Willis when Mosely Brown and David John came in.

"You need a break," David said, sliding into a chair opposite Jack. Brown sat next to him, pulled out a flask, took a swig, and passed it to Jack. "I brought some for you since I figured you still haven't gotten a bottle for your office."

After taking a pull against his better judgment, Jack leaned over and opened his desk drawer. He held the square bottle up to show his mentor. "You know why Jack Daniels is in a square bottle?"

Mosely chuckled. "Tell me."

John flopped in a seat next to Mosely and interjected, "So when they transported the booze under the car seats, during Prohibition, the bottles wouldn't roll out from under them if they got pulled over."

Jack laughed. "And I thought only I knew that!"

"Well, you still need a break!"

"What I need is a miracle. I need to get my hands on some surveillance tapes. I think the deceased had his hand in some drug dealing."

John, taking the flask and a draw of the contents, sat back and put his feet on the conference table. "Wait. As in Allgood is linked to the catfish case?"

"Not conclusively, but all I need is reasonable doubt. And these files might just lend themselves to that."

Taking the flask from David, Mosely interjected, "Be careful you don't go too off the rails. You need proof for the jury to doubt your client was the killer. Don't go chasing wild geese, or Truitt will lose it."

"Well, if Jack is right, it could go to motive. If Allgood got hooked up with the wrong people, he could have pissed them off."

"Yeah, it doesn't look like a drug killing by the cartel, though. Allgood's killer knew him and hated him. Hate is just another form of love," Mosely said in a high voice. "Well, that's what my mom used to say anyway."

Jack put his pen down on his yellow legal pad. "I get what you two are saying. But I'm thinking, *What if he was involved in the catfish case and it wasn't the cartel who offed him but one of the other people involved?* From the notes here, there's a leader named Baldy and the others, not sure how many, who did the harvesting and transporting. What if they tried to make it look like a crime of passion but being amateurs, unlike the cartel, made it sloppy?"

"Could be," John said.

"Still, too off the path. Stay focused," Mosely advised. "Hey, we actually came in here to see where you stood on football, not this case. David here went to Georgia Southern for undergrad. He had an interesting story about his legendary coach, the infamous Eek Taggart."

"Really?"

"Well, if you like football, you would be interested," Mosely said.

Jack laughed. "Are you allowed to live in Georgia and not like football?" They all laughed. "But I don't know this coach, so tell me. I need the diversion." Jack leaned back in his chair and gave a long stretch before David spoke, took another drink from the flask, and said, "Get 'er done."

"Well, as I explained to Mosely, Eek had a reputation before he got to Georgia Southern. When some rich alumni decided we needed a team, they went after Eek. Within two years, they had a program and hired Eek from Texas, where he was the defensive coordinator. Eek was about five, eight, and stout but solid, not fat. But that guy had determination you wouldn't believe.

One day, I was on the field as Eek yelled at a uniformed player, 'You want to talk determination! Stand your ground and keep standing!' The lineman said OK. So Eek barrels his head into the guy's helmet! He just bangs the helmet, and he keeps doing it. He must have run into the guy a half dozen times. And blood was flowing down his face.

By the time Eek was done, his face was almost covered in blood, and the player was cowering. Eek had to be pulled off of him because he hadn't slowed down a bit. Standing over the poor kid and looking around at the whole team as they looked on, some with amusement, but most with horror, he yelled, 'You have to be determined!' They all just stood there in shock. But that's the type of man Eek Taggart was. And he darn sure won titles for the school. He retired last year but won three national titles for the school during his tenure," David said.

"I believe it. He must have had a real hard head," Brown said, laughing at his attempt at a joke.

"He did," David agreed, "but he never gave up. A lesson for us all."

"Y'all know I am a Georgia Bulldog, and Georgia hired some young kid who went to Auburn as their coach, Vince Dooley. I wonder what those fools are thinking. To hire an Auburn boy to coach at UGA. He won't last long."

All three leaned back in their chairs. Brown, to lighten the moment, reached into his pocket, pulled out a cigar, and stuck it in his mouth. He lit a match and brought the flame to the tobacco. "You two don't mind if I smoke, do you? I have a weakness for cigars," he said.

"You're the senior partner. You can do anything you want," Jack said.

Brown laughed. "Yes, that is one of the advantages of being a senior partner." He puffed on the cigar. "So what's the investigator's status for the Allgood case?"

David interrupted. "Hold on, it's just my gut talking, but now that Mr. Allgood has departed the earth, his wife will inherit a great deal of money, which goes straight to the motive."

Mosely looked at him. "Your point?"

"It's too obvious, and from what I've heard through town gossip, Sandra could have had any guy she wanted. All I'm saying is you need to prepare for the prosecution. Layton's going to claim that's why she killed him."

Jack nodded, ignoring David's obvious and unhelpful statement. "I called Annie Masterson. She said she'd take the case. Her record is impeccable."

David piped in, "Oh Annie! She's that female investigator up in Macon. We could ask her to come down for an interview, and we would pay the expenses for the trip, of course. I think we can decide rather quickly if we all three interview her. She did work for a law firm I know, and they rated her exemplary."

"Already hired her," Jack stated, watching Brown's expression go from relaxed to shock. "Yes, Truitt said no, but I'm doing it anyway. We need the help, and it will be worth it, even if the county does not come through and pay it; if not, it can come out of my pocket."

David laughed. "You got more balls than I gave you credit for. If Eek were here, he'd say, 'You're awright, boy.'"

Brown sat forward and put out his cigar. "I'll take care of the expenses and explain it to Truitt later. Remember, boys, sometimes it's best to ask for forgiveness than permission, especially after you deliver a win. But Jack, we need that win, or the whole landscape here changes," Mosely said, motioning to the three of them.

"Well, she'll be here in a few days. I've already told her we need to know everything Allgood was involved in. From what we know, the victim was very close-mouthed about his job activities, even with Tony Tanner, his one and only friend. Plus I think something was planned for the night of the crime. If Allgood drugged his wife that night, we need to know why. What was his plan? And why did he need to keep Sandra from knowing?"

"Look. You have my support. I'm just cautioning you to be careful about making too many assumptions. Again, you have to provide doubt." Mosely went back to pushing Truitt's mantra.

David got up from his chair. "You're not wrong. Jack needs to create doubt, but sometimes the best way is to present a potentially plausible alternative scenario."

Jack nodded. "I sense the late Mr. Allgood was involved in many things, not all of them legal. The more we know about his activities, the closer we'll come to solving the case, or at least closer to finding evidence that will exonerate Sandra Allgood."

When Jack got home that night, Ruby had a huge dinner made, although it smelled more like she burned most of it, but in the center of the table sat a peanut butter cake she purchased from the Upside-Down Cupcake.

Before Jack could put his briefcase down and comment on her efforts, Ruby blurted out, "Well, I figured it out."

"What would that be?" Jack asked, going over to the stove and turning the burner off. "Looks like the steak's done."

Ruby ignored his comment. "My job. I met the editor, and he was impressed with my background and offered me to start at $200 a week as the local scene editor. I know that doesn't sound exciting on its own, but he also said I'd be backup for Brad Lavender and that with the catfish case and Allgood's murder case, well, Brad would need some help." She went on without pausing. "And I got to meet Brad today; he's from Miami so he's kind of like us: fish out of water."

Jack felt a little annoyed. Ruby had moved forward after their discussion. "OK. I'm going to go change for dinner."

"Wait. I need you to support me on this, Jack. I'm not saying no to kids."

"But your actions are, Ruby. I'm not trying to tie you to this house and being a mom. I guess I'm just disappointed because I thought we were on the same page."

"We are, but maybe not the same timeline and how it will look." Ruby dropped her head.

Jack walked over to his young bride and took her in his arms. "Baby, you have my support. Always. But support is one thing; agreeing with you is another."

Ruby hugged Jack back as tears flowed down her cheeks. She opened her eyes and wiped her tears as she looked over at the stove behind him. "Besides, do you really want *me* tied to this kitchen?"

Jack leaned back a little to look at Ruby, and he laughed. "Yeah, well, on that, we agree." He kissed his bride, but before he headed upstairs, he let out, "Cake looks good though!"

—⚬—

Jack had gotten in early the following day and headed straight for the coffee machine. Surprised to see a full pot already brewed, he searched the cabinet for his favorite cup with the largemouth bass on it.

"Good morning, Jack," Thelma said, walking in with an empty cup.

"Morning, Thelma. You're here early."

"Always." Thelma sensed the young attorney had a lot on his mind. She had seen the face of stress in that office many times before. "Is everything OK?"

Jack poured coffee into Thelma's cup and returned the pot to its holder. "Not much sleep," he said, sheepishly implying that was only because of the work.

"These cases will do that to you. Oh, and by the way, I left a phone message on your desk."

Jack gave a nod of thanks and left for his office. Truthfully the case weighed on his mind, but the growing distance between him and Ruby bothered Jack far more. His feelings about her new job had him more conflicted than he would have thought, and he wasn't sure how to deal with them. On the positive side, she found a way to connect with Pear Valley, but on the negative, it meant their plans for a family would be sidelined, at least for the short term.

Jack dropped his briefcase on an available chair and picked up the pink message slip Thelma had left him. He had received a call from the Cook County DA, Bill Willis. And as it turned out, Bill Willis was going to be in Pear Valley for a hearing in the catfish case. He wanted to see if Jack could meet this morning at 10:30 at the Gold Leaf Café.

Jack had known there was a hearing calendar set for that afternoon at four because the Allgood case had been scheduled for a status conference. Judges were not like most people who set one appointment at a time. They had what they called calendars. Then they brought in who was needed on whatever matters they felt like. The process led to many inefficiencies for the lawyers and their clients, but the judges typically did not care.

Thelma popped her head in his doorway. "You have a visitor, Jack. She says she's your investigator?" Thelma posed the last statement as a question since she was unaware the firm had hired one.

Jack, midsip, suddenly realized his mistake. He looked at Thelma over his cup and gestured for her to send her in. "And Thelma, I'll explain later, but can we keep this between us?"

Thelma nodded.

Annie Masterson strolled in wearing worn jeans and a blue, tattered blouse. She dragged her clunky boots on the floor while she ran her hands through her mop of curly brown hair, flipping it to one side. Her green eyes flashed as she smiled as if she knew a secret and wanted to tell it to the world.

"Annie, come in. Sit down. You're early," Jack said. "So tell me you've got some good news. Or at least tell me you don't have any bad news."

Annie Masterson plopped into a cushioned chair and looped a leg over the armrest. "Oh, I got news that won't get you dancin' in the aisles, but it'll taste sweeter than pecans in sugar."

"Really?"

"Really."

Jack shifted in his chair. "Well, I'm ready. Go for it. Shoot."

"Well, our dead man was in bed with a few other unsavory individuals who've been in trouble with the law. And I'm not talking about the local parking enforcement. I mean the federal law. You know the defendants in that big marijuana bust, don't you?"

"Not personally."

"Well," Annie said, "did you know that the late sheriff Cain and farmer Dan Cook had an accomplice who was a local, allegedly from a neighboring county? There were some veiled references to the accomplice being referred to as 'Baldy.'"

Jack leaned in. "And did you find out Allgood was Baldy?"

"Nope, and I doubt it's him."

Jack sat back, disappointed. "Thought you said I'd be happy."

Annie held up a hand to Jack and continued. "But what I do know is Willis, the DA, has some suspicions that Allgood was involved based on some sighting on surveillance footage."

"Yes, I know. I'm trying to get a meeting so I can see the footage," Jack said, annoyed she hadn't said much worthwhile yet. "Do they have any information about who the ring leader is?"

"No," said Annie, chomping on her gum. "No idea at this point. But Allgood had a lot of connections and was linked to several growing outfits, but no one could ever prove it. And my guess is that Allgood was smart enough to be *involved* without being a direct link."

"So did you find out about Jerry Roberts? And do you think he knew what Allgood was doing?"

"Possibly."

Jack rolled his eyes. This disheveled yet attractive woman was like trying to follow a Ping-Pong ball, and after the last few days, Jack's head felt ready to explode.

"Boss, it turns out Roberts's little wifey was sick, and he needed money for treatment not long after Allgood's old man kicked the bucket. So my guess is that Bill had him by the balls."

Jack shook his head, trying not to laugh at this slight woman who acted and spoke like a trucker. "So Jerry, to pay for medical costs, helps Allgood with the drug business, including laundering money for some illegal stuff Allgood was doing, which could have meant Bill was in bed with the catfish defendants?"

"Yes and no."

Jack lets out an.exasperated breath. "Explain."

"Ole Bill didn't get his hands dirty. But there is evidence to prove Tony Tanner could have been his runner and his go-between. There is no evidence that Cook or Cain interacted with Allgood directly. But one of the videos was from outside a club where Jernigan, the GBI agent, and Allgood were, which could have been a coincidence. Now the video does show Allgood leaving the club with a girl on his arm, not his wife, thirty minutes *before* the others left."

"Did you see the video?"

Annie dropped her leg, swung herself around in the chair, and stood. "Didn't have to. I know people."

"Think we can find the girl he was with?"

"Workin' it now, boss."

"So you think the two crimes are mutually exclusive?"

"I didn't say that. There's involvement in different degrees. I suspect Allgood focused on the cash, not the means."

"So could Tanner be Baldy?"

Annie laughed loudly. "Have you met the guy? No, he can't run his own life, let alone a drug ring." She sat up straighter and leaned in. "And here is why you pay me the big bucks. Tony got arrested by the Feds the night before Allgood was killed."

"The Feds?" asked Jack. "This was a GBI state operation."

"Yes, the drug bust was, but it was part of a bigger operation that was kept from the gumshoes in Callahan and Cook counties." Annie dropped her voice. "They suspect, at this point, the cartel, Baldy, or both may have worried Allgood might sing to the authorities to save himself. And that would have given Baldy a strong motive to kill Allgood. But that would all depend on Baldy knowing, which means someone leaked the Fed's intentions. This explains why none of this was in the files from Layton. The Feds were keeping a lid on it. State law enforcement is a necessary evil to them, and they will keep them out of anything they can. I doubt Willis or Layton even know about the Tanner arrest and deal."

Jack was stunned. He thought, as they parted, *This chick's crazy, but she's worth her weight in gold.* Jack, still in shock, said, "Annie, how did you get this information? The Feds hold their stuff close to the vest."

She smiled. "A lady never kisses and tells unless it's to her advantage."

"Lady might be a stretch," Jack said, laughing.

Annie walked to the doorway and turned back. "You're right on that one!"

When Ruby arrived, she stood outside the newspaper offices, her stomach turned like a crank on a peppermill over a hot plate of food. For a second or two, she contemplated running back home and climbing back into bed. As she gripped her briefcase, holding one pad of paper, a pen, and the lunch Jack had prepared for his effort to show support that morning, she stared up at the three-story brick building of the *Observer*.

Ruby still wondered if maybe Jack had a small point. She and Jack wanted children and had daydreamed about it long before their wedding day. Her new career might delay it some, but Ruby couldn't help but believe both could happen. The thought of a child made her glow for a moment, and she forgot the anxiety of her first day.

Denise came up behind Ruby. "Hey, welcome to your first day!"

"Thanks. Thanks for everything you did to make it happen."

Denise smiled and then half jokingly asked, "You OK? You know, eventually you have to go inside, right?"

"Yeah, just nerves."

"Meet me at the Mi-Lady Bakery around lunchtime, OK?"

"Yes, I'm in!" Ruby perked up for a second as she walked into work with her new friend and colleague.

Brad smiled as he chewed on an Egg McMuffin he had picked up at the drive-in window from the new McDonald's in town. *This will kill regular restaurants if people can just drive by and get food, Brad thought.* It had been quite a polarizing issue when word got out that fast food was coming to Pear Valley.

As he sipped his drink, Brad thought more about writing a mystery novel once his sci-fi got published. After talking with Ida the other day, his mind started working overtime. He had just about worked out the plot and scribbled a few pages the night before. His thoughts were interrupted by a beautiful blonde who walked over to his desk and offered her hand.

"Brad," she said as a greeting. Nearly choking on his Coke, Brad fumbled with his cup before he stood up and shook her hand. "Yes, well, hello again, Mrs. Sutton. Glad to see you're joining the team. I'm glad to see Evan took my advice to hire you!"

Ruby chuckled to herself and then cocked her head to one side. "You aren't suggesting Miss Walker's efforts didn't have any persuasiveness? How unprogressive of you, seeing as you're from Miami." Ruby flashed a coy smile. She could tell Brad could handle a little light ribbing.

"Right you are. I stand corrected. But you should know I was raised in Birmingham. You're going to fit in just fine around here!" Brad laughed.

Ruby, with an exaggerated accent, said, "Well, due to your efforts and others, I am the new local scene editor, and I'm also backup for when you need me. Hope that is OK?"

"Absolutely. I asked the editor if I could focus on more investigative stories and features, and he agreed. That is, if they could find someone who could handle my other stuff. You are that someone. Plus I have reviewed your resume, and you have an impressive background. I think you and I might find some things to team up on." Brad pointed to his brown bag with yellow and red lettering. "You hungry? I have a hash brown I haven't touched," he said, wiping his hands on his pants.

Ruby tried not to chuckle at his boyish demeanor. "Oh no, thank you. I am so nervous I don't think I can eat. But thanks. Being new, I'm still new here and relatively new to the town; I still don't know who's who."

He laughed. "That's not necessarily a bad thing."

Brad grabbed a seat, dragged it next to his desk, and gestured for Ruby to sit down. "OK, so today is the normal judicial hearing where all the cases are updated, including the catfish case and murder case against Sandra Allgood, but you probably know that already," he said with a smile.

Ruby smiled, giving the inference that Brad had guessed accurately, but she didn't know that information. Jack may have mentioned it, but her mind had been all over the place the past few days so she didn't know.

Brad went on. "You are in for a treat. Most people think Judge Throwbridge is unique and often humorous. Also, for any hearing information, the ladies in the clerk's office will help you out. They're friendly and will probably be delighted to see a woman covering the courts."

Ruby smiled as her nerves settled.

"This morning, you may want to go over early to the DA's office and see what you can find out. Usually, in terms of the press, it's just the paper's reporter in the courtroom. But with the big trial, there may be a few others there."

As Ruby started to leave, Brad put a hand up. "Look. It's your first day. Let's meet outside the courtroom and walk in together."

"Sounds great. I'll meet you there at quarter till four. I plan to start and see what I can ferret out from the DA or court clerk's office in advance."

"Anyone I should talk to specifically?"

"Rush Layton's secretary, Linda. She spills more information than water through a sieve. Just don't catch her at her desk. Instead, wait until she heads to the breakroom for a smoke."

Ruby gave the nod and then walked out and headed to the courthouse. She admitted to herself that she had missed the action. Her mother called every day, begging her to go to Atlanta for a visit, but Ruby feared if she did that, it would be too difficult to come back to Pear Valley. But now, she might consider a visit at some point. She had a lot she could share with Daddy and Mother to make them proud.

—⟋⟍—

Jack thought *Annie was worth her gold weight* after he showed her out. Back in his office, Jack hastily jammed a few pens, pencils, and a notebook into his briefcase and hastened to the first of his two meetings. He had a busy day before the 4 p.m. status conference.

First, Willis at the local café at 10:30 a.m. and then Layton at 1 p.m. in the DA's offices on the second floor of the courthouse.

It was quarter after ten when Jack walked into the Gold Leaf Café. He ascribed to the Vince Lombardi mantra "If you are five minutes early, you are already ten minutes late."

The Gold Leaf Café sat in the square in the middle of downtown with most other local businesses. The classic old Southern white courthouse directly across from the café housed all the town's legal units, including the DA's office, sheriff's office, and grand jury room. The granite steps led up to the giant double-door entrance. At the top of the building was a round dome on a square pedestal-type section with two clocks, one facing east and the other west. At Christmas, Jack heard, they hung lights from the dome to the business surrounding the square. It lit the area up and was a center for celebration. The scene of the traditional courthouse and square sent chills up Jack's spine. Its dignified and authoritative presence symbolized truth and justice, which is why he wanted to be a lawyer.

As Jack shut the door behind him, he saw DA Willis sitting at a corner table chatting up the waitress, who was pouring what appeared to be his second cup of coffee, given the opened paper packets piled high in the middle of the table. Looking away from gazing into the waitress's eyes, Willis noticed Jack walk in. "Hello, Mr. Sutton; glad we could meet. I have a packed afternoon so excuse my boldness, but I need to get to the point. I've discovered some information that may affect your murder defense."

"Yes, sir. Me too," said Jack.

"You first," Willis said, pouring three sugar packets into his steaming cup of coffee.

Jack, beaming with the confidence of the information that Annie had told him, said, "No, Mr. Willis, this being Brady information, you need to go first."

Well, Willis thought, *shame on me for judging this book by the gossipers. The boy's got some balls.*

Willis took a big sip of coffee and then went on to explain the information he had a concern about, what appeared to be two incidental findings of Allgood on the catfish surveillance tape. He noted that they did not suspect a connection with Allgood, but Jack had a right to know under Brady, and he and Layton had agreed to produce the tapes.

Willis then leaned in and, in a lower voice, shared, "Sutton, we have no evidence that Allgood was involved with the catfish drug ring." He stopped and looked around the room. "But we have an unidentified conspirator only referred to in conversations by the sheriff and Cook as Baldy. We have nothing else on him. However, his farm and his access fit. I'm talking with Judge Throwbridge today at four to continue our case while we investigate it further."

Jack sat back. "You don't have anything on him, but if I read you right, you think Allgood was Baldy?"

Willis smiled and then leaned in. "I didn't say that, Mr. Sutton. But you're free to interpret things any way you wish. I just have no evidence to support that." He sat back, expecting Jack to be in shock. Instead, he had the stern confidence of Perry Mason about identifying the murderer.

"Thank you, Mr. Willis." Leaning in, Jack lowered his voice. "I've recently found out that the FBI and DEA had a joint task force looking into Allgood and have an accomplice who is going to turn on him or was before he died." Jack waved off the waitress as she approached. "Sir, I concur with your suspicions that Allgood was involved in your case and that there is still an unidentified conspirator that the Feds have not identified, your Baldy."

Willis fumed but managed to mumble under his breath, "Those

fucking Feds. They keep their secrets and screw everything up." He then turned to Jack, deflecting some of the anger toward him. "How the hell did you get this information?"

Jack was not surprised or intimidated. He knew this information had hit Willis in the gut, both on what it did to his case and that some young lawyer had gotten the information before him. Jack deflected himself. "Mr. Willis, you and Mr. Layton had been straight with me, so in keeping with those lines, I have someone working on it for me, but I'm not at liberty to divulge the name yet. When I get my evidence, I'll share it with you."

After letting everything wash over him for a few moments, Willis kicked back in his chair and took a drink of his coffee, which was lukewarm by this point. "Mr. Sutton, I had my doubts that Emmitt Throwbridge knew what he was doing when he assigned this case. I stand corrected."

Jack was trying to maintain a professional appearance, but the fact Willis had called him "Mr." had not been lost on him. All the late nights, study, and work of the last few weeks had been justified.

Willis looked up. "Well, before your head gets so big we can't get out of this restaurant, why don't we go over and meet with Layton?"

Willis chugged his coffee like it was water and left a $5 bill on the table before the two walked across the street to the office in the courthouse Willis was using. Jack was shocked at the time passed; his Omega Seamaster watch, given to him by Ruby's father because he knew Jack was a fan of Jacques Cousteau who, along with his team, also wore the watch, showed five till twelve.

—∞—

Layton paced around then sat in his chair and fumed. "This is impossible," he said. "You're telling me the handwriting on the note does *not* match Bill Allgood or Sandra Allgood?"

Sitting before him, the GBI handwriting expert, Mary Letting, nodded. She had worked with the GBI for years and driven down from Atlanta to give Layton what she expected to be news he did not want to hear.

"Yes, sir. That is true. We've sampled the defendant's handwriting and compared it to the writing on the note. There is no way the defendant wrote that. It is interesting. The sample appears to be a man's handwriting, but one who possibly might have tried to duplicate Mrs. Allgood's handwriting style. It is very well done but clear to a trained eye to be a forgery. I can understand why you and your local expert thought they were similar, but too many things point to the conclusion I gave you," she said.

"Did you double-check?" he asked.

"Yes, sir. We did. We had an expert from the FBI check our work. That is why it took an extra week. They agreed with our conclusion. The FBI agent in charge, Dennis Caniglia, met with us also and asked I give you his card and suggested you call him."

Layton groaned. He did not want to begin a week with a massive headache, but it was Monday, and he felt like someone was banging on his head with a sledgehammer. To add insult to injury, he knew that Jack Sutton would be in his office later today, wanting this information.

Rubbing his forehead, he perseverated on the potentiality of what happened. "How could that be? This says that someone else put a suicide note in that house. They had to know it wouldn't match the defendant's handwriting, so why do that? And then shoot the man seven times, which again, would never look like a suicide, so why the damn note?"

"Well, with all due respect, the attempt to match her writing was, like I said, very good. They would have gotten away with it had trained experts not identified the forgery."

"Oh yeah. That makes me feel a lot better."

"Well—" Mary started.

"So it's like the killer wanted to make it look like Mrs. Allgood did it," Layton interrupted.

"But if the defendant had written it, she must have known police would check the note against samples of her husband's writing and they wouldn't match. So it didn't make sense."

Layton fumed, "No, it didn't. But do you know one of the keys to being a reasonable prosecutor?"

She shook her head.

"Dumb criminals. I have a 98 percent successful prosecution rate. You want to know why? Stupid criminals! I had one case when the defendant simply walked into a police station and dropped the murder weapon—a shotgun—onto the sergeant's desk and said, 'I shot the no-good, skunk-smelling peckerwood. He deserved it.'"

"Bet you won that case."

"Yes, I did. And this one looked just as easy. And now—"

"You still have the gun, sir."

"Yes, but the gun doesn't have any fingerprints. The shooter was a lousy shot, but she or he wiped any prints off the gun, and they did an excellent job. They were better on cleanup than performing the action itself."

"But it doesn't exonerate Mrs. Allgood completely."

"No, but it does allow for reasonable doubt now, doesn't it?"

She shook her head. "Sorry to be the bearer of bad news."

After Miss Letting left, Layton dropped down in his chair, looking at the FBI agent card. He was interrupted by his secretary buzzing in and saying, "Mr. Layton, DA Willis is here, and Mr. Sutton is with him."

Layton slammed his fist on his desk and answered, "Send them in."

Willis and Sutton walked into Layton's office. Jack had asked Annie to come, but for her to get the information, she had to be off the grid. She made Jack promise not to give her name and just use privileged sources.

"Sutton, congratulations," Layton said with a slight tone of sarcasm.

"I'm sorry?" Jack asked, assuming the DA was being metaphorical.

Layton tossed the results on his desk toward Jack as he sat down hard in his chair. "The handwriting is not a match to Sandra Allgood or Bill Allgood."

Tenting his hands while swiveling his chair toward the window, Layton lamented, "Look. I still believe she is guilty, but I don't fight battles I can't win. And to be honest, this would have been a hard win given what Willis has uncovered." He nodded toward Willis, who still stood by the door. Layton pushed his chair back and stood. "You can let your client know I will be calling the judge and dropping the charges against her at the hearing this afternoon."

Jack took his papers and stood. "Thank you. I will let her know."

Stepping forward toward Layton's desk, Willis interjected, "Wait for a minute, boys. Rush, Jack has some things for you to hear in addition to what I disclosed under the Brady material. The young fucker has been doing his homework, and he discovered the Feds have been playing fools of all three of us."

Willis looked at Jack. "Sutton?"

"Mr. Layton, the FBI and DEA have been carrying on an investigation parallel to the catfish case trying to get information on a nationwide drug ring run by a cartel out of Medellin, Colombia. They are primarily into pot but are gearing up to start importing cocaine. Because of that, the Feds had been all over the pot case. I believe they have information about the Allgood murder, but I'm waiting for that confirmation." Jack went on to explain, "Jerry Roberts had been arrested weeks before the raid and turned state's evidence. The Feds learned that he did not know Baldy; only Tanner and Sheriff Cain did. Roberts spilled that Allgood had made a move to cut Baldy out and keep more of the money."

Layton sat down and instructed the other two to do the same. "Continue," he said to Jack.

"Based on what they learned, they carried out Tanner's arrest the night before the murder, and he too turned state informant. He noted, 'The Feds planned to confront Allgood the next day because Tanner and Roberts sang.' However, they were working a deal for Tanner to identify Baldy because he was the only one left alive who could identify him. Tanner was shrewd and was waiting for it all in writing. They couldn't have cared less about Tanner or Allgood. They were small potatoes. But the big win would have been Baldy, who could connect the drug ring in Cook to the cartel network. When Allgood died, they suspected Allgood was Baldy."

Layton sat back. "But this doesn't gel. Allgood wasn't killed by a cartel member. Those boys don't stage murder scenes."

Willis interjected, "Wait. Let's back up here. Why would the Feds become convinced Allgood was Baldy? He was just an opportunist; that's what Roberts and Tanner both said. And if Allgood got greedy and tried to cut out Baldy, it would account for Baldy killing Allgood, not the cartel."

Jack went on. "Exactly. I believe the cartel identified Allgood as a Benedict Arnold, and they or Baldy killed Allgood."

After Layton had gotten over the initial shock and processed all he had heard, he looked over at Jack. "How do you know all this?"

Jack put his hands out to his sides. "I can't say. Just know I have a privileged source."

Layton, Jack, and Willis then left Layton's office and walked together up to Judge Throwbridge's chambers. They explained all they could to him without compromising his ability to continue to preside over matters. Throwbridge understood immediately and put the works in motion.

—m—

Lunchtime came quickly that day. Truitt walked into Fuzzy's, a gentleman's club on the edge of town in the old quarter's section. He found his regular lunch partners sitting around in deep discussion. "What's up, men?" The waitress was seconds behind with the senator's drink ready to go. Truitt nodded as the other two got quiet. "What?"

"Word on the street is that Allgood was involved with a woman other than his wife. He was caught on a surveillance tape that has been turned over to GBI," said Calvin.

"Shit, Cal, everyone knew that. And it wasn't one. It was many."

Calvin swirled his ice cubes around in his shot glass. "According to word on the street, this wasn't his usual one-time deal. And Sandra confronted him in public, not a week before the murder. That gives her motive."

"Where did she supposedly lose it?"

Calvin sat back, smirking. "At the Cook County Fair, Sandra lost it in front of a few hundred people. Supposedly she threatened to kill him."

"How are we just hearing about this?"

"Because it happened in Cook County, the day before the sheriff took his life. His story and the scandal overshadowed a public spectacle. But supposedly people are talking about it now. Well, mostly because she's going to trial and it's hit the papers."

Truitt sat back in his chair and downed his scotch. Truitt leaned forward. "That's hardly a smoking gun. My wife used to threaten to kill me when she was alive. I don't know a married man alive who hasn't heard those words."

"Not in the middle of hundreds of people they don't." Samuel slapped Frank on the back. "You can't win 'em all. Sometimes they're just guilty. It was a long shot anyway."

"Well, look who's counting *my* chickens! I recall a similar case where everyone thought I'd lose, but I won like always."

All the men laughed, and Samuel added, "'Cept this time you went and put your least experienced on it."

Truitt took a drink and held his empty glass in the air to signal the waitress. "Correction. The judge made that call. But I've never bet on a losing horse. Don't count my boy out."

—m—

Ruby walked into the DA office and introduced herself to Beth Shaw, Layton's secretary.

After pleasantries, Beth said in a low voice, "You just missed your husband."

"Really?"

Yes, he and DA Willis and Mr. Layton just left, saying they were going to the judge's chambers."

Trying to be as innocent as she could, Ruby asked, "Whatever for?"

"I don't know for sure, but Mr. Layton told me the 4:00 hearing was off today."

—m—

Ruby all but ran over to Brad's desk. Denise was standing beside him as she approached.

Ruby stepped in. "Brad, the hearing is off today."

"Why?"

Ruby reported, "According to Layton's secretary, DA's Layton and Willis and Jack were meeting before they went up to the judge's chambers. But then, just a little while later, it seems Throwbridge's secretary said the Allgood and catfish case weren't going to happen that day."

"Why?"

"Well, that is all I could get out of her on my first meeting."

"Then I'll let you handle the other issues that remain on the docket this afternoon," Brad said. He hesitated then added, "No chance you could get the scoop from your husband?"

"You can't ask her to do that!" Denise chided Brad.

"Thank you!" Ruby said, folding her arms and standing next to Denise.

"Look. We don't have to reveal our sources, but a good reporter has them. That's all I'm saying."

"Yeah, well, I'm not using Jack."

"Noted. So Miss Walker, why don't you accompany her and make some sketches of Judge Throwbridge on the bench? They may come in handy later."

Denise and Ruby looked at him inquisitively, but he stopped them. "We may need them as this story develops."

SIXTEEN
Suspicious Lies

Jack, knowing his client had planned to come to the courthouse for the 4 p.m. hearing, went out to the farm to intercept her. As he approached the Allgood house, he noticed Sandra on the wraparound porch in a rocking chair, looking catatonic. As Jack walked up the steps, her inward focus shifted. "Mr. Sutton, did I forget we were meeting here before the hearing?"

"No, ma'am. I came by to give you some news."

"What news?"

Jack walked over to stand in front of his client. He leaned against the railing. "Layton's dropping the charges."

Sandra's expression came alive like she had just won a prize, which in a way she had. "Wait. What? Really?"

Jack shook his head yes. "The handwriting expert from the GBI office in Atlanta didn't agree with our local person. She said neither you nor Bill had written the note."

Sandra stood still for a second before his words sunk in. She jumped up and hugged Jack. "Are you serious? Oh, how do I ever thank you? Jack, come sit down, and I'll grab you an iced tea,"

"I'm fine, thank you. But if other evidence shows up pointing to you as the murderer, then it's up to Layton to pursue it or not.

The hearing is postponed, but I'll need you in court when Layton withdraws the charges." Sandra thanked him again, but she looked as if she had something else on her mind as if the news had been overshadowed by something else. "What's wrong?"

"Why would someone come into our home, kill my husband, and leave a suicide note? Were they trying to frame me? I mean it makes no sense. And if someone killed Bill and now I'm not being charged, am I next? And then—" Sandra paused like she was lost in thought.

"And then what?" Jack asked.

"It's Robin. I haven't seen her in days, and I can't get a hold of her. Do you think she is in any danger?"

"I can't imagine why she would be," Jack responded while cocking his head to one side like he did when he was thinking. "Unless you're not telling me everything."

Sandra stood up, walked over to the porch railing, and stared at the long driveway in front. "I may not be going to jail, but I'm not totally innocent. I think Bill wanted to divorce me. And I believed he poisoned my horse to make me go mad. Let's say Bill was building his case against me as the unstable, crazy wife."

"I wish you had told me this before, but what does this have to do with Robin?"

Sandra bit her lower lip, looked down at her feet, then back up at Jack. "Robin and Bill were having an affair."

Jack didn't know how to respond. So he waited.

"You see, Bill could get anything and anyone he wanted. He used to say, 'Everyone has a price; it's just a matter of who can pay it.' Funny, he's dead, and I'm the one left paying."

Jack took a step closer. "I'm sorry." Jack put his hands in his pockets and shook his head. "Where does Robin live?"

"Why? Do you think something happened to her?"

"Has she ever disappeared before?"

"Once. But then I suspect it was out of shame or guilt."

Jack shifted his stance and stared at Sandra. "Did she confess anything about the affair to you after Bill died?"

Sandra shook her head no.

"So you never told her you knew?"

Again Sandra shook her head no.

"I'll have the sheriff check it out, just in case. But she's probably fine."

Jack headed down the porch stairs when Sandra called after him, "Does this mean I'm free to leave town?"

Jack whipped back around, perplexed. "No. Not until everything is settled. Got that?"

Sandra said a firm "Yes, I understand" as Jack walked to his car with marked hesitation—having more questions than answers, which seemed to keep happening when he met with his client.

—⟋⟍⟋—

The weight of the world had been lifted off Jerry Roberts. His wife's health had dramatically improved, and the deal with the Feds and the demise of Bill Allgood had been silver linings from the dark cloud he had been in the last few years under Bill Allgood's thumb. As a Christian man, his heart conflicted with his head on this matter, but in the end, the good outweighed the bad. Bill had sapped all the goodness out of the farm, refused to invest in it, and seemingly found joy in its deterioration. He wanted the farm to die, just like he had his father, Wade. But with Bill gone, hope appeared, and it renewed Jerry's energy to finish the vision Wade Allgood had for the farm.

He was up doing his rounds at 5:30 a.m. with his morning cup of coffee in his hand, and the first stop was the horse barn. Albeit an almost empty horse barn with only one mare being housed in the stall farthest from where he stood. He heard the shuffle of Colin's boots before he saw him. "Colin?"

With rake in hand, Colin came around the corner. "Yes, sir?"

"What's wrong with this picture?"

Colin looked at the stalls Jerry stared at. "I'm not sure, sir. I cleaned them all. I even scrubbed down all the empty ones."

"Exactly my point." Jerry moved to the first vacant stall. "I had a visit from a man yesterday asking if we would house his mare." Jerry leaned against the stall door, seemingly lost in thought as Colin awaited his next word. "Mr. Allgood is gone, and although I have no idea what Mrs. Allgood's intentions are, we need to keep this place running for Wade Allgood's sake. No more half-assing it to suit a man who knows nothing about being a farmer."

As Jerry took a long sip of his coffee, Colin shook his head. "Yes, sir."

Jerry rested his cup on the stable wall. "I'm taking that man's horse in and anyone else's. We are also leasing ten acres on our south side to the farmer that borders that land. He needs more growing space and will need our help to clear it." Jerry grabbed his cup and headed toward the other side of the barn. "Everyone's work is about to increase, so get ready."

"Yes, sir."

Jerry nodded and walked out the other side of the barn, stopping to pet the mare. "You're about to get some company, girl." As he exited and rounded the corner, Jerry headed toward the bunkhouse. But his morning rounds came to a screeching halt when he came face-to-face with two men he hadn't expected to see ever again.

Willis had contacted the FBI and DEA to let them know he and Layton needed to meet with them early the next day. The Feds were not happy when Layton and Willis disclosed what they had learned. Of course, Layton and Willis also made it known how unhappy they were with the fact they had been kept in the dark about an investigation, not only in their backyards but also involving two significant cases they were involved in.

The group went through an hour of discussion, sharing what they knew. But the FBI dumped new information on them concerning Robin Dyer. They told them she was in protective custody and cooperating. Once they had what they needed, she would be in the witness protection program.

The Feds noted she had been having an affair with Allgood. And Allgood did a lot of pillow talking, so he had let Robin in on his plan to cut Baldy out. She had tried to pump information from Allgood about who Baldy was. He would not share. She was still gathering information when he was killed.

Willis interrupted the agent in charge. "Why? Was she working for you?"

The agents all huffed at that inquiry. "No, hardly. But according to her, she started to sense Bill was off his rocker, and she feared for her friend's safety."

"Sandra Allgood? The friend whose husband she was having an affair with?"

The agent in charge shook his head. "Look. She's a shitty friend. That doesn't matter to me. But she's a material witness, and we need her alive."

Layton asked, "I get it. So you think Baldy is our killer?"

"Can't be the cartel. Not their calling card. Too messy. But it does still have the earmarks of a crime of passion."

Willis stood up and started to pace. "So it could be Robin? With that theory?"

"Look. She's not talking, and we haven't ruled her out." The agent in charge, Winston Reihnfred, got up and poured himself some coffee and leaned against the wall. "We're telling you what we know, which is limited. Do we think, based on our experience, that Allgood was done by the cartel? No, we don't. Do we think it could be Robin? Maybe, but what would be her motive? Bill funded her life. However, there are subgroups working with the cartel who had something to lose by Allgood's cutting Baldy out as well as Baldy himself."

Layton pushed. "Any idea who the subgroups are?"

"The Feds described two of 'em having a red pickup truck with stolen plates that had been spotted at the scene. But that's all we have. A few photos of the truck and can't make out their faces. Both have hats and sunglasses on in the photo."

Willis and Layton shared a look.

Winston Reihnfred leaned on the table. "Gentlemen, thanks again for the cooperation. But understand everything you learned here today stays in this room."

At that moment, there was a knock on the door. Winston's secretary came in and handed him a note. As he stood in front of the men packing up, he cleared his throat. "This just came in. Tony Tanner went missing from the safe house in Norman Park."

"Tanner?" Layton and Willis asked in unison.

"Yes, our agents have been holding him, awaiting the final terms of his deal so he could identify Baldy for us. When they went in to check on him, he was gone. You'll have to excuse me," Winston said as he gathered his files and motioned to the other agents, who left hurriedly.

Layton and Willis hung back as they thought about what or who got to Tanner.

Layton looked at Willis just as one of the agents came back into the conference room to retrieve his folder. Layton shut the door. "Look. It's just a theory, but if Baldy or the cartel went after Tanner, then they probably know about Roberts too."

The agent gestured for Layton to move aside so he could get out but added, "Gentlemen, we'll be in touch, but we're already on it."

—⁓—

The rocking and rumbling jolted Tanner awake, but his vision remained blurry. He tried to sit upright, but he couldn't find the core strength to get it done. Fighting nausea growing inside, he rolled over on the dirty floor to find Roberts hog-tied and unconscious across from him. He could hear the men speaking Spanish in the cab because they were screaming at one another. He figured between their voices and the road noise, they wouldn't hear him shift over toward Roberts.

Tanner kicked Roberts hard, bringing him to for a brief second. He did it again and said, "Roberts, wake the fuck up!"

Jerry struggled to open his eyelids and gain his vision. As he looked around and saw Tanner staring at him, he knew they were done. "What's happening?"

"What do you think is happening?"

Jerry had been forced into a no-win situation. Even though he knew Allgood was taking a huge risk trying to cut out his connection, Allgood would never listen. He had Jerry by the balls. He glared at Tanner, a man he hated from day one just as much as Allgood.

Tanner glared at Jerry. "You got taken, man. You should have left this place long ago. That mother had you by the balls."

Jerry turned his head so as to not give him the satisfaction.

"Least the little woman is doin' well. That should give you some peace."

Jerry banged his head against the side and closed his eyes. He couldn't believe he'd meet his fate with Tony Tanner at his side.

After a few hours, the truck turned off a paved road onto a dirt road, followed by the red pickup and a green Ford Grand Torino.

When the back door opened, the sun blinded Jerry for a split second before he saw the two others; he knew the men from his transports. They stood behind the dirty red pickup they had been using. An offensive lineman-type Mexican had opened the door and pulled them out of the panel truck. Jerry immediately realized they were in a swamp area and, in fact, saw a ten-foot gator sunning himself on a sand bar in the middle of the swampy pond.

"Luis, tie them to the bumper!" a man in a suit screamed as he got out of the Torino.

Joey spoke up. "Hey, amigo, we have known Jerry and Tony for years. They'll be cool; there is no need to do this to them. What do you say, Diego?"

"Amigo," he said, dragging the word out. "You're right. Mercy is good. But this motherfucker has been singing. And now the Feds are looking for your truck. Well, mi amigo, decisions have consequences for us all."

The tall one looked over at the muscular one and said, "Luis, you think we should show mercy?"

The brute obviously had been around long enough to know it was a rhetorical question. The taller one reached from his belt line behind his back. He pulled out a .45 pistol and shot Don in the forehead, splattering blood all over Joey. Jerry wet himself. Tony passed out.

Joey dropped to his knees and started begging. Diego ordered him to stand up. "When I finish with these two, you're going to take the panel truck and go to Jacksonville."

"Yes, sir, whatever I can do," groveled Joey.

Jerry saw the tall one turn his attention to him and Tony. They never thought or felt anything again.

Jack, Layton, and Willis had agreed to meet after they got back from Tifton to compare notes. They all understood if anything started pointing toward Mrs. Allgood, Jack would be forced out of the team, but they all seemed to have the same goal at this point. Find the killer and connection to the drug trial for the district attorneys and show his client was innocent of Jack.

Layton, Willis, and Jack dug into all of their files and the new material from the FBI. Willis pulled out his materials and put them on the table, as did everyone else. "I'll get us some more coffee. Start looking at those," Layton said as he stuck his head out the door to have his secretary start the brew.

Almost immediately, the combined files started to reveal a picture. Annie's work disclosed that weeks before the raid, Jerry Roberts had been brought in by the DEA in conjunction with the FBI for questioning after being pulled over in a small cargo truck with evidence of marijuana stalks having been transported in it. A check of the registration confirmed Robert's story that it was owned by Bill Allgood, and Allgood was his boss. Jerry explained that he was Allgood's foreman and had been directed to go to the Dan Cook farm in Cook County several times to pick up cargo that was clearly pot.

Roberts understood that somehow Cook had connections with Allgood that had led to the conspiracy. So Roberts would deliver the freshly harvested stalks to a farm outside of Chula, a little town north of Tifton and on Interstate Highway 75. From there, a group from the cartel took possession.

Also, according to the information they all had bits and pieces of, the DEA and FBI were cutting a deal with Jerry, who claimed he didn't know the details but understood Mr. Allgood was the middleman with another guy who had a connection with the drug cartels and could make the arrangements for the sale. Jerry assumed that Allgood and this person worked with the local farmers to arrange the illegal growing. Jerry admitted that his transporting had happened several times but never asked questions. Instead, he kept repeating that he needed the work, telling the investigators about his wife's medical condition and need for income to pay the bills.

Because of Jerry's implication of Bill Allgood and the possibility he knew the mystery conspirator, the Feds did not want to trust local law enforcement or prosecutors with the case. The involvement of the Cook County sheriff was more than enough to create distrust. While the sources indicated they felt a little bad keeping Layton and Willis in the dark, they felt they had to and, therefore, did not announce Jerry's detaining or share his information. They knew they had to move quickly because of the upcoming catfish trial and figured they would reveal all in time.

Instead, the Feds had cut a deal letting Roberts free to go obtain secret recordings of Allgood admitting his part, and Roberts would be let go and cleared of any charges. Small fish in a big pond not worth keeping, which ultimately didn't end well for Roberts.

The FBI used a prosecution-friendly drug court in Atlanta and received a warrant to tap Allgood's phone. They chose to do it through the Atlanta office because of the closeness of the community in counties like Callahan. However, after Jerry had sung to the investigators, Allgood seemed to become suspicious and became more cautious in his phone calls. Very little information was gathered. They were unsure whether Allgood suspected that Jerry tipped Allgood off or if Allgood was cautious for another reason. But at one point, Allgood called a man in Mexico; he indicated a supply of "material" that he was willing to sell to them directly.

The agents believed that the "material" was marijuana. Allgood told the man they did not have to go through their regular contact, which he revealed in the call to be "Baldy." He told them Baldy did not need to be involved, that he could go directly through him, and that he had hired new runners. It appeared Allgood was cutting Baldy out to increase his share of the profits.

That was the double cross that got Allgood on the hit list, but did it get him killed by Baldy?

Jack finished his third cup of coffee and examined the sordid tale the board showed. He looked up at Willis. "So they had that information from Roberts. What about Tanner?"

"Yes, well, afterward, the Feds nabbed Tanner. Tanner sang more than Roberts. He told them about the guy in charge, Baldy, but he swore up and down that it wasn't Allgood. He said that Allgood never got his hands dirty. He just organized their comings and goings, including pickup and deliveries, and collected the cash from Tanner or Roberts, whoever made the delivery. And that majority of the cash Allgood got turned over to Baldy, which Tanner said angered Allgood."

"So Tanner and Roberts confessed before Allgood's death?"

"Everything but the identity of Baldy. Jerry knew nothing, but Tanner knew withholding that would help him have a better deal. The Feds were set to meet with Tanner that Wednesday to finalize the plea deal for his information if it proved true, but it was interrupted by Allgood's murder."

"Do you think Roberts or Tanner went back to Allgood and warned him?" asked Jack.

"No. Tanner needed him for the deal, and Roberts was already thrilled to have a way out. Nevertheless, the Feds had guys tailing them and tapping both of their phones and Allgood's."

"So basically, Allgood was most likely done in by Baldy because he suspected or knew there was dissension," concluded Layton. Layton withheld the subgroup theory of the Feds from Jack because of the Feds' request.

Jack looked at the floor in defeat. "So you're telling me you don't think Allgood's death could have been an ordered hit."

"It may have been ordered, but the cartel did not do it."

"Remember it is usually the wife or a scorned girlfriend. It was amateur hour at best, a botched job or a crime of passion," said Layton.

Jack knew about Robin, but as far as he knew, Layton didn't. Jack wasn't sure how the information Sandra threw at him would land for her. And since his main focus still had to be on protecting his client, he kept quiet for now. So a tired Jack jerked his head toward Layton. "You're not pointing fingers back at my client, are you?"

—⁓—

The next afternoon, when Jack had walked into the courtroom, the deputy had already led Sandra Allgood to the defense table. Another "early worm" disciple, he told himself. The DA Layton stood with his hands on his hips, glaring down at his notes on the prosecution table. DA Willis sat in the chair next to him, playing with his pen as he rocked it back and forth with his thumb and index finger.

Without warning, the judge's door opened, and Emmitt Stonewall Throwbridge walked out, waving to the crowd gathered in the courtroom. He held a thicker manila folder, which he opened when he sat on the bench. He grabbed the gavel. Ruby and Brad had just snuck into the back of the courtroom to cover the proceedings.

"Everyone be seated," Throwbridge banged his gavel. He looked toward the district attorney and then at the papers in the manila folder. "Mr. Layton, I assume you have some business before the court. I've seen a lot of things in my years on the bench, but today's are rather odd. In fact, I imagine Mr. Sutton had an interesting time reading your activity."

Layton stood looking very tired to Jack. "The state does apologize, Your Honor. Unfortunately, many things were going on the past few days, and there was some confusion around this case."

Throwbridge laughed. "Oh, don't apologize, Mr. Layton. Unfortunately, it seems you have an unknown assailant who may or may not be related to the catfish case and a new drug case here in Callahan County."

Layton nodded. "Yes, Your Honor. In light of the recent

evidence that supports that Mrs. Allgood was not the author of the suicide note, along with some questions about potential drugging of her at the time of the murder, the state is prepared to drop the charges against Sandra Allgood at this time."

Sandra grabbed Jack's arm and gave him a smile.

"We have withdrawn the charges against Mrs. Allgood, and she is free to go."

The judge peered down from his chair like an eagle looking at a rodent. "You obviously have had an interesting past week, Mr. District Attorney."

"Yes, Your Honor. And one I doubt any of us will forget for quite a while. Your Honor, Mr. Willis and I would like to meet with the court in chambers privately after the hearing and would request Mr. Sutton attend."

Throwbridge nodded. The judge then turned his gaze to Jack. "Well, young man, I was surprised when Frank Truitt insisted on you for this case. But it all worked out. You didn't get to try it, but you did well by your client."

Jack slowly processed the judge's words. "Truitt insisted," reverberated through Jack's head. Recovering, he said, "Well, thank you, Your Honor."

"Mr. Sutton, your client is free to go. Mrs. Allgood, I hope you have a peaceful life. The court is truly sorry for your loss."

"Thank you, Your Honor," Sandra said.

Jack stood statue-like as the courtroom buzzed with chatter. Sandra held a hand out to Jack. Jack took a minute but replied in kind before flipping his briefcase shut and locking it. He picked it up by the handle and started back to the judge's chambers.

Sandra stopped him. "Thank you for everything, Mr. Sutton."

"Call me Jack, please. So what's next for you?"

Sandra's tears formed in her eyes as she turned to face him. "I have no idea. I don't remember life before Bill."

She paused and assessed Jack's face. "That shocks you. I get it.

Everyone in town thought I married him for his money." She shook her head. "He wasn't always a bad man, Jack. There was a part of him that filled a void in my life. Call it daddy issues or whatever, but he made me feel safe."

"Speaking of safe, I can't tell you much, but what I can say is Robin is fine. And I'm going to need you to trust me on that."

To Jack's surprise, Sandra nodded without question. And started to walk away, then turned around. "For what it's worth, I believe it all happened the way it did for a reason. Do you believe in karma, Jack?" Sandra didn't wait for an answer as she turned and left the courtroom.

Jack watched his client leave, feeling a pang of sadness, before he caught sight of Brad and Ruby. They nodded to Jack and followed Sandra out. Jack stood there thinking for a full minute before he started to walk toward the chambers. *What is Robin Dyer's role? Who was Baldy? What was Baldy's role?*

In the meeting in Throwbridge's chambers, Layton and Willis laid out what they had learned from the task force, including the other women, the cartel muscle, and the missing Tanner and Roberts. Jack had known much of it already from Annie but feigned indifference. And after the meeting with the judge, Layton, and Willis met with Jack for another hour in a courthouse conference room. Jack shared his knowledge of the red pickup and that there may have been an affair though he could not tell them Sandra was the source because of attorney-client privilege.

After the announcement in open court, Ruby and Brad bolted back to the newspaper and went straight to the editor. "You won't believe what happened," Ruby almost yelled, excited over Jack's victory, even though she had expected it.

The publisher shook his head. "I've heard many things about

Judge Throwbridge. And I've followed the goings-on in his courtroom, so I wouldn't be surprised much."

"The lab returned finding that neither Sandra Allgood nor Bill Allgood was the author," Ruby said.

Knowing the editor sat waiting for more, Brad filled in more details. "Let's don't be too hard on the DA; there may be more to the story. For now, the alleged suicide note from the victim was fake. Of course, there wasn't much doubt of that anyway since he was shot seven times. But the handwriting didn't match Sandra Allgood's writing. Also, now the police believe Mrs. Allgood was drugged that night. Perhaps she was drugged to get her out of the way while someone else killed her husband."

The editor nodded and raised his finger. "I'll look forward to reading your story. In fact, the whole town will look forward to reading your story. Now go get it done! And keep me updated on what else you can uncover before the law or another paper does."

"Right," said Ruby, jumping up.

As they walked toward their desks, Brad said, "You start on the catfish version of this, and I will focus on Allgood. Then let's exchange the first drafts, and we can each do a supplemental story about the possible connection of the cases. If my gut is right, there is more here than we know."

Ruby smiled at Brad. "Thank you." She appreciated how confident Brad was in himself. Other reporters would have hogged the whole story, but Brad's generosity endeared him to her.

"Don't thank me yet. You may be here a while tonight."

Jack walked into the office and noticed the deafening silence. It was past six, and he thought they all had gone home. The heels of his shoes clicking along the hardwood floors echoed in the empty hallway. Part of him was happy no one had been mulling around awaiting his arrival. He was ecstatic about the turn of events, confused by the unsolved portions, and angry that, given the judge's revelation, Throwbridge had set him up in the case. The last thing he wanted now was to be interrogated by Truitt, the liar.

Jack no sooner got to the conference room entrance when the door opened and out sprung Thelma and the rest of the firm clapping and cheering. "Well, boy," Truitt bellowed from the back of the conference room. You managed to pull it off! This is a big win for us on many levels."

Jack stood speechless as Mosely shook his hand and gestured toward the giant cake in the middle of the table. David asked, "Can we cut this thing now?" He shot Jack a congratulatory nod and proceeded to cut into the confection. Jack kept his eyes anywhere but toward the bombastic Truitt, thinking, *Should I stay or go? He knew Ruby would be all for leaving this town. Or would she, given her new job?*

After a round of attaboys and cake, Jack left the festivities and shut himself in his office. For some reason, he felt compelled to reread his notes from his meetings with his former client.

Mosely banged on the door and then opened it slowly. "Hey, you OK?" Before Jack answered, Mosely put up a hand. "Don't go there. You represented your client, and your requests led to the charges being dropped. You won."

"Can you shut the door?"

Mosely shut the door and sat across from Jack. "What is it?"

"Did you know Truitt had me put on that trial? He requested it?"

Mosely grew quiet and placed his hands on his knees before standing. "No. But it doesn't surprise me. You'll learn. This is Truitt's town. We just live in it."

"Doesn't that bother you?"

Mosely chuckled. "Perhaps in my youth, not anymore. I know who I am and what I can do. You'll get there only if you don't hang onto this notion that life is always so cut and dry. Good and bad, right and wrong are grayer than our youthful selves believe."

"It should be cut and dry."

"Do you recall the fishing trip and that lost treasure my friend is searching for?" Mosely asked with his hand on the doorknob.

"Yeah."

"Well, he has more luck finding that than you have of getting Truitt to follow anyone's rules other than his own. You've learned a lot with this trial. Keep it in your pocket as it might prove useful later on."

"How so?"

Mosely chuckled as he opened the door. "That I can't tell you. But as Jim and I told you on Lake Seminole, the connections will reveal themselves to you when you're ready to receive them."

—⁂—

At 8 p.m. and after a long day, Ruby and Jack met at Barbers Restaurant, the best burger place in Pear Valley. Part of that long legacy of local burger joints that would eventually die with the onslaught of fast-food establishments such as McDonald's. The locals tended to dine early so Jack and Ruby were the only ones there.

They went over the events of the day, Jack with the courtroom success and remaining mysteries and Ruby with the completed article and first byline to come in the morning press.

As Ruby sipped her chocolate shake, Jack said, "Babe, I'm proud of you."

Ruby looked up with a tempting smile. "Right back at ya." She leaned across the table and kissed Jack.

As Ruby enjoyed the last of the fried onion rings, she sat back and said, "I bet Sandra Allgood was elated."

"You would think," Jack muttered as he picked up a fry.

Ruby, thinking more empathetically, inserted, "But then again, she didn't get cleared by a jury."

"Nope, and I suspect that had a lot to do with her mixed feelings."

"Well, for Layton to drop the charges, that should say something to the Pear Valley gossipers."

"It does. Plus Layton also knows the police bungled the investigation. They should have called a doctor and had them give a blood test to Sandra, not to mention the test for gunshot residue. That would have been a problem if the case ever got to a jury and Layton knew it. Now with this other woman, the Willis videos, and the task force information reveals, it would be hard to convict Sandra beyond a reasonable doubt."

Smiling and looking proudly at her trial lawyer husband, whose feelings seemed to be as mixed as his client's, she said, "You wanted a trial, didn't you?"

"Yes, but a win is a win, I guess. As my law school professor Steve Johnson used to say, 'Clients are with you. Win or tie!'"

"Jack, it's a win," Ruby said reassuringly. "But more importantly, what about Truitt?" Ruby scrunched her nose as she said his name like she smelled something foul.

Jack braced himself for Ruby's assessment and attempted to brush it off. "Who the hell knows? I could take it as a compliment or that he lied to me."

"He lied to you, Jack."

Jack shook his head. "I love how you can be so black and white on some things but so open-minded about others."

Ruby rolled her eyes and ate one of his french fries.

"Look. He's not the greatest boss, but he was the one who gave me a shot. So some appreciation and cordiality are required."

Ruby pushed her plate away from her. "You had others willing to give you a shot, Jack."

"Not without strings," Jack said.

Ruby placed her napkin on the table, seeing where the discussion was headed. "I don't think Truitt is 'string fee.'" She pushed away from the table and stood. "I have to go back and work on some background for the follow-up story. Brad and I were going to meet there at nine. You want to walk me back to the office?"

Jack looked down. "Nah, I've got something to follow up on. I'll see you at home."

Ruby, trying to alleviate the tension, added, "By the way, I asked Brad and Denise from work to come to dinner tomorrow night. Please don't even think of protesting."

Jack forced a tired smile. "Protest? Not me."

Sensing Jack's frustration by the day's outcome and uncertainty, she said, "A win is a win, Jack."

He sent her off with a half smile.

The street lamps illuminated the way as Ruby headed back toward the paper. She relished the soft, unexpectedly refreshing breeze—something she hadn't felt in months. When she reached the block where her office building was and glanced up at the stone structure and at the top, just below the cornerstone, it read, "Pear Valley Observer." Smiling, she looked both ways before stepping off the curb to cross the deserted street just under the light of the lamppost.

The rumbling sound closed in as a pickup took the sharp turn down the main street as its passenger yelled, "What the—"

Ruby, midway across the street, looked up at the headlights coming straight at her. It swerved and went on down the street.

Brad blew through the office doors, and all the lights were out except for the one lamp on Ruby's desk. "Hey?" Brad said, leaning over the divide between him and Ruby.

Ruby jumped. "Oh Brad."

"You OK?"

"I'm fine. You just startled me."

Brad walked around the divide and pulled a chair next to Ruby's desk. "No. It's more. Look. You can't be in this business and not learn to tell when someone withholds information from you." Brad cocked his head to one side and gestured with his hands to try to prompt it out of Ruby.

Ruby turned toward Brad. "It's probably just my imagination. I mean I probably forgot to look, and it wasn't even the same truck. My mind was thinking about stuff—"

Brad made a T with his hands, cutting her off. "Wait. Time out. What are you talking about?" Ruby went to open her mouth, but Brad added, "And start from the beginning."

"I met Jack for dinner. Afterward, I walked back here to finish the article. I was headed east down Main Street so I needed to cross over." Ruby paused, lost in thought for a second.

"And?"

Silence.

"Ruby?"

"I did check. I know I did."

"You checked what?"

Ruby took a breath, and her tone elevated. "I checked to make sure there were no cars coming, and then I stepped off the curb when I heard it."

"Heard what?"

"I don't know. An old kind of truck. It sounded like it was falling apart with all the clanking and stuff. But it came at me fast. Like it had been sitting there and watching and then just took off at me." Ruby looked at Brad, who seemingly started to process her words. "I know what I saw."

Brad chuckled. "I'm sure you did. I believe you. I'm just stunned. So what did you do?"

"I ran. I'm not an idiot. I ran across the street and around up into the building. When I got in, Dusty, the nightwatchman, was about to lock the front door."

"Did he see anything?"

"I don't think Dusty can see much anymore."

"True."

"You're OK though?"

"Yeah."

"What sort of truck was it? Was it a red truck?"

"No, why?"

Brad froze. He told Ruby that the truck at the Allgoods' on the morning of the murder was discovered. "I'm walking you back home tonight. So come get me when you're done."

Ruby shook her head as she put on a forced smile.

SEVENTEEN
Business as Usual

R obin wrung her hands and paced when she wasn't reading the documents the FBI gave her to memorize. She had yet to live up to her end of the bargain. Robin knew she had to give the agents the information she had. And as she was about to be moved to her new home, she reflected on the discussion when Allgood had confided in her during one of the rendezvous.

Robin had never meant to hurt her best friend, Sandra. Truthfully, it wasn't like she was in love with Allgood. Bill Allgood gave her a proposition a broke girl like her couldn't refuse, and she took it. Her father had once said, "Every man and woman has their price," and Robin clearly had one. The only problem was Allgood never paid enough to cover her costs. She wondered if there was a figure high enough to cover losing everything.

After Allgood had been killed and her involvement looked like it wouldn't pay off, she went to Baldy and demanded money, threatening to reveal his identity. She had arranged for the money to be paid at the Fourth of July celebration. But when Sandra refused to go with her to the celebration, Robin snuck out after Sandra had gone to sleep. She wore one of Sandra's shawls and wigs to disguise herself and met him behind the bandstands. He gave her $25,000, more money than she had made in two years, and that's when she decided to run. That was until the FBI intercepted her.

"You ready?" the FBI agent asked as the plane began its descent.

"As ready as I'm ever going to be. But could you give this note to Sandra?"

"I can't. You can't have any contact anymore. It's for your protection as well as hers."

"Basically, I'm dying to live," Robin muttered as she started to cry while gazing out the window. The reflection of her face resembled a woman she didn't recognize and one she wasn't proud of.

"If it helps," the agent said, "you're not alone."

Robin looked back at the young, naïve agent. "That's exactly what I am."

Every second Friday of the month, from May to October, there was a concert in Robert E. Lee Park with the groups performing from the large gazebo. It was usually local bands or groups, some high school bands, and some church choirs. They would normally play from 8 to 10 p.m. However, during June, July, and August, from 10 p.m. to 6 a.m. Saturday morning, gospel groups and church choirs would come in from all around and have all-night gospel sings, with breakfast to follow. But the group up that Friday was high school kids who had misjudged their audience and were playing some very loud rock and roll. Fortunately, each group would usually be on for fifteen to twenty-five minutes, and this was a fifteen-minute group.

"We should have brought earplugs," Ruby said.

"I think you're right. We'll put those on our shopping list," Jack said, leaning back on his blanket. Because it was an all-night singing event, the grounds around the gazebo were full of all kinds of people and families spread out on blankets. When a band played dance music, many of the attendees would dance under the strings of white lights cascading from the gazebo to the streetlamps.

Ruby spied a dark-haired woman with a big smile dressed in red hanging back by one of the lampposts. Ruby stood up and waved her over. "Lady Daisy!" she yelled.

Lady Daisy waved back and headed toward Ruby and Jack.

"Lady Daisy?" Jack asked.

"Yes."

"I wonder if she has a poison ring with her," he said, his voice a bit unsteady.

Ruby elbowed him in the ribs. "Don't antagonize her," Ruby shot back. "Remember she is hosting a party for us on the twentieth. So be nice."

They moved over to let Daisy sit down next to Ruby.

"Thanks so much for hosting a party for us. We are honored and very much looking forward to it."

"Well, of course, young lady. Everybody wants to get to know you and your handsome, talented Jack. He is becoming a topic of conversation since he helped free Sandra Allgood. By the way, she will be at my party."

Jack just nodded but desperately wanted to run away from this conversation. He needed a night away from it all.

While a few couples took to the dance floor, Jack kept looking at the large gold ring on Lady Daisy's finger. It was a "poison ring," as she openly admitted. It was similar to the rings used by the Borgias and others in the Middle Ages to eliminate their enemies. Some people believed the story about the poison ring. Others doubted it, but as it so happened, Lady Daisy's wealthy father had died mysteriously a few years before. The family doctor said her father basically died of old age, but his death did spur a lot of rumors since it meant she would inherit his considerable fortune.

Jack's mouth opened and closed without a word. He wanted to fill the awkward silence that Ruby wasn't filling as she usually did, but he didn't know how to pick up the slack. And then it came to him. "Ruby tells me you're an expert on the history of this town."

Daisy cocked her head to one side and looked over at Jack. "What do you want to know?"

Jack saw an opening, and since his wife was lost in the music that all but annoyed Jack, he went for it with what he really wanted to know. "Did you know the Allgoods well?"

"Well? No. I met Sandra a year ago and thought she was adorable. She never struck me as a killer, but she never struck me as a wallflower either."

"Most people reside in the middle," Jack noted.

Daisy sat up straighter and let out a long breath. "I never found that. Most have a type. The killers don't take abuse, and the wallflowers don't kill."

"Well, sometimes the wallflowers kill out of desperation," Jack said, taking a long sip from his beer.

Daisy stood and straightened her dress. "By that definition, anyone could be a killer."

Jack shook his head. "Maybe."

Lady Daisy looked Jack in the eye. "Makes you question who among us might have been desperate enough to want Bill dead. There are some who say he put himself in that position."

Jack jerked back, questioning her meaning. Ruby missed the exchange as she had stood up to dance to "Joy to the World" by Three Dog Night. "So you believe he got what he deserved?"

Lady Daisy gave a crooked smile and then drew her lips together. "Mr. Sutton, the law and justice aren't always synonymous."

"So you're saying that killing a man is justified if he was abhorrent or dishonorable, for example?"

"There must be degrees associated with that statement for it to be true."

Jack shook his head. "Then you're OK with citizens operating outside the law if it serves a greater good?"

Daisy's expression grew dark. "Excuse me, but I see someone I should say hello to. I look forward to seeing you both soon," Daisy stated as she walked off toward another group of townies on their blankets.

Ruby turned to hug Daisy before she left and then flopped on the blanket next to Jack as the song ended.

"She's creepy," Jack said.

Ruby laughed and said, "What did you tell me about us blending?"

"I said blend, not hang out with people who probably sleep hanging upside down in a closet."

Ruby laughed. "Ha! She's just eccentric."

"Let's face it. Eccentric is just what you call nutty people with money. Daisy isn't her real name either. I heard it from a guy who had a financial deal with her."

"So lots of people change their names."

"Fun fact. Did you know that in the Victorian era, the term *daisy* referred to being secretive? I bet her closet is packed with skeletons."

Ruby rolled her eyes. "What were you two talking about that has you saying this?" Ruby asked, taking a sip of Jack's beer.

"She acted like she knew something. And that she thought Bill deserved to be killed."

"Come on. You know she's not alone in that sentiment. Half the town said so. You're just overthinking things, Jack Sutton. Stop being a lawyer for once and enjoy the night," Ruby said, leaning in and giving her husband a lengthy kiss.

"Well, if you give me more kisses like that, I guess overthinking works!" Jack pulled Ruby toward him, and the two fell back on the blanket, laughing.

—◦◦◦—

That Saturday, Brad went into the office. He had to do some work on his other stories, including looking at a two-year plan to put together an article campaign for the bicentennial of the state. When Fanny May Smith and Anthony Keel had brought the idea to him, he was fine with starting to think of intermittent stories that could be used over the next two years. However, Fanny May made it clear she wanted a feature story a month and wanted Lavender to do it so there was continuity. Brad had protested that was too much, but Keel made a point. "Fight if you want, but I can assure you Fanny May Smith will get what she wants in the end." It became a challenge for Brad, and he had finally said he would do one a quarter. Mrs. Fanny May said that was not enough, and they went away disagreeing.

Shortly thereafter, the *Observer* editor called him in on the matter. "Mrs. Fanny May Smith was my English teacher in high school. And I can assure you that she will win out in the end. So I'm going to save us both time and heartache and just let you know you will be doing monthly features starting this July. You better find your first topic soon."

Brad realized it was to no avail and gave a nod of acquiescence.

Mrs. Fanny May already had the idea for the first source of monthly articles. She had given him a box of old Pear Valley High School annuals and school newspapers dating back to the turn of the century. Their mascot was the Rebels, and the yearbook and school newspapers held that title.

That Saturday, he had started going through them to find some gems for his first piece. As he dug through, he stopped on a reference made in one of the old yearbooks. It was a senior comment section where a young lady had sent a note to "Baldy" thanking him for being special.

—◊—

On Saturday night, the couples dinner with Denise and Brad was to be at the Patio, the swankiest menu Pear Valley had to offer. This New Age restaurant even featured a fondue dish that Ruby loved, but it was for more than one, not to mention the oppressive summer heat, so her eyes kept scanning the menu as Jack and Denise discussed the Allgood case.

Brad had been a little late so he stood at the entrance and watched the interactions between Denise and the Suttons. Denise and Ruby had become dear friends in a very short time, and it made him happy to see Denise smiling and laughing. This town had changed him. Brad had not made many friends in Miami other than the relationship that made him leave. For the first time since he arrived, Brad thought, *This could be a place I stay in for a while.* But he hoped the news he had wouldn't sour the evening. Unsure how Jack would take the news, Brad breathed in deeply and prepared himself.

Brad dodged and weaved his way to the back table of his party, already ensconced in conversation. Denise stood up, and he gave her a peck on the cheek. He hugged Ruby and gave Jack a high five.

The Patio had gray, rustic-looking, very comfortable furniture with ample space between tables. The pergola above the tables housed many fans with large paddles to move the stifling Georgia heat around, making outdoor dining more enjoyable. Every few seconds, you could distinguish the hearty laugh of patrons enjoying their company among the soft murmur of conversation and the hum of the ceiling fans. Nestled in downtown Pear Valley, many city and county officials and departments came in since the restaurant was only two blocks from city hall and three blocks from the county commission. Many local bigwigs and a few department heads had lunch there, but during dinner, it attracted more local couples on date night. Servers bustled around the large restaurant.

As they settled in, the conversation immediately went back to the events of the last week. Brad let Jack and Ruby unearth their stories before saying anything. When a window of silence presented itself, Brad cleared his throat. "I had an eventful day doing some research for the centennial."

"Sounds exciting," Jack teased.

"Well, counselor, what I found may impact your life the most."

Jack finished sipping his wine and sat back; he could sense Brad's hesitation. "OK, out with it."

"Well, to build on what Jack has uncovered with respect to the unknown identity of Baldy, I think I may have found a crucial clue."

Jack gestured to Brad to get to the point.

"I happened to be looking through some old high school yearbooks when I came across one with reference to a nickname of Baldy."

Jack shifted in his seat. "Stop the suspense building. You're not writing a hook for your article or a novel. Out with it," Jack joked as he grabbed his wine and took another sip.

Brad took a long deep breath, surveyed the faces at the table, and spit it out. "Frank Truitt."

Jack immediately choked on his wine.

Ruby patted Jack on the back. "Are you OK?"

Clearing his throat and drinking from his water glass, Jack nodded.

Before Brad could add anything, Ruby validated Brad's finding. "Wait. Wait. At the book club a few weeks back, the ladies all said they had nicknames for Truitt and Cain."

Jack sat up and cleared his throat one more time before saying, "He wouldn't be dumb enough to use that as a code name." To Ruby's surprise, Jack all but rejected the probability as he sat back and took another drink, giving a half chuckle to the preposterous notion, at least in his mind.

Brad leaned in. "But maybe *he* didn't use it. From what you said, the tapes only used the name once or twice, and it was Warren Cain who used it," explained Brad.

Jack set his glass down.

"I wonder if Sandra knew," Denise said.

"Knew what?" Jack asked.

"Knew her husband was involved. I'm sure she didn't, but what if she did?"

Brad perked up but waited for the food to be set in front of them and for the waiter to leave before he asked her, "What are you getting at?"

Denise picked up her fork and knife and started to cut her steak. "I'm thinking if she knew and didn't use it in her defense initially, it's because she was complicit. It somehow worked for her, and she kept it a secret."

"Or she was Baldy?" Ruby said, smirking before biting her fork full of mashed potatoes.

Jack shook his head and, despite the gravity of all he had heard, laughed. "Where would you get that from? That's a stretch?"

"You know I love horses, right? Well, one of the ladies in the book club told me that Sandra's 'bald' horse died mysteriously right before her husband was murdered."

"Is there such a thing?" Denise asked.

Jack put his utensils down and cocked his head toward his wife. He wore the look that she was about to educate the table. Ruby started, "Yes, they are born with no pigment on their face, and they are called bald. It's a rare condition, but supposedly, they also have one or two blue eyes. Sandra's horse had one blue eye, and that's why she called him Blue."

"Fascinating," Denise and Brad said in unison, but they got sidetracked in laughter at their simultaneous reply.

Brad looked at Jack. "What are you going to do with this? I can't let this information rest for too long. I have a byline to write."

Jack took the check. "I'm paying for dinner, so give me the weekend to decide. Monday, I'll have an answer for you."

Brad held his hand out, and the men shook on it.

After dinner, Brad and Denise walked out arm in arm on the muggy July night.

"What do you think?" Denise asked, getting into the car.

"I don't know what to think, but I don't think it's a coincidence."

"Jack is going to be conflicted over all of this. Truitt is why he came to Pear Valley, and Sandra is his client."

"Well, this hopefully doesn't cause them to run back to Atlanta. This town needs new blood."

"Well, it's got you and me," Denise said, laughing.

Brad slowed the car and stopped at the red light. He looked at Denise. "I'm not sure if that is a compliment."

Denise shifted in her seat in Brad's Dodge pickup with its brown vinyl interior. "Yes, it is a compliment! Why would I also insult myself?"

"Touché." Brad dropped his head, trying to hide his smile, and then looked back up at the beauty next to him. "Have I told you how incredible you are? And if I don't kiss you soon, I will be the world's biggest idiot."

"We don't want that," Denise said, leaning in as Brad gently pulled her face toward his, and their lips softly brushed as the car behind them honked, startling them both back to the present. Brad laughed, shifted the car in gear, and hit the gas.

Jack was up early, drinking a cup of coffee in the kitchen and losing himself in his thoughts. He had always found that if you gave things a little time and a little perspective, they fell into place. His old high school English teacher had told him, "Things are never as bad as they seem, and they all work out, in the end, the way they're supposed to, whether you like it or not."

Jack swirled his coffee cup around, mesmerized by the cream's movement. "Well, not all things work out all the time," he said to himself.

Ruby interrupted him, approaching from behind his chair and putting her arms around him. "Who are you talking to? You looked like you were a million miles away."

Jack was startled and then turned to kiss her. "I was, honey. I was." Jack stood up and took Ruby in his arms. "Let's put some miles on Cindy."

Jack and Ruby often jumped in Cindy and drove around the county and its communities to get used to their new surroundings. They enjoyed driving among the farmhouses, tobacco barns, fields, and farms of south Georgia, stopping at an occasional roadside stand for a chance to uncover some treasures for dinner. It was a great way to clear the mind and remind each other of what was important in life.

They pointed Cindy toward a little town called Whigham on Georgia Highway 38. They had heard it was famous in the winter for a festival called the Rattlesnake Roundup. People from all over would come, and because it was winter, the snakes would be dormant in burrows. They would pull them out, not a job without danger, and then bring them to town. There would be prizes for the biggest, fattest, etc. Then the snakes would all be milked for venom for antivenom serums.

Jack and Ruby were on their way to visit Whigham before they turned onto Highway 38. On that stretch of road, they went through two little towns: Hopeful and then Climax. They could not stop laughing when they saw the road connecting them was the "Hopeful-Climax Road." They both said the words at the same time. Jack had a twinkle in his eye and downshifted Cindy. He then pulled off into the pine grove behind an old tobacco barn.

"What are you doing?" Ruby exclaimed, knowing very well what was on her husband's mind. As Jack pulled over behind the barn, she slid his seat back and straddled his legs. After some jostling that comes from contortions in a car, they turned the climax into a reality instead of just hope.

After adjusting their clothes and pulling back onto the road to Whigham, they came upon the Hurst Place Farm, where a half dozen horses were roaming along the fence line. Ruby saw the farmer in the drive and asked Jack to pull over. Having grown up around the horse set and having competed as a young child, her affection for the animals was palpable. And Jack, still in a glow from the pinnacle Ruby had just taken him to, gave in to his wife's request.

The owner of Hurst Place Farm was Jeff Sample. He was a transplant for Pittsburgh. He and his wife, Carolyn wanted to move south and found the old Hurst farm and turned it into a horse ranch where they owned and boarded horses as well as cows and goats for the town kids who wanted to have them in the 4-H or FFA (Future Farmers of America) shows. Ruby listened to Jeff with marked intensity while Jack counted the minutes until he could get back to Cindy, get her on the open road with the windows down, and cruise.

When Jeff finally ran out of things to say, they said their goodbyes and Ruby and Jack walked back to the car. Before they reached Cindy, Ruby grabbed her husband's arm to stop him. "Honey, I would like to get a horse. I want to ask Mr. Sample if he has space for one more. I could go riding on weekends. This place looks big enough," Ruby said, gesturing to the farm behind them.

Jack guided them back to the car; they got in and drove off before Jack spoke. "You've taken on working full time, and now you want a horse?"

"To ride on the weekends," Ruby said before outstretching her arms and wrapping them tightly around Jack's middle. "Come on. You know I love horses." Jack shook his head and thought about her father's words to him. *If baby doll wants, baby doll gets it.* Breathing in deeply, he said, "Well, we can think about it as long as you promise to be my Lady Godiva."

"What?"

"You know Lady Godiva from the eleventh century. She rode a horse naked through the street of Coventry."

Ruby rolled her eyes because she knew the history lesson was coming.

"Legend has it that her husband was demanding an oppressive tax from the citizens of Coventry, and in her attempt to get him to stop, she rode a horse naked through the streets in protest."

"Well, that seems a bit drastic!" Ruby laughed.

"OK, how much are we talking with a horse?" Jack asked.

"At least a thousand. I don't want a real young one. I want a steady one. I'm thinking of a horse about ten years old."

Jack nearly choked at a price. "Well, can we give this some more thought? I mean that's a lot right now."

"But I'm working, so we should have enough," Ruby said, shifting in her seat. "I remember reading *Black Beauty* when I was about ten. I already loved horses and loved them even more after reading that book."

"Babe, we'll think about it. You can stop the sales pitch! But I am thinking of you riding naked."

Ruby let out a laugh and shook her head.

Jack turned the car onto a side road. An arrow sign said, "Shiloh Primitive Baptist Church, 2 miles." "Primitive Baptists?" Jack said. "Never heard of that denomination."

Ruby laughed for a second. "Not quite snake handlers, but certainly speak in tongues. Finally, a term I know and you don't. They believe in predestination." She stuck her hand out the window and let it ride in the wind as she took in the rural surroundings. "By the way, what is this odd-looking grass?" she asked.

"That still falls under southern wiregrass." Jack let out a dramatic breath. "Feel much better now that I reclaimed my status."

She laughed. "Not to change the subject, but after last night, have you given the case any thoughts?"

Jack took a breath. He didn't want to tell her that's pretty much all he'd thought about, but he confessed. "Something about the Allgood case doesn't feel settled to me. I can't believe Truitt is involved. I mean he is a bastard, but he is a pillar of the community, a state senator for Christ's sake, and a prominent and respected lawyer. It makes no sense. And I don't think Sandra was involved either, but what you said about her horse got me thinking. I plan to talk to Annie tomorrow and then reach out to Layton and Willis.

EIGHTEEN

Uncovered

Jack had arrived at his back-porch office early on Monday morning, hoping he would not see Truitt on the way in. Jack flopped his briefcase on a side chair and then dropped his body onto his own. He swiveled around and stared out at the backyard. A miniature birdhouse hung from a giant oak tree with one small bird perched on its edge as the neighbors' kids played a game of tag. For a minute, Jack wanted to be that bird or those kids. Either reality would be totally shocking.

His phone rang, startling him. "Jack Sutton."

"Annie Masterson," she said, mocking Jack.

"Just the person I needed to speak with."

"Back at ya, boss. You first."

Jack finished the call with his dogged investigator and was all but shaking with frustration over what she had told him. Steadying his nerves, Jack picked up the receiver. "Hey, it's Jack Sutton. I need to talk with you and Willis."

—❧—

Brad's Monday started with him going back over some photos from the July 4 celebration. He had initially reviewed them to write an article about some of the funds raised at the events during the celebration. However, Annie, who had gotten a copy of the photos from Brad, called and directed him to a particular photo. After hanging up with her, Brad walked over to Ruby's desk and sat on the corner of it. "So you know how I've been pouring over the photos from the Fourth of July?"

Ruby looked up from her typewriter. "Yeah."

Brad held out a photograph and handed it to her. Ruby grabbed the photo and stared at it, not quite sure what she was looking at. She glanced back at Brad. "OK, you've got to give me a clue. It's the town gazebo, it's dusk, and it's decorated for the Fourth. I don't get it."

"Look closer."

Ruby stared at the picture and noticed a man and a woman standing a few feet in the background from the gazebo. "I can't make it out, but that looks like Mrs. Allgood. I can't tell for sure." Then looking at Brad with surprise and confusion, she exclaimed, "It's him!"

—◊◊—

Jack, Ruby, Denise, and Brad had agreed to meet in a conference room in the courthouse that Willis had arranged for them. They felt they needed to be out of prying eyes for what they had to figure out.

When they arrived, Jack told them of the favor he had asked from Annie, and he should hear from her shortly. Brad interrupted and showed Jack the photograph. Jack went through the same identification path that Ruby had. Looking up, he said, "That is Truitt, but who is he with? I recognize that shawl. Sandra wore it once when I visited her. But that's not Sandra."

"How do you know?" Brad asked.

"I know," Jack said authoritatively.

After an uncomfortable silence, Denise asked, "What are you going to do?"

Before Jack could answer, there was a knock at the door, and Ruby opened it. A woman in jeans, cowboy boots, and a T-shirt stood in front of her. "Hi, can I help you?"

"Oh sorry. I'm Annie Masterson. I'm looking for Jack. You must be Ruby."

Ruby smiled. "Oh gosh, it's so nice to meet you; you have made quite an impression on my husband. Come in, please."

Annie said hello to everyone, declined Jack's offer of coffee, and handed him her findings.

"Is this going to make me happy?" Jack asked.

"Depends on your definition of happy," Annie said, chomping on her gum.

In it was a report from an expert that Annie knew. It confirmed the handwriting on the suicide note was Frank Truitt's. Jack felt like the wind was going to rush out of him. He steadied himself and told everyone the results.

Annie added, "My source from the FBI who helped me with this also verified that they had still not seen hide nor hair of Tanner and Roberts since they went missing. He indicated that in all likelihood, they would never be seen or heard from again."

Jack really was not surprised by that.

Annie went on. "They found the red pickup truck they were looking for abandoned down by the Okefenokee Swamp near the Georgia-Florida line. It is well-known for alligators cleaning up any messes. They don't think they will ever find those two either. The theory is the cartel is cleaning up their connections with Pear Valley and looking for quieter areas to work in."

Brad interjected, "What about this photo from the Fourth of July celebration?" Brad handed Annie a copy of the photo, although she already knew what he was referring to.

Annie answered without looking at it. "Look. It wasn't

Sandra." She turned to the others. "After I talked with Brad, I wanted verification. If you look at the picture, there is a maintenance guy in the background putting up the Fourth of July decorations. I tracked him down. He knew Sandra Allgood, and he said that the woman in the picture wasn't her. Which makes sense because her staff attested to her being home and in shock over the murder."

"Well, that's good. Then who was it?"

"We don't know for sure, but the guy said the woman was wearing a wig. He could tell because his mother wore them all the time. Plus he said she was really skinny. Sandra is slim but not super skinny. And she lingered on the fringe of the park for almost thirty minutes."

Jack cocked his head, processing. Annie paused, waiting for the light bulb to come on, but it didn't.

"OK, think. Who is super skinny and hung around Sandra like a barnacle on a boat after the killing?"

Jack sat up straighter. "Her friend Robin!"

"Exactly. So I got a picture of Robin and did some digging. It seems sweet, dedicated Robin was having an affair with Allgood."

"Wait. Are you telling me Robin killed Allgood?" Ruby asked.

"I don't know yet, but I would hold off on using the photo until we have some more information."

Jack sat back and rubbed his temples.

After Annie departed, Ruby jumped in. "Jack, what are you going to do with all this evidence?"

"We have to meet with Layton. I can't just go and accuse my boss of running a drug ring with the cartel. It's just a nickname he can claim is a coincidence. And it also doesn't confirm he had anything to do with Allgood's death. As a matter of fact, there is nothing here to link Truitt and Allgood in the plot or the catfish case other than circumstantial evidence."

Brad interjected, "There have been criminals convicted based on circumstantial evidence."

Jack put his hands on his hips as he paced. "Yes, but there has to be more than what we've got for that to work. Plus we have to be careful. Our analysis of Truitt's writing is not admissible evidence until the sheriff or task force confirms it. And the picture Brad found doesn't say anything. Two people were meeting on the street. Happens every second of every day." Jack's steps picked up, and the others started to think his conversation was more for himself than anyone else.

"But what about Robin and Truitt?" Denise interjected.

"Again, no direct tie. Just like the nickname is not a direct tie. We need to go to Willis and Layton and lay it all out and let them go from there," Jack concluded for them all.

—⁂—

Jack called Willis and Layton and arranged for them to meet him in the conference room Willis had provided for them at 2:00 that afternoon. Willis and Layton arrived ten minutes early together.

Layton could not resist saying, "Do you always travel with a pack?"

Not offended, Jack quickly replied, "A wolf pack, one for all and all for one."

Jack assured them Brad, Denise, and Ruby had all been integral parts of gathering the information they were going to provide. Willis and Layton agreed to hear them out. Jack led with the disclosure of Allgood and Truitt's connection with the drug case and the theory that Truitt could be the unknown conspirator known as Baldy.

Jack then turned it over to Brad to discuss what he found out.

Brad explained his research for the bicentennial. He would show he had found the yearbook that had referred to Mr. Truitt as Baldy and let them see it.

Ruby then discussed the nickname some of the girls had given Mr. Truitt in high school so many years ago before.

Jack mentioned the early drug case Truitt had told him about, where the evidence against Truitt's client went missing under Cain's watch.

He then summarized all the findings and concluded Mr. Truitt appeared to be the coconspirator and that he was likely the silent partner known as Baldy. Jack also turned over the results of the writing sample analysis of Mr. Truitt he had gotten from some papers at the office, along with the papers that they could independently compare with that of the suicide note. He would suggest they bring back the GBI handwriting expert and see if it indeed did. Finally, he would review the photograph for them to make the connection.

Sitting around a table in the conference room, district attorneys Willis and Layton were amazed at the work the group had done and pleased it matched the information the FBI had given them. However, the new fact that Truitt was Baldy stunned them. First, because one of the most influential lawyers in the county had just been implicated with overwhelming evidence that demonstrated that he had a connection to the drug case and may have committed the murder of Bill Allgood. If the lab confirmed what they all surmised, then they would have evidence beyond a reasonable doubt, which they should be able to use to find out who actually pulled the trigger.

Layton, having regained his composure, first looked at Jack. "I guess Emmitt Throwbridge knew what he was doing."

DA Willis observed, "This information obviously affects my drug case trial that is coming up. I plan to seek a continuance from Judge Throwbridge. I will add Mr. Truitt as a coconspirator. That may affect whether we can try the case in Callahan County. The trial might have to be moved to Tift County or Colquitt County."

Layton interjected, "Mr. Lavender, Miss Walker, and Mrs. Sutton, I usually do not like the press, but y'all may be winning me over. The information you provided and delivered through Mr. Sutton will be key to our successful prosecution of these cases."

Willis took over. "We ask that all of you keep all this information to yourself. Miss Letting will be here tomorrow, and we will learn more about the Allgood murder and the catfish trial. We will update you with more information when it is available and to the extent we can. Please do not discuss this with anyone else," he said, then he looked at Brad, Denise, and Ruby. "Please, no news stories until the information is followed up on."

—ᴍ—

The next morning, Jack entered his office and dropped his briefcase on an empty chair as he started thumbing through his messages.

"Anything interesting?" Brown came from behind him, and Jack jumped. "Oh sorry, didn't mean to startle you. Everything OK?"

"It's OK. Um yeah. I'm good. How are you?" Jack asked, walking around to sit behind his desk.

"Why don't I believe that?"

"District Attorney Layton is on the phone, Jack!" Thelma yelled from outside the door.

Mosely shot Jack a funny look and then gave him a nod before exiting.

Jack picked up the receiver. "Jack Sutton." Jack sat in his chair and thumbed through his calendar. "OK, I'll be there soon."

Jack took the courthouse stairs two at a time as he fought the knots in his stomach. Layton and Willis were coming down the center stairs as Jack went through the entrance. They waved him into a conference room just off the main lobby.

"What's going on?" Jack asked.

"The handwriting expert matched the samples," Layton said before sitting down and handing the file to Jack.

Jack sat back and rubbed his forehead in contemplation. "Well, I guess that seals my fate in this town." Jack thought, *Well, at least Ruby will be happy if we have to leave.*

Ruby came over to Brad's desk. "I think we need to go pay a visit to Sandra Allgood. Maybe let her tell her story since she's no longer a suspect. I already cleared it with Evan. I didn't give him all the details, just enough that he thinks it would be great, but he wants you to go with me because he thinks a male presence would help." Ruby rolled her eyes in disgust.

Brad chuckled. "Well, you know he's stuck in 1950, right?"

"Yes, but as much as I hate it, he might be right in this case. Sandra might be more willing to talk if you're there."

Brad nodded reluctantly and then looked over at Denise, who smiled back. "OK. I'm in."

By the time Brad and Ruby arrived at the Allgood farm, the morning sun was high in the sky. "It's lunchtime. Maybe she's out."

Ruby laughed as she exited Brad's car. "Brad, you act like you're trying to avoid this whole thing."

Brad pulled the key out of the ignition and muttered to himself, "Maybe I am."

Ruby had already climbed the stairs and was about to knock when the front door opened. Sandra Allgood stood there, looking picture-perfect in her white linen pants, pink ruffled top, and paisley scarf. "Can I help you?"

Ruby absentmindedly straightened her dress and stuck her hand out. "Yes, I am Ruby Sutton, reporter for the *Observer.*"

"I know who you are," Sandra said in a soft, reserved tone while not reaching out.

"Yes, of course. You know Jack." Ruby dropped her hand and stepped back, allowing Brad to move forward.

Sandra cocked her head to one side and immediately turned toward Brad, who slowly came up the stairs. "Hi, I'm Brad Lavender. Mrs. Allgood?"

"Sandra."

Brad smiled as he stood next to a dejected Ruby. "Sandra, Mrs. Sutton and I were hoping to have a conversation with you."

"Mr. Lavender, I'm not interested in talking to the press. The Southern belles and gossipmongers need to feed on someone else," Sandra said, directing her passive-aggressive words at Ruby. Ruby's face turned bright red in response as Sandra backed up to close the door.

Brad held out his hand in a calming gesture. "Wait. We're not here to make life difficult. In fact, we want the truth to come out and give you a chance to tell your side of things, ma'am. Sorry. Sandra, the truth is the only way to combat the nasty, false rumors." Brad had turned on a level of charm Ruby hadn't seen before, leaving her slightly impressed at his skills.

"OK, come in."

The two reporters filed in and sat in the impressive living room, flanked by a majestic spiral staircase. Sandra came in and sat down. "What do you want to know?"

"Whatever you want to tell us about your life. What do you think people misunderstand?" Brad said in a tone just one notch above a whisper.

Sandra looked at Ruby. "Look. People see me as a poor girl after the sweet life. And maybe I was before I met Bill. Maybe like every little girl, I was waiting for my Prince Charming. And I got him, or at least I thought I did. In the beginning, Bill made me feel safe and loved, and for the first time, I could trust a man. Then little by little, it all fell apart. It started not long after we married. He changed. And that's when I learned about his many extracurricular activities. My life here became a prison I couldn't escape from."

Ruby leaned in. "Most will see that as a motive."

Sandra quickly shot her a stern look. "Yes, that's exactly what a good Southern belle would think."

Ruby's eyes darted to the ground. She wasn't one to back down, but Sandra's words were meant to cut.

Sandra stood and walked toward the tall windows at the far side of the room. "I may have been unhappy, but I didn't want him to die. I just wanted my freedom. I had seen an attorney outside of this county, but even he didn't want my case." Sandra turned back to look at them. "Yes, I know that adds to how it looks, but I *know* it's not true. And if I were smart enough to *trap* him early on, do you think I'd be so dumb as to try to make it look like a suicide?" Sandra took a deep breath. "To be honest, Mr. Lavender, I no longer care about how things appear. I know the truth. I didn't kill my husband." Her striking eyes locked with Brad, and he melted like chocolate in a hot vehicle.

By the time Ruby and Brad were in the car on the way home, Ruby was close to tears. Brad looked over at her and felt bad. "What's wrong?"

"You have to ask?"

Willis and Layton shared a look and said in unison, "You ready?"

"As much as I can be," Jack said, taking a seat next to Willis across from Layton.

"Well, the charges against Truitt for murder don't happen. They would be weak at best, anyway, because he had an alibi. Robin gets charged with obstruction of justice and blackmail, for starters, if she can be found, and Tanner is still missing and presumed dead."

Layton knew Robin was in protective custody and couldn't reveal it to Jack. Jack knew but played along.

"But how do we know Tanner was telling the truth?"

Willis interjected after shooting a smile to Layton. "Do you know Tanner?"

"Met him once. Can't say I particularly liked the guy."

"Well, we went to school with him. Dumb as shit but a superior marksman. He would have taken Allgood out with one shot, and he never used a revolver. Tanner's an idiot or was, but there is one thing he would never compromise on, and that's his shooting reputation. He wanted to be a sniper in the marines, but his health issues kept him out."

"So that's it? The killer or killers walk free?"

Layton gathered his files as he and Willis stood. "As prosecutors, we fight the fights we can win. We have too much work to waste our time on needles in a haystack. Allgood had a mountain of enemies."

"What about the catfish trial and Truitt?"

"It's a lot of circumstantial evidence. I haven't decided at this point, but since we've lost Tanner, Roberts, Cain, and Cook ain't talkin' well. Looks like Cook takes the hit."

The two men walked toward the door as Jack started to stand and gather his things. Layton walked and gestured for Willis to wait. "What are you going to do now, Jack?"

Jack looked Layton in the eye, puzzled. "What do you mean?"

"You're working for Baldy. We may not charge him, but it doesn't change what you know."

Jack shook his head. "I don't know what I'm going to do."

Layton and Willis shared a smile. "There's room on the other side if you're interested, counselor." Neither waited for Jack to reply before they walked out.

—⁓—

Jack walked into the office. When he arrived, Mr. Truitt yelled to him, "Boy, where have you been? Just because you won your case does not mean you don't have to work. That meeting in Adel should not have taken all day."

Jack bit his tongue and answered, "Yes, Mr. Truitt. It won't happen again."

Thelma followed Jack to his office and stayed as he settled in. "Jack, we're all so proud of you. I know Mrs. Allgood must be beside herself with joy."

"Thank you, Thelma."

To try to lighten his mood, she replied, "By the way, did you hear that Adel is so close to hell you can see *Sparks?*"

Jack laughed, knowing what she was trying to do. "Where does that come from?"

"If you're driving to Adel from Tifton down US Highway 41, you pass through Sparks city limit, where Adel city limits start immediately. They touch each other, so when you're in Adel and look back, you can see Sparks! Partly because of geographic location, but also because Adel has a reputation as a place you don't want to be on a Friday night late, or there can be hell to pay."

"Well, I'll be darned," Jack said. "You learn something every day. I'll remember that one, and I know the person I will share it with." Jack chuckled.

"Are you OK? You seem very distracted?" Thelma asked, noticing the change in Jack's demeanor.

"Fine, just thinking about this divorce case," Jack answered, picking up the file on his desk for emphasis.

Thelma nodded before adding, "Well, let me grab you some coffee."

Jack sat at his desk with the knot tying itself tighter in his stomach. He had to admit it was hard to settle into practice with so much hanging in the balance, supposition, and implication. Add to that his new day-to-day became a bit of a letdown. You could not specialize in murder cases as a first-year lawyer in Callahan County, Georgia. Instead, he had to deal with an uncontested divorce or a land dispute while wondering when or if the shoe would drop on the firm or if he would spend the rest of his years there thinking he looked the other way.

Thelma returned with a steaming cup of coffee. "Here you go."

Jack looked up. "Thanks, Thelma. I have court in the morning. Would you make sure Truitt knows?"

Thelma nodded and added, "You know, when I was a girl, my best friend passed away. For years I did nothing but think about the mystery surrounding her death. I couldn't accept that sometimes things happen without us getting answers."

"I feel like someone gave me a puzzle to solve and then took it from me before I found the last piece."

"Was the puzzle basically complete?"

"In some ways."

"Then ask yourself, 'If I find that last piece, will it change anything?'"

Thelma smiled and left Jack's office as Jack turned to look out his window and wondered, *Why is everyone here OK with accepting the results and moving on when so much is unanswered?*

In Georgia, unlike in California, you could not have a divorce for the irreconcilable differences. The person filing for the divorce had to show mental cruelty for a divorce. Jack met with his client right before the hearing and let him know that he would have to answer Jack's questions for the judge to grant the divorce and agree with them. Mr. Johnson was not the sharpest tool in the shed but indicated he understood.

Don Simone called the case. "Johnson versus Johnson. Jack Sutton for Mr. Johnson, Your Honor."

Judge Throwbridge looked up from the papers on the bench. "Mr. Sutton, please ask your client to take the stand and be sworn in." Jack felt proud to know Judge Throwbridge said his name with newfound respect.

"Your name is Willie Johnson?"

"Yes, sir."

"You're married to Victoria Johnson for more than six months prior to filing this petition?"

"Yes, sir."

"You had three children born to this marriage?"

"Yes, sir."

"You were out in Los Angeles, California, when you got a telephone call from your neighbor telling you that your wife had run off with another man, leaving your children with the neighbor. Ain't that right?"

"Yes, sir."

"You were in Los Angeles, California, on a cross-country run with your semitruck, and you had to bobtail slap back across the United States to come to see your children and protect them. Ain't that right, Mr. Johnson?"

"Yes, sir."

"And you were so distraught, you feared for your and your children's health, safety, and wellbeing. Isn't that right?"

"Hell no! Good riddance is what I thought!"

The other lawyers in the courtroom were in shock. They knew that the client had to answer affirmatively to set the legal grounds for the judge to grant the divorce.

Jack tried again. "Wait just a minute, Mr. Johnson. Weren't you fearful for your health and safety?"

"Hell no!"

Judge Throwbridge, with a hint of a smile, said, "Mr. Sutton, do you need a minute with your client?"

"Yes, Your Honor." Jack pulled Mr. Johnson aside in the hallway and said, "What the hell was that?"

"Well, I ain't upset she's gone. And I ain't no pussy who's afraid of his wife."

"Do you want to get this divorce?"

"I just said so!"

Jack explained the problem to him and then went back in. When Judge Throwbridge noted he was back, he called Jack and his client again.

"Mr. Johnson, were you fearful for your health, safety, and wellbeing, as well as your kids?"

"Yes, sir."

"Nice job, Mr. Johnson and Mr. Sutton. I hereby grant the divorce and dissolution of the marriage as requested."

As Jack finished the divorce hearing, Layton, who had been in the box and enjoying the humor of Jack's difficult client, walked up to Jack and said, "You were almost the first lawyer ever to lose an uncontested divorce. I'm sure it's a little hard handling a problematic uncontested divorce after the legal work you have been doing the past few weeks."

Jack smiled. "Something like that."

"I bet," said Layton. "Look. None of this is a slam dunk. You may have to accept that there will be no restitution."

Jack's face dropped. "I really appreciate the forewarning. But it's not in my nature to let things slide."

Layton looked around. "It's the business we are in. Like it or not."

The morning sun rose over the house, illuminating the backyard as Jack sat on the deck with a hot coffee in his hand. Ruby was still sleeping, and although he wanted to wake her and talk, he knew that would be a waste of time. They argued again last night after Jack told her he thought she should visit her parents for a week. What Jack had expected as her jumping for joy turned into an accusation that he wanted her to quit her job.

He worried about his job and the implications if what he thought was the truth really was accurate. How had everything gone so out of control so fast? But what he knew for a fact was that if he lost this job, his father would have a field day with him, and his father-in-law would all but demand his return; Jack would be a company man and living out the very life he ran from.

Jack watched as a bird landed on the feeder Ruby had just placed on the pole in the yard by her garden, which as of late seemed to be taken over by weeds. Soon after, another bird showed up, and the two ate side by side. Nostalgic for simpler times, Jack dumped his coffee over the deck, looked at the birds, said, "It's time," and headed to his car.

—⟊—

When Jack pulled up to the office that Friday morning, Sheriff Walter Jones and Deputy Rodger Franklin were standing outside. Jack got out of his car and walked over to them. "Gentlemen."

The two men nodded, and Jack stood back as they ascended the front walkway.

Thelma asked, "What are y'all doing here, Walter? Is anything wrong?"

"I'm afraid so, Thelma. Is Mr. Truitt in?"

"Yes, he is in his office. Do you want me to get him?"

"No," said Sheriff Jones. "We will just go straight back."

She protested, but they were already at Mr. Truitt's door and opened it.

Mr. Truitt looked up from the desk and said, "What in the world are you doing here, Walter?"

When Sheriff Jones started reading Truitt his rights, Truitt looked genuinely confused. "What is this about? Walter, you know me. Why are you doing this?" Truitt looked over the sheriff and yelled out, "Thelma, call the judge. And have Mosely and Sutton make my bail!"

Jones finished reading his rights, handcuffed him, and took him to the patrol car. Brad and Ruby had been tipped off by DA Layton, and they brought a photographer from the *Pear Valley Observer*. They got photos of Truitt handcuffed, but he refused to comment.

Jack, Mosely, and Thelma were all on the porch. Mosely and Thelma stared in disbelief. Mosely yelled, "Frank, I will be right down!" He turned to Jack. "You want to tell me now what's going on?"

After Truitt was led out of the office, Jack told everyone to meet him in the conference room. Mosely protested, noting he had to get to the courthouse. Jack insisted, "Mosely, you need to hear this."

Jack, Mosely, David, and Thelma went into the conference room.

After Jack divulged what had happened, Thelma cried softly, "I can't believe Mr. Truitt would be involved in either of those things. He is not a drug dealer or a murderer."

Jack was thankful Mosely spoke up. "At least, for the time being, we have a duty to our clients to keep together and look after them. Mr. Frank will be treated fairly by the court of law. We can't worry about that now; we must focus on serving our clients." Mosely stood up and walked out without a word to Jack.

David walked over to Jack. "Well, you stepped in a mess, but good," he said, patting Jack on the back before leaving behind Thelma.

NINETEEN
Celebrations All Around

It was a gorgeous Southern night. Even the humidity had broken, and the gnats must have slept in for Lady Daisy's party. The conversation about Truitt ranged from those surprised to those who said they "knew" he did it. It was amazing how many folks expressed their secret concerns about Truitt for the first time. It really seemed like revisionist history.

Mrs. Sandra Allgood came through the backyard gate at nine that evening. Everyone literally stopped and stared. Jack walked over to his client. He embraced her as she whispered, "Thank you."

Lady Daisy then came over quickly. "Why, hello, Sandra."

"Thank you for the invitation," Sandra said with a coy smile.

"Why don't you head over to Leva? I asked her to prepare you something delightful."

Sandra gave the nod to Jack and headed toward the bar. "Yes, thank you for the party. It's lovely."

"Mr. Sutton. Congratulations on your victory."

Jack cocked his head to one side, wondering what Daisy really meant by her comment. "I like to think justice was served following the law."

"I'm sure you do." Lady Daisy's lip turned slightly upward before she walked over to another guest as Mosely slid up to them.

Mosely slapped Jack on the back. "I am proud of you, Jack. You did a great job putting it all together. Like Joe Namath, you were a field general in the win."

Jack turned red and dropped his head to gain his thoughts. "I am so thankful to you and all you did to guide me along. Your affirmation and willingness to testify were what Layton needed to press charges. So I should be thanking you." Jack dropped his head and then looked back toward Brown. "It couldn't have been easy after having worked with him for so long."

"Jack, it wasn't as tough as you might think. Remember I told you sometimes you have to wait for the right moment to reveal itself?"

Jack watched as Lady Daisy showed Sandra around the garden. "What do you know about her?"

"Daisy? She's operating on a level you and I will never understand."

"How so?"

"Let's just say she possesses some capabilities you and I don't."

"You mean how she cured that kid? I heard about that."

"That's part of it."

At that moment, Layton walked up and placed a hand on Jack's shoulder. "Jack, I am very impressed with your tenacity and investigative skills. If you want to join the other side, let me know."

Mosely smiled. "Hey, don't try to poach my partner."

Jack and Mosely shared a grin and then walked to the bar together. It was a night for many bourbons.

—⚹—

That Sunday night, Jack and Ruby went to dinner at the Lower Forty. It did not have a fancy name, but it and the Patio were considered the best restaurants in Pear Valley. A waiter brought a shiny glass of red wine and placed it in front of Ruby Sutton. He returned a minute later and placed a glass of white wine in front of Jack Sutton. Both had big smiles on their faces. Ruby looked like she was about to explode in laughter.

"So the story will be in tomorrow's newspapers?" Jack asked.

"Yep! You're a hero, Jack. You made the front page! Who cares about what the White House is doing? Or what the state legislature is doing. We've got goings-on in Pear Valley, and that will be the lead story in tomorrow's paper.

"Not bad for your first month. But we need to get something straight."

"What's that?"

"I need you to know I've always got your back."

Ruby dropped her eyes. "I know." Ruby smiled and changed the subject. "So help me. I'm going to go buy Brad something. I think he likes to golf. I can get him a new putter or something or some new golf balls. Maybe a driver."

"That's true," Jack said, smiling at Ruby. He was proud of her. He raised his glass, and they made a toast. "And you thought a small southern Georgia town would be dull."

Ruby chuckled as she placed her glass back down on the table. "Which is why we are celebrating tonight," she said. The air between them grew silent for a second before she added, "And speaking of celebrating, I'm looking at a horse tomorrow. It's a gold and white mare on sale. She's nine years old. The lady came by with a picture today, and Crystal is lovely. The owner said she was very gentle."

Jack smiled. He wasn't sure about buying a horse, but if it made Ruby happy, he was open to it as he thought, *If doll baby wants it, doll baby gets it.* Her old man was annoying, but he may have a point about keeping his daughter happy. "Where are you going to keep her?"

"The Allgood farm is now boarding horses as a side business. They will room and board her, and their fee is super reasonable."

"It looks like we're settling down. We may get a horse and a dog. And in a few months, we will be attending Friday night high school football games."

A waiter brought their plates and asked, "Ma'am, everything OK with the wine?"

"Yes, I've just been talking too much." She raised her glass and smiled at Jack.

"Yes, ma'am," the waiter said.

Jack took a drink and reached across the table for Ruby's hand. "We were wondering if we would fit here in such a small town. Remember?"

"It hasn't been all that tough. Well, maybe the first two weeks," Ruby said, taking back her hand and picking up her fork. "So what now?"

"We will just have to see, Mrs. Sutton," Jack said, grabbing his fork.

After his arrest, Frank Truitt protested his innocence. District attorneys Layton and Willis met with Truitt and his attorney, Billy Lee Thornton, in the grand jury room on Monday.

Thornton had quite the reputation. He was tall and almost unhealthy thin. He had flowing gray hair that reached to his shoulders, a mustache, and a pointy goatee that looked like the one Colonel Sanders of Kentucky Fried Chicken wore. In fact, he wore a white suit and bow tie that also mimicked the chicken colonel or some imagined old retired Southern general. He had a reputation for being the best criminal lawyer in Georgia other than Peter Zack Geer. He arrived at the courthouse in Callahan County from his office in Muscogee County in a silver Rolls-Royce driven by a chauffeur.

As Truitt and Thornton walked in the door, Layton and Willis were sitting on the side of the table away from the door. To Truitt's surprise, Jack was there to watch as the two DAs, slowly and in painful detail, laid out all the evidence that had been gathered on Mr. Truitt and his men. His bank records, notes, the handwriting on the suicide note, his friendship with the sheriff and Cook, and how his partnership with Allgood went bad.

In the end, Thornton rose, motioning for Truitt to do the same. In his slow Southern drawl that many thoughts were exaggerated for effect, he said, "Sirs, thank you. I would appreciate it if the court let me confer with my client."

As they walked out, Truitt turned to Jack. "You're fired."

Jack calmly looked at him and said, "Funny, but weren't you the one who recommended me to Judge Throwbridge because you thought I would fuck it up? Guess your plan fell apart."

Truitt, inches from Jack's face, said, "Don't get ahead of yourself, boy. You got lucky."

The bailiff took Truitt back to his holding cell as Layton called out to Thornton, "Shall we negotiate a plea deal? Frankly, if your client goes to trial, he will be convicted. Tell us everything, and we'll recommend you're saved from the electric chair."

Thornton coolly left the room to head back to the holding cell to confer with his client. Layton and Willis shared a knowing smile before leaving.

Over the next few weeks, word came that Frank Truitt had entered a guilty plea to the murder and the drug charges. Georgia still had the death penalty for such crimes and gave his admission in exchange for a life sentence without parole. The revelation that

Truitt, serving as a state senator, respected lawyer, and essential community member, had committed such heinous crimes shocked and rocked the quiet town.

Early on in his career, Truitt found himself in the cartel pocket when they had offered him a huge fee in his practice. His friend Sheriff Warren Cain had taken a bribe from Truitt and lost key evidence, allowing Truitt's client to go free. Truitt had been on the take since then and had done various things when asked. Having a prominent lawyer and state senator on their payroll was a good thing.

Cain had been the one to approach Cook and Truitt about the drug-growing idea. And Cain had wasted most of his money and was looking at bankruptcy and divorce if he didn't come up with funds fast. It was supposed to be only a few runs, and then the operation would be shut down, so Truitt agreed to help his friend out as the liaison to the cartel. But greed fueled the continuation, and eventually, Allgood was brought in to expand the "growing" operation.

All was good until Allgood decided to double-cross Truitt, which would cut out his connections in the cartel as well. Truitt, fearing the response, stepped in and took care of Allgood before the cartel came after him.

Allgood was nothing if not a creature of habit. Truitt knew that Allgood would drug his wife on certain weeknights and meet Robin at some motel. So on the night of a planned rendezvous, Truitt snuck into the Allgood house and waited for his opportunity. Unfortunately, Allgood saw him and messed up the plan, leading to seven shots and a blown suicide façade. When he had to load the seventh shot, he stood over Allgood, angry at the bastard, and put one in his genitals just for good measure.

In the end, Truitt's sloppiness ruined him.

—⁓—

Annie stopped by to see Jack receive her final payment. She found him in Truitt's office. "Hey, you taking over?"

Jack looked up from behind Truitt's desk. "Hi. No. I'm trying to find a file on a client Truitt was dealing with; that's now my problem."

Annie walked around, plopped on the leather couch, and surveyed the room. "I don't get people."

"Like whom, specifically?'

"Sandra. Truitt. You name it."

Jack leaned on the desk. "Do you think that Sandra knew anything?"

"From what I found out, there is a good chance she knew or surmised what was up. I suspect she was ready to leave him, but the universe intervened."

Jack leaned forward. "The universe?"

"Yeah, sometimes we need to rely on other forces for help."

Jack laughed. "Next, you're going to tell me you use psychics or—what do they call them now? intuitive people—like that nut Lady Daisy."

Annie's mouth raised slightly on her right side.

Jack leaned back. "Are you serious?"

Annie stood up and walked toward the door, eager to change the subject. "Don't go jumping to conclusions. You know I never reveal sources. Let's just say I don't turn away help when it comes knocking either."

"I'm speechless."

"Your wife, however, surprised me."

"How so?"

"She's got a set for a Georgia peach."

Jack laughed. "That's a compliment from you. And yes, her greatest asset is that everyone underestimates her. Sometimes even me." Jack reached across the desk and grabbed an envelope to hand to Annie. "Thank you for everything. Although I don't think this will be our last job together."

"I had a blast, counselor. Until the next murder!" Annie said, waving the envelope toward the ceiling as she walked out.

—m—

Lavender took the letter to Denise's desk. She was drawing a cartoon for a feature story for the weekend edition.

He pulled up a chair beside her and sat down. "I wanted to show you this," he said, extending an envelope.

The envelope had "Fantasy and Science Fiction Magazine" on it. He smiled. He opened the envelope and pulled the letter up. He handed it to her. "I underlined in green the best part."

Denise took it and looked at the lines underlined by green. "'Mr. Lavender, our editors, found your story *Eternity in Her Eyes* to be an excellent read, a mystery that is deeply touching. F&SF would like to purchase it."

"Wow!" she yelled, jumping up and down. "That's fantastic." She tossed her arms around his neck and kissed him. "You have to give it to me. I want to read it."

"When it comes out. You will just have to wait like everyone else," Brad said with a smirk.

Denise rolled her eyes playfully. "It better be a signed copy for me."

"You know it," Brad said, backing away from Denise's desk.

Denise called after him, "That's a beautiful title."

"I wrote the story about three months ago. And I modeled the main character, the one with eternity in her eyes, on someone I know."

Denise grinned knowingly.

Brad smiled and gave her a nod.

She jumped up and hugged him again and then immediately pulled back as all eyes in the newsroom were on the two.

Half in jest, he said, "Well, we are going to have to get married, or we'll be gossiped about for years as a torrid love affair."

"Well, if we must, we must," she said quickly.

The two laughed. He said, "Tuesday work?"

Denise grinned. "Yes, I hate long engagements."

The weeks went by fast, but the harsh reality that his senior partner was a drug dealer and murderer remained a shock for Jack. So much so that as the others rearranged offices, Jack kept the porch because it just felt right for him—a young lawyer still having to prove himself. He was at his desk when he got the message that Mr. Truitt wanted to see him.

Truitt was still being held in the Callahan County Jail, waiting to be transferred to Reidsville State Prison.

Jack put the visit off for a while. The last thing he wanted to do was go visit Truitt. Jack still held onto his anger for Truitt, having tried to set him up to fail in defending Mrs. Allgood.

But his daddy and mama taught him to face challenges, and this was one he needed to address head-on for his own peace of mind.

When he entered the holding room, Mr. Truitt sat at a table with handcuffs on that were attached to the table. Truitt wore the traditional Southern prison garb of a white shirt and pants with a broad blue strip on each side of both. He looked like he had aged twenty years in the last few weeks. It was hard to imagine him as the arrogant, powerful lawyer and politician Jack had agreed to work for just those few months ago.

When Jack walked in, Truitt grumbled a quick hello. Jack noted the change in Truitt's signature hard tone.

"Hello," Jack replied, sitting down across from him at the metal table.

Silence lingered for a full fifteen seconds.

"Thank you for coming. I know I've done a lot of bad things to you and others. But I'm thankful to have the opportunity to see you face-to-face."

Jack kept his eyes locked on his former boss, trying not to show any expression.

Truitt continued. "I'm not interested in forgiveness, but I wanted you to know that I own what I did." Jack noted a touch of humility along with a maintained arrogance. "In full disclosure, when I met you, I was impressed with you and thought you would be the one who would eventually take over my practice and take care of my clients and carry the firm forward. You proved me right by how you vigorously and professionally defended Mrs. Allgood." Truitt took a long breath and looked Jack in the eye. "You may find this weird, but you made me proud."

Jack cleared his throat. "Thanks." The two shared an awkward silence. "I do appreciate you giving me an opportunity."

The guard walked in. "Time's up."

Truitt stood, gave Jack a head nod, and walked out. As the door slammed, Jack sat for a minute, lost in contemplation, then rose to leave. When he passed the front desk, he stopped. "Can I make a quick call?"

She picked up on the first ring, and he said, "I'm on my way home, babe."

Diego was ready to get out of Georgia for a while. He would miss his sister's restaurant, but he had to be in Memphis to deal with an issue there. Before he went, he had to go to Reidsville State Prison in Reidsville, Georgia, to finish all the loose ends in the Pear Valley mess. He arrived at the prison and waited for the visitation to open.

When he got in, he met with a prisoner named Javier. Javier was the leader of the cartel's men in prison. He gave Javier the instructions and passed the picture of Truitt to him. He knew Javier was a man who would accomplish things and that the Truitt loose end would soon be tied.

Over the next week, Jack couldn't take his mind off Truitt. In every other person's mind, it was resolved, the killer had been found, and justice had been done. Jack couldn't let it go. And the fact that Sandra had also called him for guidance with the Allgood finances didn't help. Given all the twists and turns Allgood worked into hiding the money he was receiving from the drug trade. It wasn't easy.

"Mr. Sutton, Sandra Allgood is here to see you."

"Send her in, please," he said. Jack was in his sleep porch office. Jack waited until his client walked in and sat in the chair in front of his desk. She looked much better and happier with her vibrant smile and raven-black hair lustrously flowing over her silky white-eyelet shirt. Sandra settled back in her chair and crossed her long legs covered by light pink linen pants. She looked like a well-put-together woman of means.

"So what did you find out, Jack?"

Jack nodded. "I am still neck-deep in your financial matters, Sandra, but I have been able to close out your past account and create a new one. All restrictions on your assets were released, and I have identified most everything, though we have a little more work to do."

Sandra nodded in understanding.

"You have a balance of approximately $37,000 in his accounts at the Callahan Bank."

"How much did you say?"

"Thirty-seven thousand dollars. That's the checking account. A savings account also goes to you, worth some $206,000. In addition, a stock account is kept with EF Hutton broker in Atlanta that has another million or so dollars in stocks and bonds. All the farmland will go to you also. You are a wealthy woman," Sutton said.

"What?"

"Yes, ma'am. You didn't know this?"

Sandra slowly shook her head. "No, not at all. Bill never let me have much money or tell me about the finances. I knew there had been financial problems in the past, but he never really involved me in that."

"Well, now you can go down Main Street, go in any store, and buy whatever you want. You can buy another house if you like. You can buy a new car if you like. Sandra, you can buy almost anything you want."

"My, my, and what did my late husband do to gain all this money?" she asked facetiously. She added with a deep Southern drawl, "According to him, his father's farm barely broke even."

Jack smiled. "Frankly, his pecan groves and other farming land amounted to some of the income. He may have downplayed that a bit. And he had a number of stocks that were handed down from his father. I will give you the complete list when I finish my audit. But honestly, the last five years or so, the marijuana business was good to him, and he was good at hiding it, so the Feds will not try to seize it."

"Which got him killed?" she then asked.

"Yes. That and his greed for even more."

"I see."

"I know everyone in town thinks I'm nothing, but I do have a brain."

"Look. I've heard a lot of rumors. I think we all have. And I'm sorry if any of them are true."

Sandra dropped her head. "I think there is some truth in almost every rumor, don't you?"

Jack smiled. "Back to your finances, in addition to the report, I will give you a fiscal analysis of all the funds. You can find an investment advisor who can guide you through the value of the stocks and bonds," Jack said.

Sandra looked toward the ceiling. "I'm going to buy a dog. Always liked dogs. I'll pick one up from an animal shelter. Give him a home."

"There will be a day or so delay until I have the accounts set up so I can transfer them into your account, but you do have full access to your checking account now, so if you have to go on a shopping spree, you can go ahead."

She nodded. "I think I will do that. I'm going to go out and have some fun. Possibly should buy the ex a tombstone too. Wondered if I could get the epitaph 'He got what he deserved" or "Karma's a bitch.' But that might sound a bit undignified."

"Well, from what I hear, it would fit him," Jack said.

Jack drove to 418 Georgia Avenue and picked up his beautiful and proud young wife. She jumped in the car and gave him an admiring kiss. She was in a small strap yellow and white sundress, looking like the Buckhead debutante she was.

"Where are we going?" Ruby asked.

"A little place just off the interstate. I heard it has the best barbeque in the South."

"Really? How do you know that?"

"The sign said when I passed it one time, 'We serve the best barbeque in the South.'"

Ruby broke up, laughing. "OK, let's go."

Jack got on Highway 316, where the speed limit was sixty miles per hour. He was in fourth gear, driving sixty-five, maybe seventy. Jack checked the mirror a few times, and no cars were in sight. Feeling like the king of the world, with Ruby next to him and Cindy owning the road, he pushed the pedal down and got her up to eighty-five miles per hour. But then he checked the rearview mirror and saw some trailing smoke coming up on him. He said out loud to Ruby, "What is that?"

Ruby turned around. "I have no idea."

The smoke got closer, so he pressed on, climbing Cindy to ninety-five miles per hour. Doing the shuffle to maintain speed among the other cars while the other drivers honked at his blowing their doors off while the smoke behind him was still gaining.

Jack pushed it to one hundred, then 110, then 120 miles per hour. The car didn't have air-conditioning, so the windows cracked, and the wind hit him and Ruby squarely in the face.

"Jack, I think you should slow down! What if it's the state police?" Ruby yelled.

"No state car can go that fast!" Jack yelled back over the road noise. He watched the car trail them, thinking, *What the hell! I'm in a 396 Chevelle Super Sport, the hottest car ever.*

He put the accelerator to the floor, truly pedal to the metal or at least carpet over the metal. The speedometer maxed out at 120, but Jack knew they were going 130 miles per hour plus.

Jack released the accelerator in disbelief as the mystery vehicle blew past him. Hanging out the passenger window was a beagle whose eyes were squinted from the wind and howled as he passed Jack.

Incredulously he said to Ruby, "It is goddamn 64 Mercury Comet. A goddamn Mercury!"

Ruby and Jack laughed out loud and then started giggling like schoolgirls. With the sun setting and the road wide open, they saw the sign for the barbeque. Jack turned to Ruby and said, "You hungry?"

"No. Follow that Comet! I like the way they roll." She laughed as the two kept going, with the road and their futures open in front of them.

ABOUT THE AUTHOR

Everette Hall grew up in rural south Georgia and the times of his youth inspire the tales of law and intrigue. Everette grew up on a farm in his early years in a home with outdoor plumbing. He and his family then moved to small town in south Georgia full of characters and stories of eccentrics. He had a love of journalism and started a local newspaper in south Georgia with a high school friend. He then went to undergraduate and law school at Mercer University in classic Macon, Georgia. He went on to practice in Atlanta and around the country in the defense of high-exposure cases civil cases. He founded a full service law firm with a national reach, spending a considerable amount of time in the court rooms around the country trying cases. He serves as national counsel for a number of clients. Part of his practice deals with international matters which has led to him serving as Honorary Consul for the country of Georgia. Mr. Hall thanks Jack Slover for several of the humorous anecdotes that inspired the writing of the book.

This novel and two others which follow in series are based on stories from South Georgia and the legal community generally in the tumultuous 70's.

Made in the USA
Columbia, SC
31 May 2024

36435812R00176